THE INFERNO BELOW

They were just entering the target area, and
he couldn't turn off before he had gone
through. He held the bucking aircraft.

From the roaring ocean of flames below,
searchlights reached up. Suddenly something
happened so close that he didn't hear it—all
he knew was a numbness in his ears, and then
the aircraft's nose dropped and he was looking at the flaming earth.

Calmly Johnny Kinsman thought, "I wonder
if this is where I'm going to die."

John Watson

Johnny Kinsman

AVON
PUBLISHERS OF
DISCUS • CAMELOT • BARD

This is the first American publication
of *Johnny Kinsman* in any form.

AVON BOOKS
A division of
The Hearst Corporation
959 Eighth Avenue
New York, New York 10019

Copyright © 1955, 1964 by John Watson.
Published by arrangement with the author.

First Avon Edition, September, 1969

DISCUS BOOKS TRADEMARK REG. U.S. PAT. OFF. AND
FOREIGN COUNTRIES, REGISTERED TRADEMARK—
MARCA REGISTRADA, HECHO EN CHICAGO, U.S.A.

Printed in the U.S.A.

CHAPTER ONE

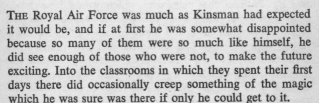

THE Royal Air Force was much as Kinsman had expected it would be, and if at first he was somewhat disappointed because so many of them were so much like himself, he did see enough of those who were not, to make the future exciting. Into the classrooms in which they spent their first days there did occasionally creep something of the magic which he was sure was there if only he could get to it.

Within weeks he was on his way to America. For the next six months there was no war, and some of them forgot why they were there. However, six months is only six months. They returned, strangers for a short time, to their own Air Force, and like small chattering boys being scattered by an impatient master, their tight little groups were split by the imminence of something much greater than their own tiny loyalties to each other.

Kinsman was sent to Avon, which was an operational training unit run by Fighter Command, and he had been there about four weeks before that night when Quigley came into his room.

He was still half asleep when he said, "Who is it?"

The voice from the doorway answered, "Quigley;" and in spite of the fact that he was heavy with sleep, Kinsman had the feeling that there was something in the way in which his visitor had said "Quigley"—a certain hesitancy in the tone, a lack of respect for the word itself, which seemed almost to infer a lack of respect for the man who used it.

"What's wrong?" Kinsman asked thickly. So far he hadn't moved on the bed: he lay there, hoping that Quigley would go away. He had been asleep for an hour, and now, as he lay there on his side with his eyes still closed, there was inside him a deep tiredness.

"You asleep?" Quigley's voice slipped lightly across the vowels, and Kinsman in his imagination could see the other's thin lips being drawn into two tight lines. Quigley usually spoke like that. His moustache was always trimmed neatly, in defiance of the fact that it lacked enough hair to make it a worthwhile ornament. His uniform was pressed, his shoes laboriously polished. This excessive maintenance of appearances was part of Quigley's argument against the fact that nature had made him tall but yet not elegant, had given him features which were fine but without that regularity which would have made him handsome, and thin yellow hair which straggled weakly across his head and along his upper lip. Even the fingers with which he had played the piano so often and so badly when they had been pupils in America were not beautiful. But Quigley not only argued with nature, he argued with almost everyone in the Flight: with authority and with himself.

For some reason he had become friendly towards Kinsman since they had arrived at Avon on the last stage of their training as fighter pilots. Once or twice they had cycled together through the lovely Border countryside in which they were stationed, and then Quigley would talk of his job and of his girl, who was the daughter of a director of the firm for which he had worked before joining the Air Force. Her parents considered that she was so far above his social stratum as to make him quite unsuitable as a prospective husband.

Quigley never drank with Kinsman. He never went into town with him or with any of the others. Instead he wrote long letters, and planned in a brooding kind of way, and walked about his business with an air of challenge which suggested that he was determined to be the last to give in to the uniformity of service life. He had antagonized almost everyone in the Flight except Kinsman. They considered him to be "peculiar," but they did say that he was a good pilot.

As Kinsman raised himself on to one elbow, he remem-

6

bered where Quigley had been. On the previous evening, while he, Kinsman, had been getting more drunk than he ever had been before, Quigley had been in Carlisle with his girl. She had come North for the week-end. Quigley had been talking to Kinsman of practically nothing else for the previous two weeks.

Because the thick, blue blackout blind was pulled down, the room was very dark.

Kinsman said slowly, "What time is it?"

"It's quite early."

There was a pause, during which the darkness settled down again. Then Kinsman, as though there was something unusual in his being there, said, "I felt bloody awful all day. I was drinking with Taffy last night. . . . Went to bed early."

This drew nothing from Quigley, standing there in the doorway. The light was such that it wasn't possible to see him from where Kinsman lay on the bed. There was just the vague outline of the open door and the smudged shadow of the tall young airman.

"Switch on the light, Quig."

There was the click of Quigley operating the switch, but no light.

"Bulb's been pinched," Kinsman said. Then he leant over to reach his clothes on the chair, where his cigarettes were.

As he was groping through his trousers, Quigley's voice came through the darkness, saying, "It's all off, Johnny. . . . It's all over. . . . I . . . I just thought I'd come in and tell you."

There was a pathetic restraint in the way Quigley spoke and when he finished speaking he did so as though to have used one more word would have required more strength than was left in him. Kinsman listened, his hand tight on the cigarette packet in his trouser pocket. Then, without speaking, he eased himself on to the bed again and up to a sitting position, with his back against the wall.

"I'm sorry, Quig. . . . I'm sorry," he said, "That's bloody hard luck."

Quigley didn't answer until Kinsman said, "Cigarette?" Then the words seemed to rush out of him, almost falling over each other.

"It's not her," he said, ". . . it's not her, Johnny. She's

7

. . . she's all right." And when he spoke, he did so in such a way as to suggest that what he really meant was that she was so wonderful that the Mother of God wasn't fit to exist in the same thought.

"It's her people," he went on. "It's her people, Johnny." And again he lingered on the long vowel, stretching the word so that it had reached Kinsman across the darkness before it had left his own mouth. Kinsman could see those fat people crowding into the room.

"What happened?" he asked from the bed.

"They've talked her into it. She doesn't really want to break it off. I know that. Since I've been away they've talked her into it."

"Of course."

Kinsman could remember those long letters he had seen Quigley writing when they were in America; written with laborious neatness of sheets of ruled foolscap. All those hours when Quigley could have been living had been wasted.

"She'll change her mind. I know she'll change her mind," Quigley said to the darkness. Then, "Her old man's a bastard. He hated me. . . . When I was in the office he hated me."

"I thought she was here till tomorrow," Kinsman said.

"There was no point in waiting till tomorrow. She told me it was all over. There was no point in going on."

"No, of course. . . . When did she tell you?"

"At tea this afternoon." As he answered there was something in Quigley's voice which suggested that he was waiting for Kinsman to ask the right question: the question which would help *him* to discover why.

Kinsman said nothing then. He could think of nothing to say that would make any difference to the misery which he sensed Quigley was feeling. And Quigley said nothing. He just stood there at the doorway in the darkness, invisible from where Kinsman sat smoking on the bed, and yet radiating pain as though his whole sensitive body was beating against the heaviness of the room.

Now Kinsman was no longer annoyed at having been disturbed. Although he couldn't see Quigley, and Quigley couldn't see him, he felt that the other was being soothed by just being there and having said what he had said. Kinsman himself was soothed.

8

Quigley's voice without the body of Quigley was the best of him. It wasn't a beautiful voice, but, listening to it without having to see the quick, distrusting challenge in the eyes, and the well-washed face, and the moustache, and the pressed uniform, it was as though all that there was of the man at the door had been filtered away until there was nothing but the sincerity in the words he had spoken.

"That's that," Quigley said quietly.

Kinsman paused, and then asked, "Was there another bloke?"

"Well . . . " The voice from the doorway hesitated before going on . . . "There's some chap. . . . He's at Cambridge. But that isn't it, Johnny. It's her people. I know it is. It's her people. . . ."

. . . Some hours later, when he had been asleep, Kinsman awoke with a start. He thought he had heard Quigley's voice. But there was no one there, and he wondered then if there ever had been anyone there. He couldn't remember having seen Quigley, but he could still hear the voice coming to him in the darkness, and he rubbed his ears and then settled down into the warmth of the bedclothes to sink again into sleep. It was strange and frightening. He hadn't seen Quigley, but he could remember every word that Quigley had said, and he could remember him saying good night when he went away. Kinsman opened his eyes again and looked up, but there was nothing there in the darkness. It would be funny next day when he told Quigley, but not then.

Next day was Sunday, and at that place, being a training establishment run by Fighter Command, where a spirit of *laissez-faire* was encouraged, no one cared whether or not you arrived at Flights until you were due to take off.

Kinsman was due to go off on an exercise at one o'clock. He arrived at Flights at twelve-thirty, and as he opened the door of the office the noise from an untidy cluster of pilots came out to meet him. A boy called Struthers, who had been with Kinsman since they had arrived at the recruits' reception centre, turned to meet him so quickly that they collided.

"Out the bloody road," Kinsman said pleasantly.

"Quigley's just bought it," Struthers said in a voice heavy with excitement. "The Flight Commander's on the 'phone to the police at Lockerbie now. He came down on the hills up there. He's been missing since nine-thirty."

And as Struthers spoke, the Flight Commander, a man who had killed many Germans, raised his head from the telephone. A long red tongue swept along the fair, silken hair of his moustache before he said, "Will you bastards be quiet until I hear what this bloke's saying!" And then to Struthers and Kinsman he smiled.

Some of the flight were sitting at the Flight Commander's desk. Before the 'phone had rung they had been playing pontoon. Now they sat toying with the cards which were on the desk before them.

"O.K. . . . O.K.," the Flight Commander said quickly in the clipped Afrikaans-accented English which he used, "I'll wait." He kept the old-fashioned telephone receiver at his ear, and said to those sitting at the desk: "All right. Where were we? . . . Who's banker? . . . O.K., Docherty —give us another hand."

Kinsman stood watching the cards being dealt. The Flight Commander turned to the 'phone to say, "Right, then. You do that. Yes. . . . We'll be sending some people up there to look after the pieces." He then replaced the receiver, and went on playing for a few minutes, until it became obvious to him that only he had any enthusiasm left for the game. He stood up, and with a jerking, impatient movement of his body leant over the deck to slap a hand on the money which was his, before saying, "Ah . . . You boys will have to learn that getting killed is part of this game. Is there an aircraft out there? Who's on the next detail?"

"I am, sir," Kinsman said.

"I'll take your aircraft. I suppose I'd better go and take a look at the prang. . . . *You* play cards, Kinsman."

The Flight Commander pushed back his long fair hair until it was underneath his hat, settled the hat comfortably on the back of his head, and then started to fasten his battledress tunic.

"Kinsman," he said then, "which one was Quigley? What did he look like?"

CHAPTER TWO

AT Cromarty, where Kinsman was posted when he had completed the course of the Fighter Command operational training unit, there were almost as many Polish pilots as there were British, Canadian, and Australian. Before he had left the Fighter O.T.U., he had lived for weeks on the brink of being sent to the Middle East or the Far East, but then Training Command had asked for pilots to fly target-towing aircraft at a gunnery school, and, possibly because a certain lack of confidence had prevented him from shining as a potential fighter pilot, Kinsman had been chosen as one of those destined to pull a target.

Had his knowledge of the ways of the Service been greater he would have known that if the posting was reflective of his ability as a pilot at all, it was only in an inverse sense. Had his ability as a pilot at Avon been greater, then, no doubt, he would have been sent to one of the crack Fighter Groups, but being little more or less than average, his name had probably been selected at random from the ninety-five per cent of his course who were in no way especially skilled.

When he arrived at Cromarty, Kinsman's confidence was as low as it had been since the morning of Quigley's death. But gradually, as he saw something of how the other pilots handled their old Lysanders and Bothas, and he began to feel that among these men were some who were brilliant in the air, there came to him the feeling that after all he was in good company.

It had become something of a tradition among the Poles at Cromarty that flying an aeroplane was worth while only if it was done with style and dash. On the surface at least they appeared to have little respect for danger, and, for them, common sense was something which Englishmen were welcome to keep.

This attitude of the Poles had gradually been adopted by the British and the Canadians, and, when Kinsman arrived at the station, the man who had the reputation of being the wildest pilot there was an Australian. Ancient Lysanders which had seen service in France before Dunkirk were thrown around the sky in grotesque gyrations which, although the pilot may have felt that the Lysander was performing with all the grace of a sleek Spitfire, looked from the ground as though some bloated old vulture had taken leave of its senses.

Cromarty was a happy station. It was the first at which Kinsman had been where he was not a pupil. Now, officially, he was a qualified pilot, and, if for some weeks he did not feel particularly different from how he had felt when he was a pupil at Avon, in time he became more confident: on the ground, and then in the air.

There was an unusual fellow, a Pole called Dilewski, who was the possessor of more than one reputation. He was reputed to be a pilot of considerable daring; his drinking was equalled only by that of the Warrant Officer in charge of Messing; and there were Waafs who could only giggle nervously when his name was mentioned.

As his knowledge of Dilewski grew, Kinsman began to realize that the Pole was different from his compatriots in that he didn't appear to have the Ghetto complex which kept them from mixing with the other aircrew on the station. Most of them, too, were haunted by the possibilities of the future, but not Dilewski. As though to demonstrate his confidence in the gods, he was always in debt, and it was when he borrowed two pounds from Kinsman that their friendship began.

Dilewski fascinated Kinsman. To look at, there was nothing which made him more than ordinary, even if his appearance had about it an air of permanent confusion. He looked like a man who was so engrossed with some aspect of living that the normal functions of dressing and bathing were more than he had time for. He never spoke

12

to Kinsman of the life he had known before the war in Poland, but occasionally he said enough to indicate that he had not been one of the officer class. Perhaps Dilewski had renounced his compatriots socially because there was resentment in his memory of how he had once lived in Poland. But with Dilewski you could never tell. It could have been that he simply preferred to drink with the Canadians, and Kinsman, and Freakley the Englishman. There was something in Dilewski which made him different from the ordinary run of them there, but whatever it was Kinsman never really knew. It seemed to stay hidden, deep in the thoughts which the Pole never learned to express in English.

There was in the Pole a kinship with the earth, a strange sureness which gave him stature as a man. He was real. He existed in *his* way. Not like the others, who made themselves into what they thought the audience expected of them.

Dilewski loved to eat in a way in which Kinsman had never known anyone use food. In the sergeants' mess he would descend on what was served to him as though he was discovering for the first time that food existed. He laughed, and he loved women, and talked of loving them, in a way that Kinsman had never known before—without shame.

On the night before Dilewski was killed, Kinsman wrote a letter for him which had to do with Dilewski's love life. He had been passing the Pole's billet on the way to his own when the matter of Dilewski's owing him two pounds occurred to him. Without knocking, he opened the door of the Pole's room.

"Ach . . . Johnny!" the Pole gasped by way of greeting.

"I'm looking for two pounds," Kinsman said.

Dilewski was lying on his bed completely naked. It was a comfortable bed on which the blankets had been neatly folded, and Kinsman noticed, too, that opposite the door there was a radio which was switched off at the moment. It was like Dilewski to have for himself one of the best rooms in the sergeants' quarters.

"Why you want two pounds?" Dilewski asked.

"Because I haven't got two pounds, because I gave you two pounds."

"I'm very worried, Johnny."

13

"So am I." Kinsman smiled when he spoke.

"Don't worry about money, Johnny." The expression on Dilewski's face was quite serious. He waved one arm above his naked body in emphasis of his impatience with financial matters. Then he asked, "Can you write a letter for me?"

" 'Course."

"I want to write to a what-you-call-it . . . a landlady, In Blackpool. . . . It's very difficult."

"Why?"

"You see, Johnny, I was going on leave with this girl. . . ."

"What girl?"

"A girl . . . my girl in Manchester. I had booked a room for us." Dilewski paused to think of the room he had booked.

"One room?"

"Of course one room. What you think?"

"What's wrong, then?" Kinsman asked.

"She can't come."

"You had a row?"

"No . . . no. She can't get away from the manufactory where she works."

"Do you want to cancel the room?"

"Of course not," Dilewski said with seriousness. "I want to take another girl."

Dilewski could see that Kinsman was confused, so he sat up, impatiently, on the bed. To Kinsman it was disconcerting to see him sitting there naked as he was, but Dilewski wasn't conscious of his nudity. He ran his hand down his long thighs, as though to touch them made him feel good. Then impatiently trying to rearrange the jumble of strange words which were in his throat, he went on, "You see, Johnny, I was taking this girl. Now I want to take another girl. How can I get this . . . this what-you-call-her?"

"Girl?"

"No . . . landlady! How do I get this landlady to take the other girl in?"

"If she was going to allow the first girl in," Kinsman said, "why shouldn't she take in the second girl?"

Dilewski allowed a long stream of breath to whistle between his teeth. "She allowed the first girl because she thought she was my wife. Last year I was there. She thought this girl was my wife!"

Kinsman laughed. Then he said, "You'd better get another landlady, Dilewski."

But the Pole didn't laugh. "I don't want to do that," he insisted. "It's very difficult to get a landlady in Blackpool, Johnny, with the war. I want you to write a letter, Johnny. Tell her that my wife is ill, and I want to bring my sister instead. You write that down, Johnny."

Kinsman roared with laughter. Then, when he could stop, he said, "But you can't do that, Dilewski. You can't sleep with your sister. People don't sleep with their sisters."

"Ach. . . . !" Dilewski's hand dropped heavily, and he subsided back on to the bed. "I'm going to sleep with my sister. Go on, Johnny. You write it."

Kinsman wrote the letter, and as he was doing so, laughing every so often at what he was writing, Dilewski lay on the bed describing in intimate detail all the variety of things he was going to do to this girl who was to appear at Blackpool as his sister. He spoke of his appetite for her in the same way as he spoke of his appetite for food, and when the letter was finished and Dilewski suggested that they go around to the mess for a drink, there was the same warm pleasure in his voice as when he had spoken of the girl. Kinsman listened to him talking of some more of the women he had known, and as he was listening he wondered why he felt no trace of disgust. Perhaps it was because Dilewski's sensuality seemed to stay within him.

On the next day Kinsman was on the lunch-time detail, because he hadn't been at Cromarty long enough to avoid it; and Dilewski was sharing it because by doing so he could catch the afternoon train for the South instead of waiting until the evening, as was usual when going on leave.

Both of them were flying Lysanders modified to pull targets for the pupil gunners in the two Bothas detailed to take the air at the same time. Rendezvous was at the most northerly point of a peninsula called The Ness, and, when the Bothas had established contact with the target-towing aircraft, one Lysander, followed by a Botha, would fly in a north-easterly direction, while the other towing aircraft would head towards the north-west, followed by the remaining Botha.

When Kinsman arrived at the rendezvous he could see Dilewski there, but there was no sign of either Botha. As he approached the place, he saw the Pole climbing his aircraft up and away from him, and then turning it so steeply that from where Kinsman saw him it looked as though the Lysander would go over on to its back. The Pole turned through a hundred and eighty degrees, and then dropped sharply to dive towards Kinsman. In his earphones Kinsman could hear the man who operated the winch in the rear cockpit shouting to him that they were being attacked. Dilewski dived straight for them.

Kinsman hesitated, wondering whether to turn to port or to starboard. He was a little afraid. Then he turned steeply to starboard and down. He looked up, feeling, as he did so, the blood draining from his head, but he caught a brief glimpse of the other Lysander turning in the opposite direction above him. Somehow Dilewski changed direction yet again, in an attempt to get inside Kinsman's turn.

Conscious of the fact that there was a man sitting there behind him in the rear cockpit watching every move he made, and yet still afraid of the violence necessary in the handling of his Lysander to combat that of the Pole, Kinsman wished the Bothas would arrive. He looked quickly to the south, but there wasn't time to really look. Briefly he caught a glimpse of Dilewski sitting high in the cockpit of the aircraft behind, and the Pole looked strangely fierce when wearing his mask. Then again there was the call of the drogue operator behind Kinsman as he shouted something which sounded like "Come on, Johnny!" and suddenly a strange, urging sense of abandon arose in Kinsman. He was unafraid because he didn't think. His hands tightened on the control column, and he threw the old Lysander over until the port wing had passed the vertical. A hand flashed to the throttle, and he dropped, in a long, sighing dive towards the green sea and the rocks.

Dilewski followed him, and down there they danced over the slender strip of beach, so low sometimes that on their port the cliffs rose above them. Once, when Kinsman dropped the big, dragging flaps, and pulled the control column back before allowing the engine to surge with power,

16

Dilewski shot past. Kinsman laughed then, and behind him his drogue operator let out a cry of joy. The grotesque, obscene-looking underbelly of the other Lysander lifted away from them as though it was being sucked towards the emptiness of the sky above. That was the first time Kinsman realized that when an aircraft climbed it climbed like an elevator, not like a rocket. It was also the first time he was really in control of the machine he flew.

The Bothas arrived. Dilewski's was first, and Kinsman heard the Pole talking to the other pilot in his slow, deeply accented voice before leading him out towards the firing line. When the Botha which was to fire at Kinsman's target suddenly appeared, it came up from behind, and had crept in so close before he was aware of its being there that he was frightened to see it, suddenly, almost accidentally, there just beneath his own high wings. Freakley, who was its pilot, waved to him as he rode the rolling streams of air, and then, as Kinsman answered the greeting, the Englishman pulled the Botha over on its side to starboard, and into the diminishing distance of four hundred yards. Kinsman headed towards the firing line.

The exercise did not take long. By the time he had flown about twenty-five miles over the sea, and then back in a reciprocal direction to the rendezvous point, Freakley's pupils had fired off all their rounds. Then the Botha came over his nose, and Freakley at its controls dropped one wing and then the other to indicate that they were finished, before diving towards the south and out of sight.

Kinsman turned laboriously back towards the northwest to head across the bay to the field where they dropped their targets. As soon as he turned he saw Dilewski again—heading in the same direction. He increased throttle and started to lose height in order to get more speed. But Dilewski must have seen him. He also appeared to lose height. From behind, the drogue operator called, "You'll lose the drogue, Johnny, if you go too fast."

But Kinsman went on; below Dilewski now, but still behind. The distance between them had narrowed somewhat, but when the Pole started to lose still more height, he drew away again. Kinsman realized he would not overtake him, and Dilewski seemed to know it too, for he started to wave his control column from side to side, so that from

17

behind his Lysander had all the ridiculous gaiety of a tipsy old woman.

Making his way into the dropping-field, Dilewski flew so low that the drogue trailing behind him was almost touching the ground. Kinsman smiled. The antics of the aircraft in front were somehow out of character with that of the sad serious man who had asked him to write that letter to a landlady in Blackpool on the previous evening.

Kinsman had descended to about a hundred and fifty feet when the Pole released his trailing target. Dilewski climbed, and as Kinsman, from behind, watched the fierceness of the climbing turn he gasped. A clutching realization of the Pole's mistake came a second after it must have come to Dilewski himself. The climbing Lysander appeared to hesitate and then it fell and fell and fell in an agonizing diving turn. Kinsman saw its wings almost level out as Dilewski tried to regain control, but it could only hit the hard ground, and it hit with a long, slithering series of pathetic collisions. A low, slowly rising hill which shouldn't have been there was tearing Dilewski to pieces.

As though only he had seen what had happened, the operator from behind called, "Look, Johnny . . . look, Johnny! . . . Dilewski . . . Dilewski!"

For a moment Kinsman forgot he was descending, and he only realized it as he felt his Lysander lurch when the target he had been trailing was wrenched from the wire which attached it to the winch in the rear cockpit. A fluttering panic inside Kinsman made him momentarily unable to decide whether or not to climb or turn or descend or what. Instinct drew him towards Dilewski, and for a moment it was difficult to realize that that was impossible. He climbed slowly and steadily, straight ahead, and then, terribly afraid, he turned. He turned towards Dilewski.

A slender black pyre of smoke arose from the staggered wreckage of Dilewski's Lysander. It was afternoon, and the air had been still, and beneath him the brown heather and the fields had looked as though they were pleased with themselves for having slowly settled there. But now the suddenness of shock had clamped Kinsman's lips. He could feel hot tears in his eyes, but nothing else of his body. The grinding groan of the big engine in front of him echoed through his loneliness. He went towards the smoke and then around it, and from five hundred feet he looked

18

down. He could see Dilewski still writhing and trapped in the cockpit. There was still life and movement in Dilewski, but only in the top half of his body. . . . Dilewski. Dilewski. Dilewski. The name came to Kinsman like a word in search of a meaning, and he went on looking down into the flames, until there was so much smoke that it was impossible to see what was burning. Kinsman was shocked as he would have been if his tongue had been torn out of his head because its laughter offended.

He climbed slowly away then from the place where Dilewski was dead. It was winter; and what there was left of that day's light had about it a peculiar unreality. He climbed and climbed through the cold air as though reaching away from something of which he was afraid, like a tourist from a brush with officialdom in a country whose laws are not his own. And then, full of fear because of what he had seen, he knew the nervous insecurity that comes from sitting on something you cannot see. He was bending, bowing, kneeling, scraping obsequiously at the feet of the treacherous master in whose face such a short time before he had laughed.

It was at Cromarty that they made Kinsman an officer, and there too he learned to fly multi-engined aircraft. In time he learned to fly with confidence. He learned many things, and he forgot many things. He forgot the boys with whom he had been trained, and in forgetting that he too had been a boy, he became something of a man. He went to another station in Training Command to teach navigation, and in teaching it he learned something of the subject; not much, but enough.

And then, when he had been long enough in the Air Force for its way to become normal, it posted him to Bomber Command. He said he was glad, and he got drunk with those who weren't going, but afterwards, when he was alone, he was neither happy nor sad.

CHAPTER THREE

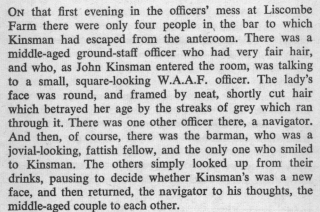

On that first evening in the officers' mess at Liscombe Farm there were only four people in the bar to which Kinsman had escaped from the anteroom. There was a middle-aged ground-staff officer who had very fair hair, and who, as John Kinsman entered the room, was talking to a small, square-looking W.A.A.F. officer. The lady's face was round, and framed by neat, shortly cut hair which betrayed her age by the streaks of grey which ran through it. There was one other officer there, a navigator. And then, of course, there was the barman, who was a jovial-looking, fattish fellow, and the only one who smiled to Kinsman. The others simply looked up from their drinks, pausing to decide whether Kinsman's was a new face, and then returned, the navigator to his thoughts, the middle-aged couple to each other.

Kinsman asked for a half-pint, and as the barman passed it over the counter to him, he suggested that the man join him. The barman uttered a curt word of thanks, pulled himself a drink and placed it on the ledge beneath the counter. Then he continued a rather sporadic conversation with the navigator at the other end of the bar.

"He's too big," said the barman.

"Got the reach, though. That's what'll count."

At that the fair-haired ground-staff officer raised his head and said, "Same again, Paddy." Then he moved across to the piano, which was in the corner, and started to play a slow, little melody.

When Kinsman had bought the barman a drink he had hoped that by so doing he would have been able to open some kind of conversation, but Paddy—for that, it appeared, was the man's name—hardly looked at him. His eyes drifted around the edges of Kinsman, and then settled on him as though the wall behind was visible through his body. There was nothing offensive in the barman's attitude: it was just that Kinsman felt as though his presence didn't seem to register with the man.

The little W.A.A.F. officer had moved from the bar, and was now standing with one hand on the shoulder of her friend at the piano. The navigator resolutely placed his glass on the bar counter, and said, "I don't see how a man can take on an opponent who's six inches taller, a stone and a half heavier, and has a longer reach."

"Ringcraft," Paddy said in a brogue which Kinsman felt sure had come from Belfast, "that's what'll even the scales . . . ringcraft."

"Is the fight being broadcast?" Kinsman used the words hopefully.

"Don't know." The barman spoke so quickly that Kinsman wasn't sure whether or not he had troubled to look at him, and by the time Kinsman had taken his eyes from the navigator, the man Paddy was deeply immersed in the business of polishing a glass.

At that the door of the bar burst open, and with considerable jostling a group of about six young men, all of them aircrew, came into the room.

"Six pints, Paddy," someone said noisily.

Without pausing, the barman began to pull six pints from the barrel.

"Paddy's not speaking to us," someone said. "He's been out with that old woman of his in the village again, and she's disappointed him."

Paddy paused, looking first in the direction of the piano where the W.A.A.F. officer was listening to her friend playing, and then said to the man who had spoken, "If you really want to know, I haven't been out with any old woman. I'm havin' an affair with Herbert in the kitchen."

"Isn't that nice?"

"Sweet," Paddy mockingly.

Kinsman moved farther along the bar in the direction

21

of the door, in order to make room for those who had just come in. They seemed to be a decent crowd. In a way it was just as he expected it would be. There was something about Liscombe Farm which was different from any other place at which he had been stationed.

As the barman placed the drinks which the newcomers had ordered on the counter, Kinsman found that he had to move still farther towards the door. He was in the corner now. Up against the wall.

The others talked of some operation on which they had been throughout the previous night. It seemed that this was their first appearance of the day.

Kinsman decided to go away. There was no common ground on which he could talk with them. Nothing that he had done in his years of flying could compare with their experience. He felt very much like a new boy. And yet he wasn't new in the same way as the average newcomer to the squadron. He had flown for over a thousand hours on various non-operational jobs. His night-flying experience was probably greater than that of anyone else in that room. But they were operational, and until he had completed his first trip, he wasn't. Acutely aware of the fact that no one appeared to notice that he was going, Flying Officer Kinsman left the room.

Outside the mess he turned left and started to walk along the road in the direction of the dormitory site on which he was billeted.

It was mid-August, and there was a pleasant warmth in the soft evening breeze which came across the fields to him. His nostrils were filled with the rich smell of the hedgerows growing high on either side of him. In his ears there was the whirring of a reaper working late on some-one's field, and then, as though to remind him that there was in fact an airfield in the vicinity, some mechanic on a distant dispersal bay started to rev. up the engines of a Halifax.

That afternoon, when he had gone to his billet, a lorry had taken him there, and he hadn't realized then that the place was in fact almost two miles from the mess. At intervals an airman, sometimes with a Waaf by his side, cycled past, proud in his possession of a bicycle. On the first occasion one of them passed him on the narrow road

22

without making any gesture of salutation, Kinsman wondered whether or not he should call the man back, but for that he lacked the courage.

There was no notice to tell him which dispersal site was which, and he walked fifty yards past number three site when finally he asked a corporal who looked as though he was making his way home from a pub.

Following the man's instructions, he walked along the pathway which led from that road to the site but he was unable to remember which of the half-dozen huts was the one in which he was billeted. Twice he looked into rooms in which half-dressed young men were folding and sorting their clothes. People always seemed to be rearranging their possessions in the Air Force.

The officers' block which he had entered was a low-roofed, wooden construction. A long, narrow corridor ran from one end to the other, and on either side of it there were three doors. The door which Kinsman opened was the first on the left as he entered the corridor.

The room was on the dark side of the building, for not only did its solitary window look towards the east, but an oak tree which had its roots on the other side of the fence practically shut out what meagre light there was on that side of the building. Consequently Kinsman was startled when the voice of a young man came to him from the direction of the bed farthest away from the door.

"Whatcher," the voice said.

Kinsman had thrown his hat on the bed which was to the right of the door, and was about to unbutton his tunic when the voice came to him. He swung around sharply.

"Hello," he said. "I didn't see you."

"It's dark in here. The light's gone. Bulb, I think. The batmen are out. The only way we can get one is if we pinch one from someone else's room. . . . Who are you?"

"Kinsman."

"You taking Barber's bed?"

"Who's Barber?" Kinsman asked.

"He bought it last Thursday. This was his room."

"Oh," said Kinsman. He searched in his pocket for a cigarette, and then said to the other, "Cigarette?"

"Got one, thanks."

Kinsman saw the lighted end of a cigarette tracing a

23

pattern through the gloom at the far end of the room as the other fellow showed him he was smoking. Becoming used to the light, too, he could now discern something of the other's features. He could see that the man who had spoken to him was lying on his bed dressed only in pyjama trousers. He could see, too, that this other fellow was dark, very dark of hair and complexion: almost foreign-looking, although he spoke with rather a good English accent.

"I just got here this afternoon," Kinsman announced.

"Where you from?"

"Rifforth."

"That's where I was. Everyone here comes from Rifforth. My name's Wakefield: what did you say yours was?"

"Kinsman."

"Did you know a chap called Johnny Crocket at Rifforth? He used to be there."

"No," Kinsman said quickly, for he was eager to be friendly, "I can't say that I knew him."

"He was an instructor. His was the last crew to be screened from here. He arrived there the day I left. I knew him at school."

"How long have you been here?" Kinsman asked.

"Six weeks."

Six weeks. Kinsman looked over at the man who had said his name was Wakefield. Through the gloom he tried to see if there was anything about Wakefield, who must have completed many operations in six weeks, which distinguished him from someone as new as himself.

"Are you in bed?" Kinsman asked.

Wakefield laughed. "I would say that I was," he said.

"I mean are you in bed for the night? Is it all right if I go to bed? I'm a bit cheesed off with things."

A kind of warmth came into Wakefield's voice when he spoke. He said, "You do what you like, old boy. This is as much your room as it is mine. What's the trouble?"

Kinsman laughed quietly. "No trouble," he said quickly. "You know what it's like, though. No one speaks to you. You don't know where anything is. And we had a bloody awful journey here in a train that stopped at every station between here and York. You feel," he went on, "as though it doesn't matter whether you come here or not."

"You mean it doesn't matter who comes here. What's happened to your crew?" Wakefield said.

"Gone drinking in Bridsea, I suppose. They buzzed off as soon as we arrived."

"All N.C.O.s . . . ?"

"No," Kinsman said, "the navigator's commissioned. He's an old fellow. About thirty-three or something. Writes letters to his old mother in New Zealand all the time."

Kinsman was in bed now, and was pleasantly surprised to find that it was much more comfortable than any he had known in the Air Force. When he was lying, quite relaxed, on his back, his hand limply holding a cigarette above his face, life, just then, took on a new complexion. There was silence in the darkening room, while from outside, above the roof, there came the soft rustle of the branches which hung low over the hut.

He was tired, but there was an obligation to speak, so to Wakefield he said, "Have you got many in?"

"Only four."

Wakefield's voice had a pleasant, resonant quality about it which, in the few minutes that he had known him, Kinsman had come to envy. Kinsman had hardly seen his room-mate, but he was sure that this Wakefield had an attractive personality.

"Haven't they been doing much?"

"I'll say they have. They've lost twelve crews in the last ten days. My navigator's been sick for the past three weeks. I've been waiting for him."

"Do they let you do that?" Kinsman asked.

"Tom Barry's a decent fellow. You met him?"

"He wasn't there when I was at Flights this afternoon."

"You'll see him in the morning. We're standing down tonight. Group's taken pity on us. You'll like him. Everybody likes him."

"Who . . . Barry?" Kinsman asked.

"Yep. . . . He's a decent fellow."

There was a brief silence then. Kinsman drew slowly on his cigarette. There was so much he wanted to know about the squadron and Liscombe Farm.

"They've lost twelve," Kinsman said slowly.

"Yes."

25

"Did you know any of them?"

"Some of them."

"What's it like?" Kinsman raised himself on one elbow, and looked over at Wakefield's corner of the room to ask the question.

Wakefield's bed made a squeaking noise as he raised himself on it, and then lowered his legs to the floor. Kinsman saw him sitting there on the edge of the bed leaning forward on his knees before dropping forward to the floor, and then standing up to stretch himself. When Wakefield had fully stretched his body he walked over to the door.

"Pardon me, old boy. Must have a run off. Eh . . . it's bloody. Just now it's bloody. They've really got their fighter defences organized."

Wakefield opened the door of the little room, and walked to the entrance of the hut. Kinsman could hear him standing there urinating on the ashes outside. It was a friendly sound. Kinsman was feeling much better about the place already.

When Wakefield came back into the room he was carrying a light-bulb, which he fixed into the socket in place of the one which had failed. With the light on, that room was transformed: from being a place of quiet shadows it became almost gay. Kinsman, when his eyes became accustomed to the light, could see that it was a pleasant place. Someone had spread a grey blanket over the table which stood under the window, and had almost succeeded in giving the room a warm, furnished look. On a small chest of drawers over by Wakefield's bed there was a photograph of a smiling girl. The girl was very dark, like Wakefield, and quite beautiful.

"My sister," Wakefield said.

"She's nice."

"*I* think so."

Wakefield was standing leaning against the wall by the light-switch, as though allowing the newcomer to get an impression of the room. Kinsman, looking at him, saw that he was slightly taller than he was himself. It was possible, too, that he was a few years older. Wakefield could have been twenty-four or even twenty-five. He had a clean face, clean and good-looking in a way which suggested

26

that he wasn't English. Kinsman thought then that he might have been Welsh. He had a lithe strength about him, so that as he looked at him standing there, Kinsman wouldn't have been surprised to see him leap across the room like a young tiger.

"What's that?" Kinsman asked. He was looking at a photograph pinned to the far wall by a sheath knife.

Wakefield laughed. "That was Barber's girl friend. She wrote to him one day saying that she was going to marry someone else, so he threw a knife at the picture. No one got around to taking the knife down."

"Is he missing?"

"No, lost an engine on take-off."

"Oh."

"Want the light left on?" Wakefield asked.

"Not particularly. Not unless you do." Kinsman liked his new room-mate, and he was anxious that Wakefield should like him.

The room was dark once more, but Kinsman had lost the desire to sleep. This Wakefield was the kind of man he'd expected to meet at Liscombe. Everyone who was at Liscombe Farm or any other operational station had to come from the kind of place where Kinsman had been instructing or under instruction since he had joined the Air Force. There they were training types. The best of them lived for the day when they would be operational. None seemed to realize that operational types had been training types. Kinsman, lying there, wondered what it was that made the difference.

Wakefield said, "How many hours have you got in?"

John Kinsman waited. Then, casually, he said, "About eleven hundred."

"This your second tour?" There was something which might have been called mild alarm in Wakefield's voice as he asked the question.

"No . . . no, I've been stooging in Training Command."

Without much enthusiasm, Wakefield then announced that Kinsman had done twice as much flying as he had himself. And then, as though to remind the newcomer that mere flying experience wasn't everything, he said, "What you've got to watch nowadays are fighters. Gerry's got a fellow in France just now who claims to have over a hundred and forty victories. All of them at night."

"Terrific," Kinsman breathed.

"And the thing is," Wakefield went on, "evasive action is almost as bad as the bloody fighters. Our streams are so concentrated that you're more or less bound to hit something if you throw a kite around."

Kinsman was beginning to think that his chances of being posted alive from Liscombe were slight. But there was no fear in him, no conscious fear. He was lying in a comfortable bed, and his body was warm and dry. The immediate present was comfortable. He was tired, pleasantly tired. Within a few days he would know the thrill of being operational. That was a wonderful thought. Once he was operational, there would be nothing else in his whole life ever that would really matter.

Before him stretched an interminable number of weeks and months. Somewhere there ahead was Christmas. If he was still alive at Christmas he would really be operational. But Christmas was so far away. He had still to live through summer and autumn and half the winter. But it was good to feel that there was no need to think of the day after tomorrow when there was tomorrow. No need to think even of tomorrow when there was now.

Aunt Lizzie had been under the impression that he had been having daily brushes with the enemy ever since he left home. He smiled to himself as he thought of the letter he had received from her shortly after his Uncle Willie had died. "Just to think, son," she had said, "that you are up there getting yourself shot at by these Germans every day in the week and nothing happens to you and he dies lying there upstairs in the room. Providence works in funny ways."

"Got a good crew?" Wakefield asked sleepily.

"Very."

"You've got to have a good crew. One night last week a fellow's crew baled out over France and left him to bring the aircraft back himself."

"Quite a thing bringing back an aircraft yourself," Kinsman said slowly.

"It happens." Wakefield's voice, normally deep, was even deeper as he spoke. It was slightly thick, as though the muscles of his throat objected to being used now that it was time to sleep. "A bloke came back from the Ruhr without a navigator or maps. That, in my opinion, is really something."

"What happened to his navigator?"

"An incendiary from one of our own aircraft chopped his head off over the target area. The blood spurted out of the chap's body and ruined the maps."

"Do you mean," Kinsman asked, "that someone's bombs fell on him?"

"It can happen."

Kinsman raised himself once more on to his elbow. "What," he said, "was your roughest trip?"

"Versailles. You wouldn't think it would be, but it was. The target area was rotten with searchlights and fighters. We lost five that night."

As though completely satisfied now, Kinsman sank back on to his pillow. As he relaxed his lips closed.

Half asleep, he thought of those who were about to become operational with him: Fred Day, the bomb-aimer, Geordie and Chico the gunners, old Bob the navigator, Les with the round soft face who was the wireless operator. And Wintrop. Wintrop was gutless. The first thing he must do when he saw the Flight Commander the next day was to get rid of that engineer. He was bad for the others, and they were all good lads. Even old Bob, in his way.

The cigarette he had been smoking felt hot against his fingers, and Kinsman rolled over to stab it out on the floor. All those boys, even old Bob, liked him as a skipper. He felt that. He was a good pilot, too. He knew that. Suddenly he wondered how he would face up to operational conditions, and then, just as quickly, he dismissed the thought that he might not, as being silly. Kinsman had a strange feeling then.

All those things that Wakefield had spoken of could happen to other people, but not to him. He ran his right hand down his naked left arm. Then he touched his thigh as though expecting the flesh to be covered with fire-resistant paint. He was sure that nothing was going to happen to him, for he couldn't imagine it. And yet he was no different from Wakefield or any of the others, except that he didn't know as much about the job as they did.

There was no point in thinking about it.

" 'Night, boy," Wakefield said slowly and roundly in his rather beautiful voice.

" 'Night, boy."

CHAPTER FOUR

"You're Kinsman."

Kinsman smiled. "Yes, sir."

"Eh . . . eh, welcome to C Flight."

There were two other officers in the office. One, slumped forward and leaning on his knees, was sitting by the window. The other, a tall, lean-looking man of about Kinsman's own age, was behind him writing with chalk on a blackboard which was hanging on the wall.

It was the one who was writing who said, without pausing in his labors, "I think the Flight Commander's going to make a speech."

"No . . . no, I'm not."

The 'phone rang.

"You take it, Dennis," said the Flight Commander, and Dennis, the man who had been writing on the board, moved forward to the desk and lifted the 'phone.

"Well, now . . . eh, Flying Officer Kinsman," the Flight Commander went on. He was a little man, slightly under the average height, and slim. He wore a brown moustache which was half grown and didn't look as though it would ever reach maturity, and this ornamentation he stroked nervously as he spoke to Kinsman. . . . "Your log-book. You left it yesterday. That's right. Now where . . ."

Dennis replaced the receiver. "Widdowson is in the circuit, sir."

"Well, now," Squadron Leader Barry said, laughing,

"isn't that decent of Widdowson? He's finally decided to come back to us."

The officer who had been sitting by the window, and who, so far, hadn't spoken or moved, now said without raising his head, "He'll probably forget to put his wheels down."

"No doubt," said the Flight Commander dryly.

Kinsman didn't speak. He felt awkward standing there listening to them joking about something of which he knew nothing. He smiled until he felt the smile on his face.

"Well, now, Kinsman," said the Squadron Leader again, "there's the question of your familiarization trip. Bora here could take you round."

From the direction of the Squadron Leader's glance Kinsman learned that Bora was the silent, thick-set fellow sitting beneath the window.

"How about this afternoon, Bora?" Barry asked. Then, as Bora slowly raised his head to speak, the Squadron Leader had another idea. "No . . . I tell you what . . ."

The 'phone rang.

". . . take it, Dennis, will you? I tell you what, Kinsman. I'll take you round this afternoon. I'm free this afternoon. Am I, Dennis?"

Dennis turned his face away from the 'phone as though the thing offended him. Then, after an almost imperceptible pause, he said, "Widdowson, sir, has pranged."

No one spoke. Then Barry stood up. He said loudly, "The clot!"

At that Bora came to life. He opened his mouth and burst into coarse laughter which sounded something like a very deep "Heh, heh, heh."

"Get the Hillman, Dennis. Does Winco know? Tell the Winco, Dennis. We'd better get out there. Where is the prang, Dennis?"

Dennis, who, so far, had not moved, said, "It seems he overshot on oh-three runway, sir."

"But he *can't* have. Not in that lovely new aircraft."

The Squadron Leader was almost at the door with Dennis and Bora when he remembered Kinsman, who was still standing there before his desk.

"You coming, Kinsman?"

"Yes, sir."

When they saw the Halifax it was lying across a crater which looked as though it might have been caused by a bomb which fell there a long time ago. Behind the Flight Commander and the other two Kinsman walked slowly around the machine, fascinated by the sad, sick air of humiliation which seemed to hang over the twisted fuselage.

The great wings, now purposeless, were half a dozen feet from the soft clay in which the nose was embedded. The four guns of the mid-upper turret pointed helplessly upward. With the others, Kinsman walked around to the front of the Halifax. There they saw that all four propellers were hopelessly buckled. It looked as though the aircraft had almost bounced across the crater but had just failed to reach safety. From where he stood, Kinsman could see the huge tail, tilted at a defiant angle, high above the rest of the plane. To him the machine seemed to be saying that the error was human, and not its own.

No one else appeared to be particularly worried about what had happened. It was all just part of the day's routine. This was the kind of thing that would be talked about for weeks on the other stations at which Kinsman had been, but he had a feeling that here it would be forgotten by tea-time.

Kinsman was staring at the great, black-painted aircraft when he heard a voice, laden with authority, behind him. He turned to see the Group Captain addressing Squadron Leader Barry. Along with the others, Kinsman saluted smartly. The Group Captain, his eyes on the little Squadron Leader standing before him, was saying something about bloody awful, and as though to deflect something of the great man's wrath, the Flight Commander said, "Anyone badly hurt, sir?"

The Group Captain, whose precise function was that of Station Commander, was a tall, heavily built man. Like Squadron Leader Barry, he wore a moustache, but it was long and silken, and when he forgot to stroke it back it hung low over his moist, sensitive lips. Group Captain Savory had a very fine complexion, and the dark beard which appeared to float just beneath the surface of his skin gave his face a peculiar, velvet-like appearance.

"They bloody well deserve to be hurt," the Group Captain said. There was no particular note of anger in his

33

voice. In fact the C.O. displayed so little emotion that Kinsman half expected him to smile.

"Looks like a bad show," Barry said lamely.

"Tom, I'm going to arrest this man. First of all he decides to spend twenty-four hours in Norfolk instead of coming back here. Then when he does come back he messes up my beautiful aerodrome. Arrange to have someone pick him up when the M.O's finished with him."

"Is he fit enough, sir?"

"Nothing," the Group Captain said in the same restrained, almost toneless voice as he had used before, "ever happens to that type. He's all right. Just damned sorry for himself. That's all."

At that Group Captain Savory saw the senior engineering officer examining the Halifax closely, so he turned quickly to join the engineer. Squadron Leader Barry and his three officers saluted, but the Group Captain ignored them.

"Poor old Widdowson," said Dennis.

"Really, Dennis. He is a bloody fool. It should be almost impossible to do a thing like that in this weather. The old man's quite right. You can't have people going around doing this sort of thing."

Kinsman had the feeling that little Squadron Leader Barry was too tired to care much. The indignation in his voice was forced, as though he felt that it was his duty to be annoyed at what had happened.

Bora said, "It's lunch-time, ain't it?"

Those were the first words he had spoken. He had seen the crashed aircraft and expressed no comment whatsoever. On his shoulder Bora wore a tab which said that he was an American, but to Kinsman he looked more like some kind of Southern European who spoke English.

"Yes," said the Squadron Leader, as though the idea had been his own, "let's go to lunch. There's nothing much we can do here."

Kinsman tried to open conversation with Bora on the way to lunch, but Bora, sitting thick-set and heavy beside him in the back of the Hillman van, answered only in monosyllables.

That afternoon Kinsman completed his familiarization trip with Squadron Leader Barry. Three times he took off over Widdowson's crashed Halifax, and three times he made reasonably good landings.

When the trip was completed, Barry, as they were walking back from the locker room to the Flight Office, said "You like the Mark III, Kinsman?"

Kinsman said he loved it.

"You've got a fair bit of time in, Kinsman."

"Yes, sir."

"I'm losing Dennis shortly. He's only got two to do. That'll leave me short of a deputy."

"Oh," said Kinsman.

They had reached the office then, and Barry said, "Did you sign the book, old boy?"

"Oh, I don't think I did."

"Always sign the book, old boy. Mustn't forget that."

On the way back to the mess, Kinsman couldn't get his mind away from Barry's words about Dennis ending his tour. Could he have meant that he was thinking of promoting him? It was unthinkable. Impossible. That would make him a Flight Lieutenant.

The evening of that day was sunlit. With Wakefield, Kinsman walked to the pub in the village. They talked of flying, and, with three good landings in a Mark III Halifax behind him, Kinsman felt much more confident. They talked of Widdowson's disaster of that day. Wakefield had been in bed when the accident happened, so Kinsman had to tell him all he knew. He talked until he thought of how shocked he would once have been to have seen an aircraft lying there broken. He thought of how long he would have wondered about Widdowson. Once he would have tried to imagine the boy's fear when he realized he was going to overshoot and it was too late to go round again. Now it was a shock to realize that he was thinking it almost funny that Widdowson should be spending that night in the guard-house.

When they returned to their billet, they were only a little drunk. Wakefield, although the night was warm, insisted that they should light the fire, and there were considerable confusion while he searched their room for anything that might prove inflammable. Kinsman fell asleep before the fire was lit, and, after calling his room-mate, a two-pint bastard, Wakefield continued his fire-raising activities with one of Kinsman's shoes.

CHAPTER FIVE

"I_F you look over my shoulder," John Kinsman said, "you'll see the one I mean."

Wakefield, resplendent in his number one blue, carefully placed his half-pint tumbler on the bar counter before taking his friend's advice.

"You mean the little one?"

"Yes, the little one with the teeth. She's very nice. Look at the way she smiles."

"Kinsman, there isn't time for that kind of higher appreciation. Give me them big and fat and . . . and foolish."

Wakefield emptied his glass with one long swallow.

"Is it all right us being here?" Kinsman asked.

" 'Course it is. Groupie's here. Everybody's here . . ." Wakefield paused. Then he said, "Where did she come from?"

"Who?" Kinsman asked.

"The one with the teeth."

"She was dishing out coffee at de-briefing the night we came back from Brest. She was the first thing I saw," Kinsman said.

"Trust our Johnny Kinsman. I've been here two months, and I've never seen her before."

"What's the matter with you? Go and dance with her."

Wakefield spoke to the man who was acting as barman. He asked for a large whisky and a small whisky. Then,

36

without turning his head, he said to his friend, "Have a look and see who she's with."

Kinsman ignored him. "What," he asked, "is all this large whisky and small whisky stuff?"

"My need is greater than yours. I can't afford to be buying you large whiskies."

"She's talking to Pop Barry," Kinsman said, "trust our Flight Commander. He just looks simple."

Kinsman laughed then. He raised the whisky which Wakefield had bought him to his lips, and, having emptied the glass, continued to laugh.

"What's so funny?" the other asked.

"You're funny. Why all the fuss about this female? This place is full of them. At least a dozen of them are ready and willing to eat you all up, and then start on me if I let them. What's the matter with you."

"I don't know," Wakefield said slowly. "I thought I'd cured myself of all decent feelings. But that girl frightens me."

"She's very nice," Kinsman said slowly, as though he really meant it.

"That's what it is. That's what frightens me. Let's get to hell out of here. Let's go back to the mess."

"No," Kinsman said, laughing. "I like it here."

The walls of the long, narrow hall were whitewashed. Normally the place served as the airmen's dining-hall, but now the station band occupied the platform which ran across the end of the hall. Girls in the uniform of the W.A.A.F. danced on the red stone floor with N.C.O.s who wore aircrew brevets and the faces of boys.

The harsh, fast rhythm of the band made their legs move jerkily, always in an opposite direction from their shoulders. Over the place there seemed to hang the influence of alcohol. Not so that anyone was yet overwhelmingly drunk, but it was there in the clink of glasses, and in the occasional loud, uninhibited laughter which would reach across the room, and in the energy expended by ageing corporals and aircraftmen first class and officers who had been brave in the other war.

To Kinsman the place never seemed to stop going round. People were all around him. People pressing close to the bar to get drinks. People pushing past on the floor, locked in each other's arms, dancing. It was a beautifully

37

confused world in itself, full of excitement and yet not dangerous. It was warm and it was happy, strangely of the moment in which they were living.

There was a fat girl standing in front of where Kinsman and Wakefield stood with their backs to the bar. She appeared to have been pushed there. One second, dancers were swirling past, and the next there was a gap, and this girl was standing there. Delicately balancing his glass in his hand, Kinsman swung around on his heel to place his drink on the counter.

"Guard that with your life," he said to Wakefield. "I'm going to dance."

"I thought we were going."

"Not yet. Wait till I dance."

The fat girl was literally snatched from Kinsman's arms. Just as he was about to tap her on the shoulder, an airman, whom it appeared she knew, burst through the crowd on the floor, and with a joyful cry of "Molly!" took her up in his arms.

At that someone grabbed Kinsman by the arm and swung him around. It was his bomb-aimer.

"Fred, you old bastard!" Kinsman gasped.

"Have a drink, skip."

"I've got a drink."

"Well, have another one with us."

"Who's us?"

"The lads. Chico and Geordie and Les. We're all here."

Kinsman laughed. "I thought you had gone into town to see your friend."

"I did. But she was hanging out the window when I came along the street to tell me that her husband was home on leave. I've been betrayed."

The mid-upper gunner had joined them then. He was Geordie, and he had a face which, when he wasn't flying or about to fly, was bright and red and healthy, full of laughing expression. Now in mock sadness he said, "Fred's proper upset. It hurts him to think of the woman he loves sleeping with her husband tonight."

"Tonight nothing. He'll be at it right now," Fred said in his slow, curiously gentle voice. "It's enough to drive a man to drink. I'm a sensitive man. I feel this kind of thing."

38

The gunner, Geordie, laughed. "Not as much as Sandra feels it."

"Who's Sandra?" Kinsman said.

"The woman," Fred said slowly, "that I love."

"Woo woo!" Geordie exclaimed. And he jumped high in the air, holding his backside with both hands as he did so.

Fred ordered drinks and Kinsman asked where the little rear-gunner was.

"There he is," Geordie shouted, and they turned to see little Chico, neatly pressed and his hair heavily oiled, dancing carefully with a plump little girl on the other side of the room. Chico always looked as though his mother had inspected his ears before he came out.

It was then that Kinsman turned to speak to Wakefield, but Wakefield was gone.

"Where's Wakefield?" he asked no one in particular.

"I saw him," Geordie said. "There he is. There, he's over there with the big shots."

Between the moving heads and shoulders, Kinsman could see his friend talking to Squadron Leader Barry and some others. The Group Captain was there, and that W.A.A.F. officer had been there too. But Kinsman couldn't see her. Then Wakefield moved slightly to his right, and she was there, smiling, Kinsman could see, to Wakefield.

"He's doin' all right," Fred said quietly. "Wouldn't mind a little bit of that myself."

Kinsman didn't hear him. He just stood there looking at the girl. There was a smooth regularity about her features, a kind of well-proportioned symmetry as she stood balanced sensibly on her heels looking up at Wakefield. Her hair was brown and worn with simplicity, and on her face, and in the way she moved her lips when she spoke, there was a look of tiredness. Kinsman wondered, as he looked at her, what it was about this girl that made Wakefield and himself find her attractive. There were better-looking women in that place right then. She wasn't seductive. It was something to do with the way she had of looking at you, as though she knew a great deal about you. And, vaguely, Kinsman had the feeling that, knowing you, she would be prepared to forgive you for all that you might be.

Then he saw her smile, and was surprised at the amount

39

of life that came into her eyes. Her beautiful teeth and her eyes seemed to light up her whole face. It was a beautiful smile, and yet, somehow, it retained a trace of sadness that perhaps was only there because Kinsman felt it there.

"Skip, your pint," Fred said.

Geordie leaned over and placed a hand on Kinsman's shoulder. "I think," he said slowly, "that our little old skipper's had his woman pinched by someone that was supposed to be his pal."

"Balls!" Kinsman exclaimed, laughing, and he walked towards Wakefield who, with one hand in his pocket, and the other limply holding his glass, talked to Squadron Leader Barry and the girl as though he had never said to Kinsman that he had been afraid of her.

Kinsman had almost joined them when Wakefield placed his glass on a window ledge and took the girl officer by the arm. He saw Kinsman, and on his lips there was the faintest of smiles, but he didn't speak. The girl looked at Kinsman as he approached, knowing that he was her partner's friend, and as she looked at him she smiled as she would have smiled to anyone else in the hall. They were on the floor and dancing when Kinsman joined the Flight Commander.

"Well, Kinsman, having a good time?"

Kinsman nodded but was silent, as though to reply would have been unnecessary.

"Who's that girl, sir?"

"Code and cypher, I think. Damned nice type. Julie something or other."

Julie. It wasn't quite the kind of name he expected her to have, but somehow, as soon as Pop Barry had said it, it was right for her.

"Looks as though our friend Wakefield's off his mark," Squadron Leader Barry said.

"Doesn't it?"

"The Group Captain's off his mark too," Barry went on.

"With her?"

"No. He's gone home. Mrs. Groupie doesn't allow him to stay any longer than an hour. His time's up."

Kinsman laughed. Pop Barry was a strange little man. One of the strangest things about him was that he was rather a good Flight Commander. The first impression you got of him was that he was an ineffectual, timid creature who was out of his depth. And that was partly true. He was old enough to be afraid on the ground as well as in the air. But he was saved by the fact that he was afraid for all of them. For some reason he had transferred to the Air Force from the Army after being evacuated from Dunkirk. Now he looked on the job he was doing as a man would look on a bride of two weeks who had betrayed him before the honeymoon was over.

Barry had taken to the air at an age when most men would have known better, and consequently had never succeeded in convincing himself that flying was a sensible thing to do. The air, to Barry, was an unpredictable tyrant, and for that reason he was probably more sympathetic towards the weakness of those who failed to master it than he should have been. When someone who had completed many operations failed to return from one of his last, Barry would pace up and down the control room staring at the captain's name and staring at it, as though by so doing he could will some sense into this business of war in the air.

Kinsman had been saying something about hoping the weather would break in order that they could get off the ground, when suddenly Barry interrupted him to say, "Oh . . . oh, by the way, Kinsman, your thing will be through in the next day or two. I think tomorrow, in fact."

"What thing, sir?"

"Your . . . your promotion, old boy. You're going to be Acting Flight Lieutenant Kinsman."

"Why . . . why . . . thank you, sir. Thank you very much."

"Nothing to do with me, old boy, really. You're just a more obvious choice than the rest."

"But I thought it was all off," Kinsman said. He was still trying to comprehend what Barry had just told him, and the words were spoken in order to allow him to think.

"It was," Barry said slowly, "until poor old Trotter bought it the other day."

Flight Lieutenant Trotter had been posted to the squadron a week after Kinsman had arrived. Trotter had held the substantive rank of Flight Lieutenant, and when posted to Barry's flight would automatically have been appointed a deputy Flight Commander, for he had done all

41

this before, and was returning to operational duty after a year's rest.

Kinsman said that it was too bad.

"It was such a damned silly place for a man like that to buy it. Brest, of all places. A silly little pansy daylight op like that, and Trotter buys it. I still can't believe it. There's nothing sensible about this business. There's no logic in it. You would think, wouldn't you, Kinsman, that it would take more than an op like Brest to kill a man like Trotter?"

"I saw him killed," Kinsman said. "Direct hit."

"I just can't understand it," Barry went on.

He stood there, looking past Kinsman, his face screwed up, as though by intense concentration he could find some sense in the job he was doing.

"Come and have a drink with me on the strength of what you've just told me."

"Of course . . . of course, old boy," Barry said eagerly.

Kinsman pulled his Flight Commander over to the bar where he found his crew still standing.

"Is this your crew, Kinsman?"

"Unfortunately, sir, yes."

"Did I get you an angineer?"

"Not yet, sir. We're still trying to forget the last one. We took a spare man with us to Brest."

Kinsman's crew was hushed by the presence of the Squadron Leader. They stood waiting for Kinsman to say something. But it was the Squadron Leader who said, "Your captain's been promoted. He's going to buy us all a drink."

"Promoted?" Fred gasped.

Kinsman was embarrassed. He said, laughing, "As from to morrow morning there'll be two rings on my sleeve. In future I want you all to stand to attention when I board the aircraft."

Above their laughing protests Kinsman called for more drinks, and they drank with no one mentioning again the reason for their celebration. Pop Barry's eyes were wandering in the direction of the dance-floor. He was a man who gave the impression of never being able to keep his mind in the same place as his body.

The bomb-aimer, Fred, asked the Flight Commander when Flight Lieutenant Kinsman was going to be allocated

42

an aircraft of his own, and vaguely, half turning his head, Barry answered that they would probably get Dennis's aircraft. Vaguely, because just then a girl was approaching them.

Her name was Paddy and she was the Wing Commander's typist. In an aggressive way, she was good-looking with dark hair and dark eyes. She was quite a tall girl, probably slightly taller than Squadron Leader Barry, and she had a way of looking at an officer which ignored his rank. To Paddy, all creatures who wore trousers were just men, and all men who weren't officers didn't exist.

"Hello . . . sir," Paddy said. There was the merest suggestion of a pause before she said "sir".

Kinsman turned to meet the girl, and, realizing that he was there, the Squadron Leader said, "Kinsman, do you know L.A.C.W. . . . eh . . . eh. . ." Barry couldn't remember the girl's surname.

"Paddy," she said, turning to Kinsman.

"Hrrmm." The Flight Commander coughed.

"Don't people in C Flight buy girls drinks or dance with them or anything?" the girl went on.

"Er . . ." The Flight Commander laughed and tugged at his moustache. He turned to Kinsman. "Do we, Kinsman?"

"We very seldom buy them drinks. But we dance with them," Kinsman said, and, handing his glass to Fred, who was standing behind him, he took the girl Paddy in his arms and proceeded to dance towards the centre of the floor.

This girl was all the excitement of that place in one warm tunic.

She danced close to him so that as, at intervals, she raised her face to speak to him, he could feel the smoothness of her forehead on his chin. The smell of her hair, and the faint, suggestive smell of gin, and the softness of her moving back which he could feel under his fingers: the noise, other people's laughter, the monotonous music, the inexpert movement of his own legs, the occasional rub of her knees against his, seemed to draw all of existence, at that moment, between his own arms.

She looked up at him as they moved across the floor.

"All right, skip?" Fred asked as they passed him.

43

"Who's he?" There was a suggestion of distaste in her words.

"One of my crew."

Her eyelids dropped. Then she said slowly, "You're new here."

"Not all that new," Kinsman answered. He didn't like her. Not the part of her that spoke.

She went on. She said, "You've got nice eyes."

There was no answer to that statement. She liked his eyes, but she didn't like Fred. His fingers tightened on her back, and he squeezed her hot palm more firmly. Stupid woman. Stupid with a wisdom that told her how to bring him down to a level where she was taller than he was.

"Let's go somewhere," he suggested.

"Where?" She smiled. "I like it here." She went on as though he wasn't altogether up to date with the facts. "This is the Station Dance."

"Oh," he said slowly.

She wriggled as though to break free from the closeness in which he held her, and he could feel her, soft, against his body.

"Boy," she said, "It's hot."

"Let's go outside," he suggested, "and cool off."

Paddy's lips curled as she looked up at him. "That's not the way to cool off," she said. "Buy me a drink."

So he bought her many drinks, and occasionally they danced. Each time he held her in his arms it was more difficult to let her go when the music stopped. Once they were standing at the edge of the floor and he tried to kiss her. She turned her head away, so he kissed her on the neck.

"Hey . . . hey, Kinsman," she protested, and when she tried to break free he staggered forward, almost pulling her with him to the floor. She became angry when he said she was an American because she spoke like an American. He'd learned to fly in America, and he knew how American women spoke, and she spoke like an American. Kinsman couldn't have known that Paddy's accent was the result of having had two Canadian boy friends.

As the evening wore on, the people in that place seemed to move faster, and Kinsman's neck more slowly. Occasionally he glimpsed some of his crew, and once he saw Wakefield. Wakefield was still with the officer girl. Wakefield was a funny bloke. He starts off the evening by saying that he wanted a woman, and ends up with that girl. She was a nice girl. She was a nice girl all right. But she wasn't a woman in the sense that she would let you get very far. Wakefield would be mad as hell when she shook hands at the entrance to the W.A.A.F. site, and thanked him for the lovely evening.

Kinsman had decided that this Paddy was dumb in a cunning kind of way. She gave the impression of thinking that because she knew the details inscribed forever on the record sheet of every aircrew officer on that station, that she also knew what made the world go round. But in spite of the fact that he was carrying as much alcohol, internally, as he could, without being sick there and then in the middle of the dance-floor, Kinsman gathered from the glances he received from those watching him with the girl that he was on to what was known as a "good thing."

She insisted on referring to those whom she should have addressed as "sir" by their Christian names. Once she spoke like that when the American, Bora, was with them and Kinsman winced. As soon as Bora was gone, he tried again to get her to leave the dance, but she wouldn't. Kinsman looked at the clock above the platform, and as far as he could see he would have to wait about forty minutes before he could be alone with her. It was a delicious thought.

Four bars of the National Anthem had been played before Kinsman realized that it was time to stop dancing. It was Paddy who pulled his tunic and told him to stand to attention. Then the crowd broke, and Paddy said eagerly, "Wait for me at the door."

She started to leave him, but he caught her by the arm.

"Wait a minute," he said. And he laughed. "Where you going?"

"To spend a penny."

He released his grip on her and said, "Don't be long."

Paddy never did come, and some hundreds of people had filed past him before Kinsman realized it. The realization came with a sudden quickening of his pulse, and he became aware of the fact that inside the hall there was near-silence. He looked in to see a small knot of airmen still standing at the bar where the barman was busy gath-

45

ering glasses together. He felt as though the tight-rope from which he had been dangling over emptiness had started to slip. He walked quickly into the dining-hall, so that he could hear the echo of his own footsteps, and had almost reached those standing at the bar when he saw that two of the men there were Geordie and Fred of his own crew. Instinctively he started to ask if they had seen the girl, but he caught himself before the sentence had gone too far, and asked instead if they intended to stay there all night.

His eyes wandered to all corners of the room lest by some odd chance Paddy might have fallen or something and was unable to get up. But there was no sign of a body. He walked over to the kitchen entrance, too, where she had headed, but she wasn't there.

"What's the matter with you?" Fred asked when he came close to them again.

"Where can we get some beer?" Kinsman asked.

"Some beer, he says!" said Geordie.

"We could celebrate."

"What?"

"Anything. Just celebrate. I feel like getting drunk."

Geordie laughed. "You are drunk."

"Everybody's drunk," Kinsman muttered.

Fred said they might get some beer from the sergeants' mess.

So they started towards the sergeants' mess, Kinsman and Geordie and Fred, and they were almost there, just passing the officers' mess, when Kinsman asked three other officers to join them.

How Fred got that beer no one knew, but when he and Geordie reappeared they were carrying what looked like a case of the stuff. Then someone brought a car which had been parked in front of the officers' mess, and they were on their way to Kinsman's billet.

The man who was driving the car drew up outside the billet with a terrifying screech of brakes, narrowly missing Tom Barry's little sports car which was parked there in the dark shadow of the hut.

Within two minutes of their arrival, Kinsman and his friends had awakened the entire block. Wakefield wasn't there, but there were loud shouts of protest from farther along the hall. Fred placed himself in peril of twenty-eight days in the glass-house by telling those half-asleep officers who had shouted at them to "wrap up". They didn't wrap up, but their protests were pointless, for those in Kinsman's room were occupied with the business of opening bottles. Then, when the first bottle was empty, someone had the idea of throwing it into a fire-bucket at the other end of the room. The bucket was empty, for it was actually Wakefields's ashtray, but with the first successful crash of thick glass the idea grew. It was decided to stage a contest, and three bottles crashed into the fireplace in quick succession. That was when Fred suggested that if they tried urinating in the bucket from the other end of the room there wouldn't be so much noise. But Kinsman wouldn't allow that.

"This is my home, Fred," he said. "And it's Wakefield's home too. It's my home . . ."

The door had opened, but no one had noticed that. The first indication of the Flight Commander's presence, was when he shouted in his rather high-pitched voice. "It's my home too, Kinsman, and the neighbors here are making the most God-awful row!"

"Hurre . e . eh!"

They descended on Barry in a body, and dragged him, in spite of his protests, right into the room. Someone thrust a large bottle of beer towards his mouth, and most of it was spilled over his shirt-front, Barry's tunic having been hurriedly pulled on when he thought investigation was necessary.

Gradually the room filled with officers from the other rooms in the block, and when the stock of beer looked like running low Fred disappeared with the officer whose car had brought them up from the mess. The first Kinsman knew of his bomb-aimer's disappearance was when the latter was making his triumphal reappearance with a fresh supply of beer.

"How does that fellow do it, Kinsman?" Barry asked.

"Don't know, sir. It's just Fred. Fred's a great chap."

Barry laughed. "This is a damned good party, Kinsman. I only hope the old man doesn't get to hear of it."

"He won't hear of it, sir. Won't say a word about it."

Wakefield! There was Wakefield standing over there in the doorway trying to fight his way into his own room, and laughing in the direction of Kinsman as though he thought the whole thing very funny. Finally he managed to push his way into the room, and Kinsman could see that he had the girl with him, the girl officer, Julie.

"Where'd you come from?" Kinsman shouted.

Wakefield waved and called back that they had come with Fred in the car. Then he turned to the door and spoke to someone outside. At that another officer came into the room leading a girl. He was a fellow with a double-barrelled name, Boscombe something or other. But the girl who followed was Kinsman's friend of earlier in the evening, Paddy. A dishevelled Paddy with a blank, slightly drunken expression on her face. When Paddy saw Kinsman standing there her eyes dropped, and then she looked up at him, pouting her lips defiantly.

Kinsman gave Wakefield two bottles of beer, and said to the girl who stood by his friend's side, "I'm afraid you'll have to drink it out of the bottle."

"Love to," the girl said, smiling.

Kinsman looked to Wakefield, waiting to be introduced.

"What's going on?" Wakefield asked.

"A party, I think."

Wakefield laughed. "In aid of what?"

"In aid of me. I decided to get tight."

"Did you supply all this beer?" Wakefield went on.

"No, it took the genius of Fred to get the beer. But I'll probably have to pay for it."

The girl tugged at Wakefield's sleeve and said, "Is this him?"

Wakefield nodded, and said to her, "The name, as I told you, is Kinsman, but I think he'd better call you Assistant Section Officer Holmes."

"Pay no attention to him," the girl said to Kinsman, "I'm Julie—Julie Holmes."

"You didn't tell me," Wakefield said then, "what all this is in aid of."

Kinsman's eyes had wandered in the direction of Paddy, and when he tried to look back at Wakefield there was a distinct suggestion of uncertainty in the movement of his neck. To Wakefield he said, "Love. I've been disappointed in love. I decided to get tight . . . no . . . I decided to get tighter. Who brought that tramp here?"

"Which particular tramp?" Wakefield asked.

The room was so full of people drinking that it was difficult to see Paddy for a moment. Then Wakefield said, "Oh, Paddy! Boscombe-Ferkin brought her here in the car with us. He was standing at the entrance to the Waafery with her when your Fred fellow stopped."

"She's a bitch!"

"No, no . . . she's Paddy," Wakefield said quietly, and then he hurriedly asked the girl Julie if she liked the beer.

At times there was so much noise in that room that it felt as though the roof would have to come off in order to allow its escape. Some more bottles were broken—accidentally now—and then somehow, someone broke a window and a little later Wakefield leant against the slender chimney which ran from the stove to the roof and the thing almost came crashing down amidst them. Kinsman insisted to Squadron Leader Barry, when the little man suggested that the party was possibly getting a little out of hand, that such incidents were necessary to an affair like this. They gave it atmosphere.

The girl, Paddy, managed to avoid Kinsman until they were accidentally thrown together. Squadron Leader Barry was there and Wakefield and Julie. They were all standing in a little group when Paddy appeared amidst them. To Kinsman she said shyly, "Hello."

He looked at her, and then pushed back a dark lock of hair in order that he could see her more clearly before saying, "You're a prize bitch!"

She slapped his face, and the shock to Kinsman was such that the bottle he had been holding fell with a crash to the floor.

"Bossy!" Paddy called to the man who had brought her to the party. "Did you hear what he called me?"

"What was that, Pat?" Bossy said vacantly. "Yes . . . yes, I heard him. Well, you are in a way, you know, aren't you?"

"That's what I told her," Kinsman said. And he laughed. They all laughed then, Wakefield especially thought the incident very funny. He became almost hysterical.

When it died, the party seemed to die slowly. People started to sit on the beds. Someone opened the window. Squadron Leader Barry went to his room. For Kinsman it ended when he fell asleep sitting with his legs across his bed and his back against the wall. Paddy was sitting there too, with Fred attempting to take the place of the officer who had brought her there. But Paddy, by now, was tired.

The energy of the place seemed to escape through the open window with the noise. Then Julie, conscious of the fact that she and the girl Paddy were very much out of bounds, insisted that she escort the airwoman to her billet, and Wakefield likewise insisted that he accompany both of them to the W.A.A.F. site. So, together, he and Julie helped Paddy to her feet, and when all three of them were gone, the only noise that was left came from Bora. Bora the silent, who had been awakened two hours previously by the sound of crashing beer-bottles, was now loudly protesting to someone who was sitting on the cast-iron stove that the only reason the Americans bombed Germany by day was because they didn't know how to fly at night.

Kinsman's back had slipped down the wall until now he lay stretched out on top of his bed, while Fred had slipped to the floor, his knees up to his chin and his long, thin, ugly face low on his chest. At intervals Fred muttered loudly, "You're a traitor, Bora, that's what you are. You're a traitor."

Two batmen attended to the needs of the officers who lived in that block. One of them was a little stocky Scotsman who was known as Jock, and he it was who tried with the greatest difficulty to wake Kinsman on the following morning. The desolation of that room did not dismay Jock. He had been there for three years. When he entered the room he stepped over the body of Fred who lay on the floor alongside his captain's bed, and said, "Sur . . . sur, there's a call on. All C Flight crews to report to the Flight Office immediately."

Kinsman stirred, turned over, and immediately fell asleep again.

"Sur!" Jock went on.

Wakefield awoke at that. "Did I hear you say there's a call on, Jock?"

"Aye, sur. All crews to be at the Flight Offices. . . ."

"Not now."

Just about then Fred opened one eye and started to drag himself up to a sitting position.

"Ten o'clock, sur. All crews." Jock winked to Wakefield, who was in better condition than the other two.

"Who said this?" Wakefield asked.

"They said it on the 'phone, sur."

The batman once more had to turn his attention to Kinsman. He shook the sleeping officer and called loudly, "Sur, there's a call on. There's an ops on, sur."

Life came gradually to Kinsman. His mouth was dry and when he closed it, he felt as though his lips had died during the night. Gradually he became aware that things were not as they should have been. He raised himself on one elbow, and it was then that he saw Fred and the broken window and the glass on the floor over by Wakefield's bed. Kinsman groaned, and allowed his head to sink back on to his pillow.

But Wakefield could laugh, and in a loud voice said, "Have a drink, lads!"

No one answered. Fred was rising slowly to his feet, his long, hard body looking almost as though it was uncoiling itself. He spoke to no one. Kinsman, though, opening his eyes once more, saw his bomb-aimer leaving, and felt a sudden pang of friendship for Fred. His head bowed, not, of course from any feeling of remorse, but just because it felt heavy, poor Fred looked very sad. In spite of how he felt, Kinsman laughed, and managed to say, "Fred, you look bloody awful."

Fred didn't turn around. He merely said, "See you down at the Flights, skip."

"What's happening?" Kinsman asked Wakefield.

"Do you mean what's happened? . . . You and half the squadron got tight in our room."

"I don't mean that. What's happening now?"

"There's some kind of call on."

"Can't be now," Kinsman said.

"Ten o'clock," Wakefield said.

"A daylight, do you think?"

"Maybe. . . . Maybe the M.O.'s going to lecture us on the perils of going with women to whom we haven't been introduced."

"What time is it now?"

"It's the morning after." Wakefield laughed. Then, seriously, he said, "We've got half an hour or so . . . unless you want to rush down to the mess and have some of that nice, greasy fried bread that they give you for breakfast."

"Shut up."

Kinsman found a cigarette, but the taste, when he lit it, was unpleasant. Through the broken window he could see the tree which grew there, gently rustling in the morning breeze. He wondered how long it had been since he had realized that trees still existed. He stretched his whole body along the bed, leaving his arm dangling over the side. He was alive.

Kinsman wondered what Aunt Lizzie or old man Faighley, who had employed him at the *Western District News*, would have thought of the life that he was now living. No matter what they thought, though, it was a good life. You didn't have to plan. You didn't have to think. All you had to do was live. And it was good to live, and to be so aware of living. In the old days he could never remember being aware of just living. Now, if you had a good billet and some friends, and a few hours to yourself, you were happy. There was no need to plan or wonder if, by getting drunk, you were affecting your whole future. Now he had a job he could do well. In those days he was nothing, only a little boy who was afraid of almost everyone; and home and Aunt Lizzie and Mr. Faighley and even the memory of Dawson and Robby, his friends who had gone with the Territorials at the beginning, were so much a part of those days.

Kinsman sat up quickly, and shouted across to Wakefield, "What was the name of the girl you were with last night?"

"Julie," Wakefield said.

"Julie what?"

"Holmes. Assistant Section Officer Holmes to you."

"I used to be madly in love with a girl called Holmes. Her name was Chris Holmes. Let's have breakfast."

"Breakfast?"

"That's what I said—bub . . . breakfast."

"You sound like Bora.

"I like Bora!" Kinsman said as he got out of bed.

CHAPTER SIX

"Aye, aye," said Wakefield. He waited for some reply, and then went on, "As they say in your native land."

Still Kinsman, walking beside him on the road that led to briefing, said nothing. So Wakefield tried again. He said, "Your own, your very own, your native land . . . or something . . . what's the matter?"

Kinsman spoke. He said, "Nothing. I'm merely trying to appreciate the solemnity of the occasion."

"How can you do that when we don't know how solemn the occasion is going to be? The solemnity, I should say, of this occasion will be determined by the direction of that little red line which stretches across the map on the wall towards which we are now progressing."

"Why can't you shut up?"

"But I can't. I'm not one of your dour—"

"Doer."

"Doer, door, dower Northerners. I come from a sun-kissed land where men march to war with laughter in their eyes, and a kiss, a kiss left on their lips by the woman they've left behind."

"Who kissed you?"

"No one," Wakefield went on, "but I wish someone would. I feel as randy as an old drake. I always do before an op. . . . Do you think there's something peculiar about me, Mr. Kinsman, sir?"

"Does your nose light up in the dark?"

"No, I can't say that it does."

53

"Do you ever feel an impelling urge to walk into the briefing-room on your hands and knees?"

"No."

"But you do have this feeling of . . . of . . ."

"Randyness, Mr. Kinsman, sir."

"Always before an op?"

"No, sir, more especially before an op."

"For boys or for girls?"

"For girls."

"Pity," Kinsman said seriously. "I'm afraid there is something peculiar about you, Wakefield."

Wakefield swung his left arm in the direction of his friend's midriff. A small van pushed through the airmen scattered over the road behind them, and then hooted loudly as it was about to pass them. A girl's face appeared at the open window. It was the face of Assistant Section Officer Holmes. She asked them if they wanted a lift. But they declined the offer.

"I like her," Kinsman said.

"You like her. I *love* her."

Kinsman laughed, and then said, "You love everything from afternoon tea to that dog you're always talking about."

Wakefield laughed, and started to sing lightly something about "How can I tell you that I love you?" and then broke off by saying something about writing songs for a living if the prospects of living were such that the problem might ever arise.

When they arrived at the briefing-room, most of the squadron were already there. Kinsman's crew had seated themselves on a form which ran along the back wall of the long, narrow room. They greeted him noisily as he sat on the bench, leaving Wakefield to look for his own crew amidst that sea of dusty blue uniforms.

"Have a gander at that lot," Fred the bomb-aimer said to Kinsman.

He looked towards the huge map which hung on the wall above the raised platform from which briefings were conducted. The red tape which reached out from base appeared to make its way to the south-eastern corner of the Ruhr.

Kinsman went through the motions of laughing. He looked at the navigator—the humorless, silent New Zealander, Bob—and said lightly, "If Bob can find it we can get there."

"And back, skip," said Geordie, who was the mid-upper gunner.

"Don't worry about that, Geordie. We can always walk back. The war'll go on for a long time yet."

Little Chico, who manned the rear turret, bounced up and down on the bench and said, "That's right. I've got on me clean underwear so that I won't be embarrassed if they take me prisoner."

"Don't be talking like that," Fred said.

Kinsman looked at Fred. Long, thin lines ran down the bomb-aimer's face on either side, from his lean nose to the edges of his jaw-bone. Fred stared straight in front, ignoring those on either side of him, his eyebrows pulled down low over those grey eyes of his. Someone who didn't know Fred might have described him, in the language of juvenile fiction, as "hawk-like". But there was nothing of the hawk in Fred, and if there ever had been, his years in London's Police Force had killed the bird. But there was strength in Fred. Real strength.

Without turning his head, Fred said, "Here's the Winco."

Unevenly, the squadron rose to its feet. Wing Commander Carr, his tall, soft-looking, almost shapeless body slightly stooped as he talked to the Group Captain by his side, walked quickly between the aircrews. Someone near the front shouted, "Hurrah!" There was a buzz of laughter. The Group Captain sat on the front bench, where the senior Intelligence officer and the met. man were already seated with the engineering officer. Wing Commander Carr, betraying the impression created by his appearance, leaped lightly on to the platform and turned to face the squadron.

"You've all seen where we're going. . . ."

A voice: "You wouldn't nob it."

There was a gasp of laughter from the squadron. The Wing Commander smiled.

"The target is a synthetic oil-plant at a place called Sterkrade. Some of you will remember having been there a month or so ago. . . ."

Kinsman expected some wag to comment on this, but now they were silent. They had settled down.

The Wing Commander went on, "It seems they require another visit from us." He smiled. "And that's what they're going to get. H-hour is 01.15 as far as this squadron is concerned. The whole thing should be over in seven minutes." He went on to talk of the flight plan, reminding them that it was absolutely essential that they should rigidly obey the instructions given to them, and pointing out the reasons for the route which zigzagged its way from the coast to the target. The Wing Commander finished his briefing and then, after wishing them the best of luck, stepped down from the platform to allow the senior Intelligence officer to take his place.

That gentleman told them what Intelligence had learned of the activities of the plant they were about to attack, and then went on to discuss what was known of the enemy's fighter defences in the area through which they would be flying. Then the little met. man spoke of the weather they could expect on the trip; the engineer officer, a greying man of about fifty who wore a long-service medal on his tunic, advised them on engine handling. Briefing was over, except for the Group Captain's customary moral-boosting speech.

The Group Captain mounted the platform with considerable presence, and the Group Captain said, "Well, chaps, errr . . . you've heard all the gen. Looks like a good trip. Errr . . . have a good trip. Rather wish I was coming with you. Best of luck!" And, having said these words, the Group Captain stepped down from the platform.

There was much scraping of benches on the hard stone floor as the squadron stood up. Briefing was over.

The locker room occupied part of a building opposite Station Headquarters. Liscombe Farm had been built early in the war. It was a dispersed airfield, designed so that it could not easily be knocked out from the air. There were bits and pieces of offices and workshops scattered all over the aerodrome. But no one seemed to have found an excuse for using all of that concrete building in which was housed the locker room. That part which was empty looked like a great high-roofed barn, and it was there that Kinsman found his crew waiting, when he had dressed in flying-clothes.

Fred commented adversely on the blue seaman's jersey

which had been given to Kinsman by a pilot in the Fleet Air Arm. Now it was worn over his battledress, and, but for the parachute harness which pulled it between his legs, it would have reached down to his knees. Kinsman sat on the floor with the others and leant against the wall as Wakefield walked across the concrete floor and sat down beside him.

Wakefield said, "Watcher."

Kinsman lit a cigarette, gave one to his friend and then threw the packet to his crew, who sat on the floor alongside him, leaning against the wall. They all grabbed one except the New Zealander, Bob. He was busily marking figures on a chart which was spread out before him on the floor, for Bob took his job very seriously.

Wakefield, seeing what Bob was doing said, "It's a bloody good thing someone in your crew knows where they're going, Kinsman."

"Isn't it?" Kinsman said, smiling.

Fred looked at Wakefield and then said to Kinsman, "What happens to you if you hit an officer with an Aldis lamp, skip?"

"You'll get ninety days if you hit me," Wakefield said quietly.

Outside, the buses had arrived to take the crews to their aircraft on the perimeter of the airfield. An N.C.O. stood at the door shouting out the alphabetical letter by which each aircraft was known, as space became available on a bus for the aircraft's crew. Wakefield and Kinsman, being in C Flight, had to wait until most of the others had gone, for their aircraft were Sugar and Zebra respectively.

The room was so bare and, because there was insufficient light, dull. The crews, some of them dressed, some still dressing, were straggled all over the place. It was quiet, and then, occasionally, there would be a burst of young, boyish laughter that came close to hysterical giggling. Some, like Kinsman, Wakefield, and the former's crew, sat around the floor; others leant casually against the whitewashed wall; one or two walked impatiently up and down, as though they were unable to stand still. The noise of their being there echoed back at them from the high grey walls.

They were silent until Fred, after taking a long pull on his cigarette, said, "It ain't exactly glamorous, is it?"

"Glamorous . . . Christ!" Geordie exclaimed.

"Oh, I don't know," Wakefield said, "this captain of yours cuts a fine figure with his seaman's jersey. Look at him."

"I like to look my best at a time like this. . . . We'll be going out in a minute. . . . What was that letter he called?" Kinsman said.

"Peter."

"R . . . S . . . You'll be in the next bus, Wakey. You'd better gather those boys of yours together."

Wakefield raised himself to his feet. When he stood up, he eased the parachute harness from between his legs. Then he turned to look down at Kinsman sitting there on the floor.

"Now are you sure, Kinsman, that there's nothing I've forgotten to tell you?" he said.

Kinsman looked up at him and smiled. Then, quietly, he spoke. He said, "Shove off, chum."

"That's what I'll do," Wakefield answered solemnly. "That's what I'll do." He started to walk over to his own crew, but after a few paces he turned back to say, "Good trip."

"You too, boy," Kinsman answered.

Wakefield walked away, and then Kinsman could hear the N.C.O. at the door calling out the letter of his friend's aircraft.

"Roger. . . . Sugar. . . . Tommy!" the man called as Wakefield and his crew gathered up their gear and walked out to the bus without looking back.

Suddenly Kinsman hated to see his friend go. Somehow, with Wakefield there it was possible to laugh at the job they were doing.

He was cold, so he stood up and fiddled with the harness of his parachute. He adjusted the thing, and then readjusted it.

"We're next," Fred said.

Now the large, barn-like room was almost deserted, and outside the sky was darkening. Soon it would be night and he would be out there alone. Kinsman thrust his hands into his pockets. It was reassuring to feel the warmth of his own body. He lit another cigarette, and sucked deeply on the thing, as though trying to taste more keenly the flavor of the tobacco.

"Fred, give me one of those sweets," Kinsman called.

"Can't, skip."

"Why?"

"Can't eat the rations until we've been through the target."

"Oh."

"I've got some from the last trip," little Chico said. "Here, skip, have one of mine."

Kinsman took the sweet and placed it in his mouth. He looked to the door. The bus that was to take them hadn't arrived. He wished to God the thing would hurry.

"No bus?" he said to the N.C.O. at the door.

"Something must have gone wrong," the man answered, "It should have been here by now."

Kinsman looked down at himself. Again he tested his harness to see it wasn't too slack. His trousers were comfortable about the crutch. He wriggled his toes inside the warm, fleece-lined boots. He was very much alive. Everything was in order.

Then the bus came, and they left the empty building. With two other crews they climbed into the vehicle. The man who had been supervising the dispatch of crews to dispersals slammed the door tight, and the driver, probably feeling the urgency of the occasion, revved the engine fiercely as they rumbled off. No one spoke. They sat on benches which ran along each side of the interior of the bus, each one of them avoiding the eyes of the fellow opposite, silent. Then they arrived at Yorker's dispersal bay, and that crew got out. As soon as they were gone, Chico and Geordie and Fred all started talking at once.

Zebra, which had been Dennis' aircraft, crouched over them like a huge black frog. The bus drew up underneath one of the great wings, and when he jumped after the others on to the concrete bay and looked up at the big plane, Kinsman wondered that the thing was capable of flight. The corporal and his three ground-crew came out to greet them from the hut which they had built with empty petrol-cans and corrugated iron.

"All ready and rarin' to go?" Kinsman said to the corporal, whom he had never seen before.

The man, who was a quiet man, seemed to look him over, and then said that everything was as it should be. Kinsman felt that this corporal was judging him in relation

59

to Dennis. Dennis had flown Zebra since it was new, and now the corporal, who was in charge of the aircraft's day-to-day maintenance, while not exactly displaying resentment in his attitude to Kinsman, seemed, without saying a word, to be telling him that he had some sort of tradition to live up to.

"When are you off, sir?"

Kinsman looked at his watch. "We've got about twenty minutes."

The airfield had started to come to life. From away down at those bays nearest to Flying Control came the sound of revving engines, and from where they stood they could just see the first aircraft taxi-ing out to take-off point. The gunners, Geordie and Chico, were now in their turrets checking up on the movement of their guns, and Bob, the navigator, was sorting out his maps and equipment in the little office he would occupy in the nose of the aircraft under Kinsman's feet.

Kinsman didn't go into the aircraft. He looked at the sky, and then across the green airfield to the straggling trees on the other side. The light was going fast, and the thought came to him that it would be almost dark when they took off.

There was an upturned petrol-drum at the door of the ground-crew's hut, and Kinsman walked across the soft, muddy grass to sit on it. He was lighting a cigarette when he saw an airman inside the little hut and bent over the tiny fire which they had rigged up to work from the power of an aircraft battery. Kinsman offered the man a cigarette, and he came out to smoke.

"What are you?" Kinsman asked.

"Rigger . . . sir."

"Like it here?"

"Not bad."

Fred ambled over to where his captain was sitting then, and placed his parachute on the grass preparatory to lighting a cigarette.

"I wouldn't do that, Fred," Kinsman said. "You might need that thing, and it wouldn't be much good to you wet."

"There they go," Fred said.

Kinsman followed the eyes of his bomb-aimer, and saw

the airfield controller's lamp flashing green. A big black Halifax was rumbling towards take-off point.

"The only good thing about watching A flight go off first," Fred said, "is knowing that they've got to wait up there for us."

The Halifax which was about to take off was turning on to the runway. Then, its nose headed into the wind, it stopped. Kinsman sat with his elbows leaning on the parachute which was across his knees, his eyes half closed for protection from the smoke which rose slowly from the cigarette between his lips. The Halifax's engines came to life, and then died away again. Then again they were revved up.

"There she goes," Fred said.

The plane started to move slowly forward. Then the noise of its engines rose in intensity, until they were drowned in the noise of all the other engines which were being prepared for take-off. The Halifax now racing towards them raised its tail, its engine screaming as though in protest at the effort that was being asked of them. The pilot anxiously tried to lift it from the runway before it was ready, and the great thing settled slowly back on to its wheels. Again he lifted it; it settled again, but not back on earth. It was airborne, its nose was down, and it roared for the hedge at the end of the runway. Kinsman watched it pass him, and then let his eyes go back to the controller. The green light was flashing to the next aircraft which was moving into position.

"We'd better get cracking," he said.

The gunners, having checked their guns, had come out of the Halifax to smoke, but now, seeing Kinsman and Fred walking towards the hatch, they quickly extinguished the cigarettes they had lit, and rushed to the grass at the edge of the bay to empty their bladders. Kinsman followed them, and did likewise.

"Fit?" Kinsman asked as he stood alongside him.

The gunners said nothing. The three turned to see that Fred was urinating against the wheel of the Halifax.

"Heh!" one of the gunners called.

"That's for good luck," Fred said dryly.

Kinsman followed them into the belly of the aircraft, and then made his way along the fuselage to his controls.

61

He fixed his parachute in its holder and then, climbing into his seat, secured his safety straps.

"All right, Bob?" he called down to the navigator.

Something which sounded like a grunt came back from Bob below.

"All O.K., Les?" he then asked the wireless operator.

"Right, skip."

The ground-crew outside was moving the starter battery into position underneath the port wing. The corporal called to Kinsman that they were ready when he was. A roar came to his ears from the aircraft in the next bay, and he realized that he would have to move fast with the engine check. From where he sat there, high up in the Halifax, he could see Wakefield's aircraft. It looked as though Wakefield had already completed his checks for the engines of his plane were ticking over smoothly.

The engineer, who had never before flown with Kinsman, had been making sure that all the petrol-cocks were in their correct positions. Now he leant over Kinsman's shoulder, and said, "All ready when you are, skip."

"Right, eh . . ."

"Dick."

"O.K., Dick. See if they're ready outside."

The engineer looked out and announced that the ground-crew were ready to start the port inner engine. Kinsman switched on the ignition.

"Contact!" the fitter called from underneath the port wing.

The engineer pressed one of the four starter buttons which were on his instrument panel, and the engine spluttered harshly. Then reluctantly, it came to life. The same procedure was repeated with the three other engines. All engines running, Kinsman checked that the intercom system was working properly. Then, when he was allowing the engines to reach their minimum temperature for running up, he looked at his watch.

At briefing, each captain was designated a time at which he should taxi out for take-off. Each aircraft, it was planned, should taxi out at one-minute intervals. In this way it was hoped that the whole squadron would be airborne in about twenty-five minutes. Kinsman saw that he had six minutes until he left the dispersal bay. A curious impatient tightness seemed to be inside him, and as he waited for the engineer to read the cylinder-head temperature gauges, he willed the things to rise.

When the wireless operator had switched on the intercom there had been some talking between the crew, but now they were silent. Each man was ready, and alone. The engineer, standing by Kinsman's side, looked back and forth at his instrument panel. Once their eyes met, and Kinsman winked at him. The other fellow smiled an embarrassed sort of smile. Kinsman thought it strange that a man should be embarrassed at a time like that.

Yorker, the Halifax in the next bay, was taxi-ing out, so Kinsman ignored the temperatures of his engines, and started his check. Rather hurriedly he ran up each engine, and checked that the mag. drop was within the specified limits in each case. Finished, he looked out to see the ground-crew standing by to pull away the big blocks of wood which had been in front of the wheels. Then, very smoothly, and almost silently, the Halifax moved forward. It felt good to see the ground-crew standing down there with thumbs upraised in salutation. It gave Kinsman a feeling of strength. There was no wondering or hesitation in him now. Now there was a job to be done, and he was doing it as he had been trained. The aircraft sounded good, and the crew were with him in eagerness. In minutes they would be airborne, and all this waiting would be over.

Now there was a procession of aircraft in front of him, all heading for take-off. The light had almost gone, and Kinsman, braking his Halifax so that twenty yards always separated him from Yorker, which moved along the perimeter track in front of him, could just see the gunners in Yorker's turrets caged like unhappy animals.

This was his third operation, and his second at night. Last time it had been a much gayer affair. They had gone off in daylight. Each aircraft had progressed to take-off as though taking part in some triumphal procession. From mid-upper turrets and astro-domes the crews had thrust flags and mascots. His own Fred had flown a pair of ladies' cami-knickers as they passed the crowd outside Flying Control, and when Kinsman had protested on learning what the crowd were laughing at, Fred had insisted that he had gone to great trouble to acquire the mascot. He went further, and claimed that he had had the things specially stained for the occasion.

One after the other, with thrilling monotony, aircraft roared down the runway into the wind, and when Kinsman had taxied close enough to discern the figure of the airman wielding the signal light from on top of the black-and-white hut at the end of the runway, there were only two Halifaxes in front of him.

It was so dark now that it was impossible to read the letters on the side of the fuselages of the planes in front. Then one of them turned slowly on to the runway, and as the light from the flarepath caught it, Fred, who was now standing beside him, said, "Wakefield."

It was Wakefield's aircraft. His letter being S, he should have been off by now. Kinsman smiled into the mask which covered his face as he thought of his friend being held up. He brought the Halifax to a stop as the fellow in front stopped his. Then he looked towards Sugar. It was so hard to believe that it was his room-mate who was controlling that thing. It looked so inhuman, like some great beast that was deciding for itself what it should do. The big black Halifax with the caricatured figure of a blonde painted on its nose now looked grotesque as Kinsman saw it in the yellow light of the flares.

Wakefield had steadied the Halifax, having pointed its nose into the wind. Then Kinsman saw his props almost disappear as he revved up the engines on the brakes. Then, as though someone had given a rather matronly lady an undignified push, Sugar moved forward when Wakefield released his brakes. Briefly, Kinsman saw the figure of someone at the controls as the Halifax started down the runway. It was Wakefield, sitting straight and tense and masked.

The engineer was now behind Kinsman, watching the dials on his instrument panel, and Fred had come up from the nose to assist his captain at take-off. The Halifax in front had received a green, and as it turned on to the runway into Wakefield's slipstream, Kinsman started into his final cockpit check. His hand reached out to each control as he said to himself, "Trim . . . mixture . . . pitch . . . fuel . . . flaps." All controls were in the correct position. But now the Halifax which had taxied along from dispersal in front of him had started to roll forward, and, hurriedly, he went through the cockpit drill again. His fingers moved gently, almost lovingly, over the control column and the throttles.

They gave him a green, and he said, "Here we go."

The Halifax in position, he revved up the engines to about fourteen hundred r.p.m. Then, having received his final green, he turned to Fred. Fred was looking at him as he turned, and with his eyes, which were all of his face that Kinsman could see, the bomb-aimer signalled that he was ready. Slowly Kinsman eased the throttles open.

As he had turned on to the runway, he had looked at the sky, and, momentarily, he had felt something of a sinking sensation as he thought of how lonely it would be out there. By now all he could see were the two lines of yellow flare-path lights, reaching out almost to join together out there in the dark.

To counteract torque, he opened his port throttles more fully than the starboard. She swung to port in spite of that, and he almost jumped out of his seat on to the starboard rudder control. The weight of the whole aircraft seemed to be on his right foot. Then he eased the stick forward to raise her tail. She wouldn't have it, until they gathered speed and the slipstream brought the tail up. The pressure eased on his right rudder. The roaring of the engines increased as his right hand opened the throttles. Fred had one hand, cupped, behind Kinsman's which was controlling the engines.

The throttles were fully open, but Kinsman held the Halifax down as she strained to leave the ground.

"Clamp!"

Fred slammed the clamp on the throttles, and Kinsman now had both hands on the stick. He took her from the ground, and seconds later the lights of the flare-path slipped beneath them, and there was nothing out there but darkness.

"Wheels!" Kinsman breathed into the intercom. He purposely kept his voice quiet to disguise the tension which was in his throat.

They were airborne, and, as he watched the speed build-up on the instrument panel, John Kinsman switched off his intercom, and then sucked breath deeply through his mouth.

At ten thousand feet the stream flew south until they

passed over what the navigator said was Reading. Then they started the long, slow climb to their operational height. Flying over England on the way south, Kinsman had felt as though he was taking part in some kind of gaily lit carnival. All around him there had been the red and green navigation lights of other aircraft, but now, one by one, the lights were extinguished, until by the time they reached the South Coast there was nothing to see at all.

For a long time the crew had been silent. Kinsman, at regular intervals, had spoken to the gunners, but below him old Bob, the navigator, had been busy with his charts, and Fred was busy too. Kinsman had never quite discovered how Bob occupied Fred so completely on the way to a target, and he didn't like to ask, for he had a feeling that it was something he should have discovered at operational training unit. The wireless operator, since they were maintaining R.T. silence, busied himself with a book.

Ahead there was three and a half hours of flying before they reached their target. Then, it seemed such a dismally long time. The aircraft had been trimmed and retrimmed until it was climbing at exactly two hundred feet per minute, and was maintaining an air-speed of one hundred and seventy miles per hour. Again and again he had looked at the instruments on his panel, and each time they were reading exactly as they should have done.

Reminding him that he wasn't alone there, there was a crinkle in the intercom, and he heard Bob's voice asking Fred to see if he could get a landfall as they were crossing the coast.

Fred's voice came back saying, "Do you think I'm a bloody owl or something?"

There was silence again.

The two downstairs switched off their intercom, and their voices faded away. It was as though these two who were so familiar to him had visited him there briefly, and then gone away into the darkness outside. He checked the grid on the compass. He checked the oxygen supply. He checked the gyro compass. Again he trimmed the aircraft, and, taking his hands from the control column, allowed the big Halifax to fly by itself as long as it would. He had worked out something of a routine for himself, and, after he had gone through it, he looked at his watch. If fifteen minutes had passed, he called up the rear-gunner. He held no conversation with Chico. All he said was, "Hello, gunner."

"Skip?" Chico always said.

"O.K."

"All O.K."

Then, five minutes later, he would speak to Geordie in the mid-upper turret.

On the way south to Reading they had climbed through some wet-looking cloud, and the thought had passed through Kinsman's mind that conditions might not be so good when they returned to England. When they were approaching the enemy coast, and still climbing towards their operational height of twenty thousand feet, they went to a thick layer of cloud.

Kinsman sat straight up in his seat when they hit the first grey wisps of the stuff. For some time they had been climbing through a sky that was black and still. Only the occasional dangling sway of the Halifax, and the steady drone, droning of the four Hercules engines, told him that he was moving at all. There was nothing with which he could compare his speed. Reality existed only in the feel of the rudder-bars against his feet, and the warm, clinging rubber of the oxygen mask which was strapped across his nose and mouth. Out there, was nothing.

But now there was cloud, and, as its first filmy edges swept past him, the figure at which the needle on his air-speed indicator was pointing became real. The Halifax entered the solid gray mass, and as it did so Kinsman's first instinct was to duck. He did that. And he gripped the stick more tightly. He had no idea as to what type of cloud this was. At briefing they had made no mention of dangerous formations on the route, for he would have heard the met. officer if he had said anything about the dangerous cloud which was called cumulo nimbus. He was bound to have heard him.

Inside Kinsman, there fluttered a terrible desire to turn away from this stuff. But he couldn't. There was no particular reason to be afraid just because he could see nothing of the sky above, but, somehow, instinct made him want to turn away. That was impossible.

All he could do was sit there. The Halifax's route had

been laid down for it, and his job was to see that it stayed on that route. He experienced a feeling of helplessness. It was as though he was hanging on to the tail of this thing, and being dragged through the sky whether he liked it or not.

Kinsman had been peering into the darkness since take-off, lest another aircraft should cross their path. Now he stared ahead, seeing nothing except that thick grey wall of cloud, rushing at him with furious speed.

Bob's voice came to him. "What speed are you at, Johnny?"

"A hundred and seventy, Bob."

"You should be at one eight five."

Kinsman caught a curse in his throat, and then said quietly, "I'm trying to get clear of this cloud."

"We've got a course alteration coming up in three minutes," the navigator told him.

"All right. Give me it."

"One two zero. I'll tell you when to start turning."

The overcast through which they were climbing was becoming lighter in color, and Kinsman had a feeling that they would clear it soon. In that stuff he seemed to feel that the Halifax's nose was up. With the overcast thickening and then clearing slightly, getting lighter and then again darker, Kinsman felt that his aircraft was clawing its way up into the sky. The roar of the engines seemed to be greater in that cloud world than it had been in the limitless darkness through which they had been flying before, and Kinsman placed a hand on the throttles, as though to check his engines in their enthusiasm.

"Start turning now," Bob said.

Kinsman turned the Halifax, while still climbing, on to its new course. It occurred to him that by now they must be well into enemy territory, so he switched on the microphone which was fitted into his oxygen mask.

"How are we doing, Bob?" he asked.

"We were a minute and a half early there. We're on the long leg now. If we don't lose it by the time we reach the next turning-point I'll give you a dog leg." Bob's voice trailed off as he told Fred who, now, was acting as a kind of assistant navigator, to hand him some instrument or other.

The engineer had just announced that he was about to change tanks, when Bob again asked Kinsman at what speed he was flying. Kinsman told him that they were maintaining one six five, and still climbing.

"Lord! Why?" Bob said.

"Trying to clear this cloud. I'll go back down when we clear it."

Bob started to say something about the flight plan, but he was cut off. "Balls to the flight plan. I'm the flight plan," Kinsman said. And there was silence.

They were flying now in a kind of half-world, where the cloud was different from that through which they had climbed. It was almost like mist. Kinsman wasn't sure whether they were still in it or not. A tiny flash of fear shot through him when he wondered whether or not they were on the right course. For a long time now, since before they had crossed the Channel, he had seen nothing of the ground. They hadn't said at briefing that the weather would be like this. Or if they had, he hadn't heard them say it. Since just after Reading, though, he hadn't seen another aircraft. He felt so bloody lonely. If only he could see something. The ground. A light. The flash of ack-ack guns. Anything.

Soon he did see. There was a yellow flash which lit up the mist ahead and slightly to port, below. Almost before Kinsman could think, the mid-upper's voice came over the intercom saying, "Somebody's bought it."

Then there was a similar flash straight ahead, and the mid-upper, Geordie, spoke again. "Aye, aye," he said.

"Where?" Fred was speaking. "I didn't see anything. Oh, yes. Err . . . hello there!"

They all joined in then, and it was impossible to disentangle their words. Kinsman yelled into his microphone, telling them to shut up, and there was silence. Allowing them to calm for a moment he said then, "I didn't see any flak. It might mean that there are fighters about. Keep your eyes open, gunners. How long have we got to go, Bob?"

The navigator hesitated, and then said gruffly, "One hour and fifty minutes in one minute's time."

Fred had a thought, so Fred said, "I bet you these two silly bastards shot each other down."

"All right, Fred," said Kinsman, silencing him.

The trip was coming to life. Kinsman eased himself forward in his harness, and searched the misty sky ahead. Both his hands were now on the stick, and he knew a sensation of tenseness which he enjoyed. It occurred to him, too, that they must be on course after all, or he would never have seen those two aircraft going down. It seemed stupid now to have thought that they might have gone wrong.

They were clear of the mist, and once more flying in a clear black sky. The engineer came forward from aft of the bulkhead, and indicated to Kinsman by the raising of the thumb of his right hand that the tanks had been successfully changed. The trip was going well. Below on his own side, the port, Kinsman could see the lights of a small French town. He had never been in a French town.

"Bob," he said.

Bob answered him.

"What would the name of that little town down there be?"

"Oh, I don't know," Bob said curtly. "Could be any one of a half a dozen."

When they turned on to the leg that ran into the target, the navigator announced that they were still half a minute early. Kinsman said that they would leave things as they were and go in slightly early, for he had a horror of flying across the stream in order to lose time.

Fred, the bomb-aimer, had gone into the nose to check his bomb-sight, and the engineer, after Kinsman had turned on to the course which would take him to the target, went back beyond the bulkhead to check the master fuel cocks before the run in.

Kinsman called his gunners. "All O.K., gunners?"

"O.K. . . . . O.K.," they came back to him.

"How long is this leg, Bob?" he asked the navigator.

"Seventeen minutes."

Kinsman was flying at twenty-one and a half thousand feet. His bombing height was twenty. The extra height he was planning to use up by putting his nose down just before he started his bombing run. He intended to get through as quickly as possible. With his nose down he could increase his speed by about twenty knots, and while that didn't make much difference to their chances of getting through, it made him feel better to think that he was travelling fast.

"Keep your eyes open, gunner," he said. "If we're going to see any fighter activity, we'll see it now."

He had hardly spoken when he saw the first of the Pathfinders' flares. Still a long way ahead, a beautiful candelabra of green light burst lazily in the sky, a few thousand feet above their aiming point. As he saw the thing, Kinsman felt a sudden quickening of his pulse. Now he had something on which he could focus his purpose. . . . After hours of flying in the darkness, wondering most of the time if they would find the target they had been sent to attack, there it was, right there in front of him. He could understand things now. Kinsman had never quite ceased to wonder at the intricacies of navigation. He understood the principles of Bob's work, but there was something in him which never allowed him to take it for granted the fact that it was possible to take an aircraft off the ground in England, and fly it a thousand miles to a tiny spot on the map of continental Europe, and actually find that spot. Bob had found him the target. It was up to him to bomb it, and then get through it.

Fred spoke up. "There she is," he said. "Ain't it lovely?"

"See anything else, Fred?" Kinsman asked.

"Nope."

Kinsman had the nose of the Halifax down now, so that its speed had increased slightly. He had set the throttles, and once again tightened the clamp. The revs., too, he had slightly increased. With high revs. the engine seemed to run more sweetly.

"Your mike, Fred. You've forgotten to switch it off."

"No, skip, my mike was off," the bomb-aimer answered him.

"Who's got their mike on?" Kinsman asked.

No one answered.

More flares were dropping now, and they were drawing close enough to the target to see something of the glare, which was starting to light up the ground. A few straggling clouds, low, were floating over the target ahead of them.

"All set, Fred?"

71

"Yep. . . . There they come. See them, skip?"

Kinsman saw. Around the target area the enemy had started searchlight activity. Great menacing beams were beginning to sweep that part of the sky through which they would have to fly.

There was still a buzzing in Kinsman's intercom receiver. Again he asked Fred if he had his microphone switched on, and again Fred denied that he had. So Kinsman started with the tail-gunner, and asked each member of the crew individually. He asked Chico, and Geordie, the mid-upper; Les, the wireless op, Fred and Bob. Each one denied that the mike was switched on. The sound of heavy, labored breathing had been coming to Kinsman for some minutes, and gradually there was more desperation coming into whoever's breathing it was that he was listening to.

"Engineer!" he called.

There was no reply. The only sound that came over the intercom was the labored breathing he had been listening to.

"Engineer!" Kinsman called again.

There was something wrong with the engineer. They were running up to the target, so it was impossible to ask either of the gunners to come out of their turrets. Fred was fully occupied, and so was Bob, so Kinsman told the wireless operator to go back to the engineer and see if he was all right.

"Take a deep breath before you go back," Kinsman said to Les, "and see that you're not back there too long without plugging in your oxygen supply."

Les muttered a low acceptance of the command, and Kinsman heard him sucking in oxygen before he switched off his mike. Then he was vaguely aware of the boy passing him on the way back down the fuselage. Les, Kinsman somehow felt, was terribly afraid.

The target was now ablaze with lights of many colors. P.F.F. were dropping green flares, and the Germans, as Kinsman had been warned at briefing, were sending up flares from the ground which were of a slightly different shade of green. Now a couple of dozen searchlights were sweeping across the sky, and the first of the flak had started to shoot up to the attackers.

72

Chico, in the rear turret, came up saying, "There's fighters about, skip. Somebody behind us just bought it. . . . Look . . . look. . . . You see him, Geordie? See him?"

"Where? . . . Where?" the mid-upper asked excitedly.

"All right. Wrap up! You ready, Fred?" Kinsman said.

"All set."

"We should start the bombing run in about five minutes," Bob announced.

Kinsman tightened his hold on the control column, and then relaxed it again. He was sitting straight up in his seat, his eyes ceaselessly searching the sky in front. For now there was the added danger of collision as the stream narrowed its way into the target. The sky was becoming still brighter, so that he could see the shadows of three Halifaxes flying ahead of him and slightly below.

"It's getting warm," Fred said.

Kinsman switched on, and with a laugh in his voice which he didn't really feel said, "Isn't it?"

"Coming up," Fred said then.

"I'm ready when you are," John Kinsman replied, but the words were bitten off, for just then there was a blinding flash on the port bow and very close. A great dirty yellow-and-red blaze of blinding oily light seemed to envelop them. Kinsman closed his eyes, and instinctively ducked. For a moment the force of the explosion killed the sound of his own engines, and his right hand shot out to the throttles. Someone asked if they had been hit, and without knowing whether they had or not, Kinsman reassured them by saying that they hadn't.

"Well, some poor bastard copped his packet," Fred said.

"No, Fred, it was a booby. It was a booby, Fred," Kinsman said. Purposely he kept his voice low, and he spoke slowly, almost pausing between each word.

There was silence in the aircraft, and Kinsman seemed to sense the fear that was in all of them, and sensing their fear allowed him to overcome his own. It was like getting drunk with them at the local, and then sobering up when he realized that someone would have to see them home.

Les came through on the intercom. Kinsman heard him switch on his mike, and then take a few deep breaths before he spoke. When he spoke the little wop said, "The engineer seems to be suffering from lack of oxygen, skip. He's nearly out."

Kinsman asked if he could drag the engineer to the couch just behind the main spar.

"I'll try." That was all Les said. His own breathing sounded difficult, and as the boy spoke Kinsman felt a warm pang of love for him. For he knew that young Les was very frightened back there.

Flying in there with the nose slightly down was like flying through a picture-frame to become part of the picture it enclosed. Kinsman sat on the sound common sense of his pilot's seat, and looked down on something which was mad, quite mad. The earth and sky beneath had run together in the natural darkness, like a collection of left-over colors on an artist's palette, to become a dirty purple. The whole of existence was shimmering and grimacing like some ridiculous old whore as the bombs dropping from the Halifaxes winked through the garish green and red flares of the Pathfinders. Searchlights waved their long yellow arms crazily back and forth.

"Ready, skip?" Fred said. "We should start in about half a minute."

Fred hadn't switched off when the aircraft started shuddering under the recoil of the mid-upper's guns. Kinsman had never heard his guns fired before, and for a second he thought they were being hit. Then, when he realized that one of the gunners was firing, he grabbed the control column tightly and yelled, "which way do I turn?"

There was a pause. Kinsman kept his aircraft straight and level, and ducked now as flak burst so close on their starboard that the aircraft rocked in protest.

"It's all right, skip. I thought we were being attacked. But it's O.K." Geordie spoke as though the words came to him with difficulty.

"Skip!"

"Yes, Les."

"I've got him to the bed."

"How is he?"

"He's breathing hard. I've turned on his oxygen full blast."

"Bomb-doors open!" Fred called. And Kinsman opened the doors, acknowledging, as he did so, the bomb-aimer's request. Then he said, "Les! Leave him there and come on back up here."

74

Fred cut Kinsman off. He said, "Bombing run. . . ."

"O.K."

". . . Now!"

Kinsman held the Halifax as tightly as he could. Now, over the target, the flak was thick, so that even in that night sky it was possible to see the black angry puffs of the heavy stuff. As they flew into the smoke that was still lingering at their height from explosions of some minutes before, the smell of the cordite crept into the cockpit of the Halifax to penetrate their tightly fitting masks.

Fred said, "Left!" and Kinsman turned.

Ahead and slightly above, three Halifaxes and a Lancaster became visible to Kinsman. There must have been about seven hundred aircraft attacking that target then, but he could see only four of them. Chico's voice came piping up: "Two blokes have just bought it behind." And then he shut off quickly, as though afraid that Kinsman would blast him for breaking into the circuit.

"Left . . . left," Fred said.

In Kinsman there was a kind of elation. As he sat there with every muscle in his body intent on the job of holding that aircraft, he drew a curtain between his eyes and his brain. Even when he saw one of the Halifaxes ahead burst slowly into flames, amidships and then glow with growing enthusiasm like a half-lit taper, he didn't realize that the men in that thing could well have come from his own squadron. The thing had no meaning for him at all. It was just an aircraft burning slowly and deliberately in the sky ahead of him and slightly above. The slack-looking figure of what Kinsman took to be an airman, fell from the fuse-lage before the Halifax disappeared in a blaze of light.

"Right! . . . Too much. . . . That's it. . . . Hold it!"

Kinsman's teeth were clamped together, and the sweat which gathered between his mask and his nose irritated so that he had to take one hand from the stick to move the mask. It wasn't possible to move his body. He just had to sit there, holding that thing, and saying to himself, "We're making it. We're getting through. I'm living. Right at this second I'm alive." It was as though long fingers had drawn all of John Kinsman's existence to the fine point which was that moment, and now he had to experience everything that was life, then.

"Steady . . . left a little . . . steady."

"Skip."

Kinsman drew his lips apart to answer the gunner, but little Chico went on, "There's a guy right above us with his bomb-doors open. Can you go over a bit?"

"Steady," Fred said.

There was a Halifax above and about to drop its bombs on them, and all hell was coming up from below, but Fred was saying "Steady." It had to be steady.

John Kinsman looked straight ahead. Not once as he held his aircraft did his eyes move. Now the Halifax was hurtling through that target like some lifeless clay pigeon. Kinsman tried to imagine his life coming to an end right then. He closed his eyes, and then quickly opened them again, as though ashamed of his own weakness. Never once did he turn his eyes outside the limits of the helmet which framed his face. Within his clothes he didn't move. For there was no place to hide, except in them.

"Bombs away!"

There was something which sounded like triumph in Fred's voice as he called the words to his pilot, and Kinsman, in his enthusiasm, called back, "Good old Fred!"

The captain's elation was infectious. Instantly there was a burst of chatter on the intercom, but for Kinsman the tension was not yet over. He was watching the little light on his instrument panel which told him that his camera was functioning. It was still necessary that he held the Halifax absolutely straight and level, otherwise they wouldn't obtain a photograph of their aiming point, and Intelligence at base would be unable to check the results of their trip.

The damned light kept blipping in and out until Kinsman thought it would never stop. But at least he now had something more to do than sit there waiting to receive a direct hit amidships.

"How was it, Fred?" Kinsman asked. As he spoke his eyes never moved from the light on the instrument panel.

"Bang on! I'm sure I saw our bombs bursting."

"Like hell."

"I did," Fred insisted. "They went right across the target."

"Fred."

"Aye, aye, skip."

"Stay down there and guide me through those searchlights. I can't see where they're coming from. . . . Bob, what's the course out of the target?"

When Bob spoke there was cheerfulness in his voice for the first time since they had left the ground. He said, "Turn on to one-two-five."

"That'll take us to Russia." Kinsman answered.

"We've got to go east before we turn. . . ."

The light had gone out. The camera had stopped turning. Kinsman momentarily relaxed his grip on the control column, and then, in a brief diving turn, changed course.

Fred's voice came from the nose, giving his pilot a running commentary on the searchlight activity which was all round them. On their starboard and slightly above, they could see a Lancaster caught in a cone of about a dozen searchlights and trying desperately to escape. Like some wild animal waking up to find itself caged, the Lancaster dived and turned. But the enemy's searchlights never let go until long steams of flak had poured into the centre of the cone, and the Lancaster was burning.

Kinsman, with Fred guiding him through the few pockets of near-darkness which were in that sky, was relaxed. Again and again, he asked the gunners if all was well, and as each time they reassured him that there were no enemy fighters to be seen, he began to have the feeling that they had passed through the worst of what the enemy had to offer. Before they were clear of the area, though, there was still a wall of searchlights to go through, and from where they were at that moment it appeared to be impossible to get through without being coned.

The searchlights drew nearer and nearer until Kinsman said, "What do you think, Fred?"

"I'm watching the green ones," Fred answered. "We've got to watch that we're not coned in the green ones. The others seem to follow the green ones. I see a lot of our kites. There's a fellow in front on three engines. There's smoke coming from one of his engines."

"I've just seen one of our kites back here," the rear-gunner announced, "but he's not going the same way as us."

"When do we turn, Bob?" Kinsman asked.

"A minute and a half."

"What's the new course?"

All of the crew seemed to share the feeling with Kinsman that now, being through the target, they had tasted the worst of the opposition, and Bob, when he spoke to Kinsman, did so in a tone of voice which was quite different from his usual curtness. He said, "It's almost an about-turn, Johnny. You go on to two-two-one."

A course of two-two-one degrees would have taken Kinsman away from the searchlights towards which he was heading, but not in a minute and a half. He started into the turn immediately Bob told him the new course. He knew he would have to turn tightly, so he went into a steep bank to starboard, and his wing had just gone down when the rear-gunner almost screamed the words: "Corkscrew port! . . . corkscrew port! . . . Now . . . skip. . . ." The rest of little Chico's words were drowned by the furious chattering of his four guns.

Johnny Kinsman automatically reversed the direction of his turn, and in doing so almost turned his Halifax on to its back. Instead of turning to starboard, he was suddenly over and diving wildly to his port. The violence of the manoeuvre, and the fear inside him, made him feel sick. He had a momentary vision of the fires below being where the sky should have been. His sense of balance disappeared, and the fear of the attacker was joined by the fear that he had lost control of his aircraft.

He was vaguely conscious of the mid-upper gunner shouting something to his opposite number in the rear turret, and then Geordie's guns seemed to be firing as well. Kinsman, diving, saw the altimeter whirling around as he lost height. His automatic pilot had gone crazy. It was quite useless to him, and all his training told him to ignore it. No matter what he saw or felt, he was diving to port. He had to work things out in his own mind. When he had lost three thousand feet, Kinsman put all his weight on the stick to turn it to starboard, and then, when it was over, he pulled back until the blood drained from his head and before his eyes there was only a kind of misty blur. The recoil of the guns was still causing the big Halifax to shudder, and, feeling it almost groan, Kinsman relaxed his pressure on the stick. It was then that there was a kind of silly bang which sounded as though some little boy had kicked an empty can in a deserted street.

Kinsman groaned, and in spite of the fact that the control column was far back in his belly, so that the Halifax felt as though it was standing on its tail, he ducked.

They had been hit. He knew that they had been hit, but the Halifax was still climbing. He felt a stupid, sudden surge of tears to his eyes, and he had a crazy desire to call out that it wasn't fair. It wasn't right. Then Geordie's voice came over the intercom through the mike which had been switched on since the fighter attacked them. There was no speech from Geordie—only a mad kind of babble about his head, his head. Geordie screamed and laughed, and all the noise that came from him gradually dissipated itself into a long, high-pitched, hideous wail.

Kinsman somehow said, "Gunners!"

There was a pause before little Chico answered. Then he said, "I can see him, skip. I can still see him."

"Look out for searchlights," Fred shouted. Fred's voice had lost its customary rough assurance. But his warning had come too late. Almost as he spoke, Kinsman found himself blinded by the fierce glare of a searchlight's beam.

He had to remember—he had to remember what he was doing. He was climbing to starboard. And he mustn't look at the artificial horizon. He mustn't. He was climbing to starboard. Starboard. He couldn't see. All that terrible light was coming back at his eyes from the perspex of the cockpit.

"We're going to be coned, skip," Fred called.

Kinsman didn't answer. His teeth were clenched so that the breath was trapped in his lungs. And then, violently, he threw the Halifax to the port and down; and as gravity pulled at them, his mouth opened in spite of his own will, and the sound of his breath being expelled was like the sound of a long sigh.

"Fred, Fred," Kinsman called as they were going down. He had to speak. There was an urgent excitement inside him that was like pain, and he had to speak. Without thinking at all, he said, "Are we in it, Fred? Are we in it? I can't see, Fred."

"Yeah . . . yes, but he's lost us. . . . Keep going, skip. Keep goin'."

Kinsman opened his eyes, and as he did so he had the strangest feeling that they had never been open before. They were in darkness again and he could see.

"Chico . . . Chico!" he called.

The rear-gunner's voice seemed to pipe up from away far behind. He said, "I can't see him, skip. He's away. I'm sure he's away."

Kinsman brought up his port wing until he sensed they were diving on an even keel. His gyro compass was spinning madly, and his magnetic compass would be useless until it settled down. He looked to port and then into the darkness to starboard. Out there to starboard, somewhere, was base, so he started into a steep turn in that direction. As he turned, he looked down and back from where he sat on the high end of the turn, towards the earth; and he could see the burning target they had left, flickering in silent protest, like some poor, dumb, outraged child, while above the flames, the long, helpless arms of the searchlights, exhausted, waved back and forth in muted anger.

"Looks like the whole bloody world's on fire, don't it, skip?" Fred said. "Can I go back and see what happened to Geordie?"

By the time they had reached the enemy coast, Kinsman felt as though the night had once again closed in to take them in soft, protecting arms. In spite of the fact that the mid-upper turret had been shot away when Geordie had been killed, the flying qualities of the Halifax were unimpaired. Young Les reported that his set was unserviceable, but that didn't worry Kinsman particularly. The engines appeared to be undamaged, and all his controls were functioning. And although the W.T. set was unserviceable, the intercom worked perfectly well. But Geordie was dead. Fred had told him that Geordie was dead.

Fred and young Les had pulled the gunner's body from his turret with great difficulty, and they had laid his body out on the couch amidships. Fred had said he looked horrible. He'd been hit in the face and in the chest. Fred said he was very dead.

It was a strange night. There was no light now whatever. Outside the cockpit it was quite black, and Kinsman saw no cloud or anything of the ground. He looked at his instrument panel as they neared the coast, and the altimeter told him that they were flying at sixteen thousand feet. But there was no physical sensation of being at that height, or of flying at a speed of two hundred miles an hour.

Since shortly after leaving the target area they had seen no other aircraft, and now the feeling of intense loneliness that he had known in the earlier hours of the trip had returned to Kinsman. But now every turn of the propeller blades was taking them nearer base, and, as he eased the nose down while trying not to lose height to quickly, he knew the thrill of feeling that he was speeding towards home. Once or twice he caught himself trying to urge his aircraft on by pushing his buttocks forward on the seat.

"Chico," Kinsman called.

"Skip?"

"Are you all right?"

"Yes, sure. I'm all right."

There was something in the little gunner's voice which made Kinsman feel sorry for him, so he said, "You did a good job, boy."

Chico laughed.

After they had left the target, and after Fred and Les had brought the dead Geordie from his turret, Kinsman had sent Fred back to see if Chico was in fact unhurt. He would have liked to have brought the little gunner out of his turret for a time, but he couldn't do that.

"Course alteration coming up in two minutes," Bob announced. "You go on to three-two-five."

"Is this the coast?" Kinsman asked.

"Yes," Bob said hurriedly.

Kinsman told himself that it would soon be all over. Soon, in an hour and a half, it would be all over, and he would be trying to get Zebra on to the ground in one piece.

He altered course when Bob told him, and as he turned on to the leg which would take him across the North Sea to the English coast, he felt as though he had stepped out of an overwhelmingly warm bath.

Over the sea, the big black Halifax flew smoothly through the night with each member of its crew working quietly at his own job. Back in his lonely turret, little Chico moved his guns from side to side occasionally as he felt himself coming close to sleep, and Kinsman could feel the movement of the guns as the drag on the turret caused the Halifax to wallow slightly from side to side. John Kinsman, now that the aircraft had little need of his help to keep it flying, was trying to appreciate the fact that his mid-upper gunner, Geordie, was lying there amidships, dead.

Geordie had been a strange, unhappy, frightened fellow. His fear had affected him as they had gone through their operational training as a crew, until by the time they had been posted to a squadron there had been little left of the Geordie that Kinsman had first known. And now he was dead. Little over an hour ago he had been alive, brimful to the neck with fear, and now he was lying cold and dead. Kinsman had a fleeting picture of himself as an undertaker taking Geordie home in a big black, old-fashioned hearse.

He should have been sad, and yet he wasn't. At home he used to be sad when he had looked at Uncle Willie, and the thought had come to him that soon the old man might die. Just to look at his Uncle Willie and the grief that was always written on his Aunt Lizzie's face, had made him sad. And now he was sitting there at fifteen thousand feet in a darkened night sky with half a dozen feet behind him, the cold dead body of something with which he had shared life for six months, and he felt nothing. Except relief. It was Geordie who was dead, and he was alive.

"Chico."

"Skip."

"What's Geordie's wife like?"

"Don't know. She lives in Leicester. She's going to have a kid."

Kinsman set the information Chico had just given him alongside a memory of a girl he used to know who was called Chris Holmes. What kind of person would she be now? He wondered how she would have reacted to someone bringing her home a dead husband.

Outside the cockpit, there was still nothing to be seen. He was still trying to ease some extra speed from the Halifax, and it was good to watch the needle on the air-speed indicator creeping up by five miles an hour, and then try to hold the speed he had gained while he checked the rate of descent. The adjutant would write to Geordie's wife, and so would the Winco, but he, too, would write. He would tell her that he had known Geordie for a long time, and that they had all been proud to have known him, and to have flown with him. Kinsman looked up as it occurred

82

to him that a letter like that would call for words that were out of the ordinary. But he couldn't think of them then. He'd get down to it tomorrow or soon.

As he looked up he could see that a layer of stratus cloud was above them, and he said to the navigator, "Bob, it looks like there's weather about."

There was a grunt from Bob by way of reply, and that was all. Bob wasn't aware of the significance of weather in the way that Kinsman was, and that was part of the reason for the degree of tension which existed between them.

Soon after that Bob came through, asking Kinsman to tell him when he saw anything of the English coast. The navigator said that they should cross close to a well-known marker beacon. But by that time Kinsman was in cloud. It was smooth cloud, and not in any way threatening. He had been flying for long enough to have become thoroughly adjusted to the night, and flying on his instruments had become as natural to him as flying by his senses.

They were losing height fast now, and Kinsman had a kind of instinctive feeling that the coast was near. If Geordie had been alive, he would have landed at the first available airfield, but there was no point in taking his gunner's body to any place other than his home base. He asked Fred again if he was sure that Geordie was dead.

Bob, with some anxiety in his voice, asked again if his pilot could see anything, but now, down at five thousand feet and in wet cloud, Kinsman could see nothing. They were completely enclosed in a grey, wet blanket. It was thick, smothering cloud, and Kinsman felt as though it was sticking to them. The rain was running down the outside of his cockpit, and the sound of the engines seemed unable to escape from the aircraft, so that it came back at them in great breakers of noise. Fred came up from Bob's side to stand with Kinsman. The big bomb-aimer stood leaning with one elbow against the side of the cockpit, and then he turned to shout to Kinsman, "Bloody, isn't it?"

Kinsman smiled. Always he had to reassure them. In his mind, then, he knew of the hazards that were confronting them. If this weather was bad all the way down and back to base, they were in trouble, especially since they no longer had the use of a W.T. set. But they didn't know all that.

Fred leaned over close to Kinsman's ear, and then

pulled back the pilot's helmet before shouting into his ear, "Won't be so good if it's like this all the way down."

Kinsman smiled, to Fred and to himself. He'd been wrong about Fred.

Gradually the Halifax lost height. They were down to three thousand feet, and still in rain. And there was as yet nothing that Kinsman could see. He moved uneasily in his seat, alternately checking his instruments and waiting with his eyes for a lighthouse, a beacon—anything to shine up from the ground. There was nothing.

"Do you think we've crossed the coast, Bob?" he asked.

Bob, looking slightly more worried than usual, came up the two steps from below, and nodded his reply.

They were now below three thousand feet, and if they were over land, that was too low—especially when they didn't know exactly where they were. Kinsman decided to turn on to a reciprocal course and let down towards or over the sea. It was safer to break cloud over the sea.

The navigator had taken Fred's place by his pilot's side, and Kinsman, taking his eyes from the cloud in front to look at Bob, smiled as he saw that Bob's round, red face was puckered in bewilderment. Bob became conscious of the fact that John Kinsman was smiling at him, and turned to smile back. The less sure Bob was of his navigation, the more friendly he was towards the rest of the crew.

"Skip," Chico called.

"Yes."

"Are you looking for the sea?"

"Why?"

"I've just seen it."

Fred, who was standing behind the navigator and looking down on the starboard side, grabbed Kinsman, by the shoulder, and when the pilot turned his head, pointed excitedly downwards. Still Kinsman could see nothing, but the cloud was thinning. The altimeter was approaching a thousand feet, and as he saw the needle slowly creeping down, there was an exciting little flutter in his stomach. His right hand was reaching for the throttles, ready to give the engines power should he need to climb hurriedly. He couldn't go much lower, for the cliffs which they should be approaching were almost four hundred feet high. Then he saw what Chico and Fred had seen. The black sea, angered somewhat by a wind, so that white tops broke at intervals, was below them.

Kinsman's right hand came back from the throttles, and he tripped the control column tightly as he almost dived underneath the overcast.

Ahead, right ahead, was a slow flashing light which Bob said was a marker beacon on Flamborough Head. Flamborough Head was only seven miles from base.

Almost over the coast, Fred's voice came over the intercom saying "There's Brid . . . there's Brid . . . skip."

Kinsman laughed. He switched on and said, "Fred, I'm sure that's a light in your Maisie's bedroom window. Her husband must be home."

Fred made no reply, and neither did anyone else, and Kinsman, wondering why, remembered Geordie. In his relief at breaking cloud, he had momentarily forgotten about the mid-upper. There was reproof in the silence of the others.

"Engineer," Kinsman called.

"All set for landing, skip," the engineer said, without waiting to be asked. In minutes the Halifax roared over Liscombe Farm.

It was raining heavily, and the moisture running down the outside of his cockpit made it difficult for Kinsman to see. Because their W.T. set was useless, they couldn't contact the tower. He searched the circuit for other aircraft, but he could see nothing.

"See anything, Chico?" he asked.

"Somebody's just going in. He's just touching down now."

Bob had gone back downstairs to his desk, but Fred was still standing there. The bomb-aimer shook his head, indicating that he could see nothing. Then he lifted the flap of Kinsman's helmet, and said, "We must be late after having gone back out there."

Kinsman nodded at that. They were flying above what he took to be the runway in use, in an up-wind direction. The circuit was clear as far as he could see, and in spite of the fact that he couldn't get permission from the control tower, he decided to go in.

They turned on to the down-wind leg when Kinsman remembered something. "Fred," he said.

"Skip."

"Did you check your bomb-bay?"

"A long time ago," Fred answered.

On the down-wind leg, with rather more speed on the indicator than he should have had, Kinsman selected flaps down. His flaps fell down, and the nose of the Halifax reared alarmingly. Kinsman stiffened. He thrust the stick forward, and then, when he had a grip of it, he started winding his trim forward.

As they shot up, he lost the lights of the Drem, and he had a sickening senation of stalling. Then, automatically, he cut the engines, so that there was a moment of unwelcome silence inside the aircraft. The nose fell, and he caught the descent with power. He was in control as they lumbered awkwardly into the turn across wind.

"Something wrong, skip?" Fred breathed.

"Hydraulics," Kinsman said sparingly. "They must have been damaged when we were hit."

At five hundred feet Kinsman turned on to his final approach. He dropped his wheels, late. Ahead was the yellow flare-path, two beautiful long lines of bright lights.

A red Aldis lamp was flashing at Kinsman.

"He's giving you a red," Fred said, with disgust in his voice.

Kinsman continued to bore down towards the earth. At two hundred feet the red light was still flashing, and Kinsman took one hand from the wobbling stick to hold the microphone to his mouth.

"Fire a red Very, Fred!" he called.

Like Kinsman's own right arm, Fred fired, and the red Aldis lamp was extinguished. At fifty feet they received a green, but Kinsman made no comment. His hand was on the throttles, easing them back slowly while his left hand held the nose down. Then gradually he allowed the tail to sink, and as the big Halifax settled back he eased the throttles farther back until all four engines were merely ticking over.

The wheels touched a moment too early, and Kinsman, unsure, wondered if they would hold. They held.

Fred slapped Kinsman on the shoulder, and called, "We're down, skip, we're down."

Bob jumped up the steps to beam at Kinsman, who was still trying to keep the Halifax running straight. Kinsman heard the engineer laughing. Chico maintained that the landing was ropy.

"Where's our dispersal?" Kinsman asked.

"What about taking Geordie to Flying Control?"

"No point," Kinsman answered; "they'll take him."

He tried to turn the Halifax completely around when they reached the bay, so that it was facing the perimeter track, but something seemed to have gone wrong with the brake pressure. He decided not to risk it. So he switched off, and sat there unfastening his harness and listening to the engines reluctantly closing down.

CHAPTER SEVEN

"Once," Julie Holmes said, "there was a bottle of whisky in that cupboard, but Millie drank it."

"And, no doubt," Kinsman said, "She ate the bottle after she drank the whisky."

Millie looked up from her desk at the other end of the room in Station Headquarters which was occupied by Code and Cypher. "That," she said in her slow, deep voice, "is unkind."

Kinsman leaned over and extinguished his cigarette in the ashtray on Julie's desk. "The hospitality in this office," he went on, "has reached a new low. No tea. Nothing to drink. You two don't appreciate us. Coming, Wakey?"

"I'm staying. It's enough that I can sit here and look at Julie."

Millie, who was Mrs. Sefton, and in charge of the office, again looked up and said, "You look at me, Johnny. Then you'll both be happy."

"I've been looking at you. That's why I want a drink."

Kinsman stood up then, and, smiling, again asked his friend if he was coming, but Wakefield insisted that he would stay and be alone with Julie.

"Alone," Millie protested. Millie was forty, and it was said that her husband was a professor of physics at a Midland university. "How can you be alone when I'm here?"

"Millie," Wakefield said lazily, "when one is in love one has eyes only for the person with whom one is in love. No one else exists."

"Has one? Er, doesn't one?" Julie said.

"Take an occasional look at Millie there, and that'll keep you from getting too serious," Kinsman said, and was gone.

Half an hour later, Wakefield was walking to the mess for tea with Julie and Millie. He had hoped that Millie would have allowed them to walk alone, but Millie stayed with them. She was a large woman—almost as tall, walking beside him, as Wakefield—and yet, strangely enough, there was nothing in her appearance which suggested masculinity. For a woman of around forty she had a very fine complexion. Smooth and pale, marred only by an excess of lipstick, her face, with its large brown eyes, even larger than they should have been in proportion to her general size, had always an expression of gentleness about it. Wakefield liked Millie.

He said to her as they walked with Julie, "An old married woman like you should know better than to spoil a beautiful moment like this."

"I thought," Millie answered, "that you like married women."

Wakefield thought he saw Julie flush slightly when her friend spoke, and suddenly he felt the color rise in his own face. He coughed, and fished in his pocket for a cigarette. Millie went on talking until Wakefield had regained something of his composure.

In the mess he brought tea for the two women, and then Kinsman joined them, so that gradually Wakefield was able to pry Julie loose from her friend.

"This communal life," he said to Julie, "has its limitations."

"More compensation than limitations," she replied. "If we weren't living here, I'd have to make tea for you."

"And maybe your mother wouldn't allow you to bring me home. How right you are! I like it here."

"I haven't got a mother."

"Oh . . . I'm sorry," he said.

"You're off tonight," Julie said.

"Do I take it that you're about to ask me out?"

Julie laughed. "Out where?"

"Anywhere. There are lots of exciting places around here. We could go around the perimeter track or something."

89

"Wakey, you must think I'm a jeep."

"Here's this bore Kinsman coming to break into our rather beautiful conversation," Wakefield said.

Kinsman laughed. "I don't want to talk to you," he said, "I want to talk to Julie."

"And how welcome you are," Julie said. "This friend of yours is trying to talk to me into an expedition around the perimeter track."

"Don't go, Julie. I'm going into Brid. . . . Dinner and dancing at the Imperial, and if we miss the last bus, a taxi home."

Julie laughed. "Well, I . . ."

"Too late, old boy," Wakefield insisted. "Seriously, Julie and I have arranged to go into town tonight."

Millie had risen from her chair and turned around so that she was standing looking down on them. Something in Wakefield's voice made Kinsman hesitate to speak, and maybe something in his eyes and the nervously twitching flesh at the corners of his mouth.

"Millie," Wakefield said, "Johnny Kinsman here's just suggested that you come into Brid with us tonight to make up a foursome with Julie and me."

"Love to," Millie said pleasantly. "Thanks, Johnny. We can go in my car."

Kinsman didn't say anything. He just smiled to Millie. And as he smiled, he stood on his friend's foot. Shortly after that, they left the mess together, and made their way to their billet in order to shave and wash.

"I repeat," Kinsman said, as he shaved in front of the tiny mirror, "you're a bastard. A first-class, extraordinary kind of bastard. You claim to be my friend. I share a room with you, my socks, my shirts, my money. . . ."

"I'm always quite prepared to share anything of yours," Wakefield said from the other end of the room.

"But in spite of all that . . ." Kinsman went on ". . . Damn! I've cut myself . . . in spite of all that you ruin the first evening I've had off in a week by pairing me off with an old horse like Millie."

"It was just my little joke," Wakefield said quietly. "Millie's all right. You'll be all right with Millie. I nurse a sneaking regard for Millie myself. . . ."

"Well, why the hell don't you sneak into town with her, then, and leave me alone? . . . Wakefield! . . ."

"Don't be angry, Johnny boy."

"Chum, I could have had half a dozen women in town tonight."

"Half a dozen in the same night!"

"Any one of half a dozen . . ."

"Do Millie . . . er, have Millie. Do have Millie," Wakefield said, laughing.

"I'm not even sure that Millie's a woman," Kinsman insisted.

"Have her, anyway." Wakefield started to sing ". . . I'll get by . . . as long as I . . . *have* you . . ." Then he roared with laughter

"You're a bastard! An arch-high, cardinal bastard."

They dressed and cycled to the mess, and all the way there Kinsman expressed the hope that something would make it impossible for Millie to go into town, but when they reached the mess, her little Hillman car was standing outside. Inside, Wakefield suggested that they have a drink, for in spite of the fact that the car was there, there was no sign of the two women. He had a feeling that Kinsman was genuinely annoyed at having to spend an evening with Millie, so when Paddy had given them a drink along with his customary comment about the place for aircrew being in the bloody air, he said to Kinsman, "Johnny, do you know why I asked Millie along tonight?"

"I've been telling you for the last hour. You're a bastard."

Wakefield hesitated. Then he said, "I wanted you to be with us, and it seemed better if someone like Millie—someone she knows well, was there. . . ."

"What's the matter with you?" Kinsman said.

Wakefield finished his drink before replying. "I don't know, Johnny. For the first time in my life I think I've . . . I'm almost scared of being alone with a girl. Does that sound silly?"

"Yes."

At that the door opened and Millie's head appeared in the entrance. She said, "The W.A.A.F. party's all present and correct."

"Drink?" Wakefield asked. But Millie shook her head, so they left the bar.

King George V had once had lunch at the Imperial

when he had visited Bridsea to open the floral gardens, and ever since, the place had been the centre of what social life there was in Bridsea town. Even in the "off" season the Imperial was in business, mainly because its cocktail bar was recognized by the town's publicans, bookmakers, fairground proprietors, and widows as the place in which to be seen.

In 1935, recognizing the Jubilee of that monarch who had once graced their dining-room, the proprietors decided to redecorate in cream, black glass, and chromium. That had been a mistake. For by the time Wakefield with Julie, and Kinsman with Millie, came to sit in the dining-room, where once His Majesty had sat, the décor of 1935 had taken on a grey mist of ridiculous shabbiness which all the prosperous enthusiasm of the well-fed farmers and their wives, and the quiet, self-conscious appreciation of the clothing manufacturers who had brought their secretaries from Leeds, could not dispel. The Imperial had been destroyed by the war without Bridsea ever having been hit by an enemy bomb. The most exciting thing, in fact, that had happened in Bridsea was when one of Liscombe's aircraft had crashed on the promenade when carrying a full bomb-load, and as well as tearing up the promenade and part of the sea-wall, had destroyed Joe's fish-and-chip parlour and one wing of the Green Room.

"I haven't been here before," Julie said.

Kinsman, sitting opposite her and beside Millie, said, "Well, this is the place to be. As you can see, all the best people get here sooner or later."

Millie had finished her third double whisky of the evening. "I've been here," she said, "for half an hour, and neither of you two characters has asked me to dance yet."

Kinsman said that the band was tired.

"The music's too slow," Wakefield added, "and if the violinist moves his arm any faster his dinner-jacket'll rip."

"Dance!" Millie insisted.

Kinsman stood up. "After all," he said to the other two, "she is my partner."

In spite of what he had said to Wakefield before meeting the women, Kinsman was enjoying himself. Millie he liked. He liked her more when he saw her open the top button of her tunic and casually scratch her right breast.

There wasn't much room to dance, and he was glad of that, for Millie was tall, perhaps slightly taller than he was.

"Your friend's in love with her," Millie said when they had moved away from the other two.

John Kinsman didn't answer. It wasn't the kind of thing he expected a woman like Millie to say or be interested in saying.

The drink inside him made him laugh.

"Millie's grip tightened on his tunic, and she said, "I'm forty, Johnny, and you're about twenty-two. Love's about the only thing in life that's really worth a damn."

"I forgot," Kinsman said, "you're married."

"Twice."

"I see."

"No, you don't. I married the same man twice. For love."

Kinsman's eyebrows were pulled down over his eyes when he looked into her face. "Do you still love him?"

Millie laughed then. "No," she said. "He's old now. No good in bed."

The music stopped and had started again by the time Kinsman had escorted Millie back to the table. The other two had left to dance.

Kinsman listened to Millie and looked at Julie Holmes dancing in the arms of his friend. On her face there was a kind of half-smile as she looked over Wakefield's shoulder. Her expression was just as he had seen it on the night of the dance in the airmen's dining-hall. When Wakefield's back was to the table where Kinsman sat with Millie it was just possible to see Julie's eyes. Somehow, in spite of Wakefield's tall, straight, hard-looking body, Julie was stronger. There was life in the soft cream of her hands, and in the delicate shading of her eyes that kind of understanding which to Kinsman was always slightly disconcerting.

Julie, someday, would be plump, Kinsman felt. There was just that degree of roundness about her cheekbones and her buttocks which suggested that there would come a day when she would be happy in being someone's wife. Now she was lovely. Maybe even when she was old and thirty-five she would have a kind of loveliness. When she

was a wife, she would be the wife of a banker or an archi-
tect, or someone like that. He could forget about her, for
how could her understanding reach out to the poor simplicity of his Aunt Lizzie living back at home alone in
Clover Road, and the job he had before joining up.

"I said," Millie went on, "I feel like another drink."

"Good . . . good. Let's have one."

"I was just thinking."

"About your friend and Julie?"

Kinsman turned to Millie and smiled, and Millie smiled
without implying that she was happy about anything. Her
teeth were very long, remarkably long, Kinsman thought
again.

"This isn't a time for love," Millie went on. "To be in
love now is to be out of step with events. This is a time
for passion."

"Is it, Millie?"

"It is."

"I'm glad you feel that way about things."

"Pay for these drinks and shut up," she said.

Kinsman paid as Wakefield and Julie arrived back at
their table, and he started to make some remark which pe-
tered out half-way through when he saw how Wakefield
looked at Julie as she sat down.

Once during the evening Kinsman danced with Julie,
and all the time she was in his arms he was aware of
Wakefield looking at them. The day before, an hour before, he would have pulled Wakefield's leg by holding
Julie closer than was really necessary, but not now. The
time for laughing was past, and he couldn't decide
whether that was because of the love for her which he
knew was in Wakefield, or that which he feared might be
in himself.

Dancing with her, he was silent until she said, "Are you
enjoying yourself, Johnny?" She said it in such a deliberate
way that it sounded as though his answer was important to
her.

"Yes . . . of course. Of course," he said hesitantly. "I
like Millie."

"Millie's wonderful," she said.

In their dance they turned, so that, almost at the same
instant, Kinsman was aware of Wakefield sitting there

watching them, and Julie's body touching his: her thigh, and as she missed a step, the softness of her breast.

"I'm sorry, Johnny," she said.

Only his body was in that room when Kinsman thought, "If there was only time to love you. If only I came from your world and there was time to love you. Even if Wakefield has no more time than I, he is from your world."

The music stopped abruptly, for it was that kind of music, and Kinsman halted awkwardly, so that he stumbled against her.

"I'm sorry," he gasped. "I'm a rotten dancer."

"No, you're not," she said. "I like dancing with you."

But that was the only occasion during the evening that Kinsman danced with her. To him it was as though Julie allowed herself to be carried along on the current of Wakefield's enthusiasm. To each one of them, Wakefield was so obviously in love with her. Kinsman wouldn't compete with him. Instead, with the passing of each minute, he withdrew more and more within himself. He looked at Julie again and again, and he thought it strange that he should have lived this way, so that, in those moments, people like Wakefield and Millie and Julie and himself should know so much that was common to each one of them. Once, removing the need to talk by holding a glass to his mouth for longer than was necessary, he thought of Robby, a friend of long ago, and wondered how he would have fared here. These people, this Julie—even Wakefield, whom he thought he knew—had come from somewhere which to each of them was real, but which to him was nowhere; just as the village, and Aunt Lizzie, and the *Western District News,* to them was nowhere. They were like thistledown, blown along by the whim of each breeze, sometimes gathering in little clusters as they made their way towards the cliff over which the grass sloped.

"We're thistledown," Kinsman said.

"Hurrah!" Millie exclaimed as loudly as she dared. "Johnny's getting tight."

Wakefield had been leaning close to Julie, talking. He looked up. "Are you tight?"

"Course not. Millie just wishes I was tight," Kinsman said, laughing.

"Do you want to go, Johnny?" Julie asked.

"Go? Of . . . of course not. What's the matter with you people?"

Kinsman stood up and held on to the table as he leaned over towards Wakefield. "I don't want to go. I want to yell. I want to wake this place up. I want to shake the whole town up."

"Oh!" Wakefield smiled.

Millie said, "Let's go back. We can have a drink at my place."

"Can't we shake it up? Can't we make a noise?" Kinsman asked.

He wasn't drunk. But suddenly he wanted to exhaust himself. He wanted to do something that was mad. Something that tomorrow he could laugh at. Julie's eyes turned to Millie, and Kinsman saw her. There was an expression in those eyes which told him that he had made her uneasy.

"Don't worry, Julie," Kinsman said. "I'm all right. I'm just trying to shake this Wakefield out of his awful seriousness."

"Of course he is," Millie insisted. "We'll go back and have a couple of drinks at my place. As long as you don't make a noise that wakes up old Fanny Fusspants, we'll be all right."

Julie shrugged her shoulders, and they left. Wakefield drove back to Liscombe. They passed the mess, and went on up the road which led to the billets. Millie suggested that it might be better if she drove into the W.A.A.F. site so, about a hundred yards before they reached their destination, Wakefield stopped the little car and got out from behind the wheel to join Kinsman in the back where he had been sitting throughout the journey from Brid with one hand in Millie's, and the other just above her right knee. His eyes, though, had never left the back of Julie's neck as she sat beside Wakefield. Julie's neck was lovely. It looked so very white and clean.

Millie's room looked like the kind of place that someone lived in. Unlike any other room he had been in since he joined the Air Force, it was carpeted, and as well as the standard light which hung from the ceiling, a bedside lamp shone from a table which had been arranged beside the bed. A dyed sheepskin rug adorned one of the three armchairs, and an embroidered bed-mat was arranged on the bed. The table was covered with a deep green cloth, and on it there was a large mirror, before which, carefully arranged as though ready for any emegency, was an assortment of creams and brushes. As Kinsman looked around the room, he could see that the place was littered with the remnants of some other former existence. There was an attempt here to transplant some previous ordered comfort. Warmth, he thought, must be important to Millie; and he wondered why.

Wakefield said, "This isn't a billet, Millie. It's a bedroom."

Millie smiled. "It's quite nice," she said, "but wait till you see Julie's. She lives in luxury."

Wakefield flushed when she said that. He glanced at Julie, and then to Kinsman. Millie appeared not to notice. She brought out two bottles from under the table by her bed.

Julie didn't drink, but Wakefield did, and Kinsman had a whisky. When Millie poured his drink she poured an extra large one. Talk appeared to be difficult, so Kinsman, after sipping his drink, asked who was represented by the photograph of the bald-headed man on the wall. On the face of the man there was an expression which suggested that the camera had caught him just before he broke into a smile. And the photograph had been taken from slightly below eye-level, so that now this half-smiling, bald-headed creature was looking down on them.

"That," said Millie, "is him."

"Your husband. . . . ?" Kinsman asked.

"My husband."

"He looks as though he thinks we're all rather funny," Wakefield said.

"Julie," Kinsman said then, "what right has a husband to laugh at his wife's guests?"

"None, Johnny. None, I should say."

"Maybe he's just laughing at you, Millie, because you've got two men in your room. Maybe he's saying to himself, 'The old girl's rather overdoing it tonight.' . . . Maybe that's what he's saying."

"What do you mean, 'old girl'?"

"I think we should turn him to the wall," Kinsman went on.

"No, Johnny. Don't be silly," Julie said. "George is nice."

"Have you met him?"

Julie smiled and nodded.

When Wakefield had finished his drink, Millie asked him if he wanted another, but as she spoke she saw the almost imperceptible movement of Julie's neck, so that when Wakefield refused, she didn't press the matter.

"Who's drinking?" Millie asked.

"I am," Kinsman said.

"We'll have a party," Millie said, laughing.

"I think I'll go, Millie," Julie said. "Tomorrow's almost here."

Wakefield moved in his clothes, unable to decide what to say, so Julie took him by the arm, and said, "Come on, Wakey, we'll go. We're not in their class when it comes to drinking."

Millie went out with them, leaving Kinsman sitting there alone in the sheepskin-covered chair. When Millie returned, Kinsman was staring up at the photograph of the man she had said was her husband.

"Drink up, Johnny."

Kinsman raised the glass to his lips. "I . . . I don't know that I want to drink any more."

" 'Course you do; there's plenty."

Millie sat on the edge of the bed and reached for the bottle. Kinsman raised his glass in the direction of the photograph. "Why," he said—"why do you have that up there?"

"Because I like George, and . . ."

"And what?"

"I've known him a long time."

"I don't feel as though I've known anyone a long time," he said.

"Neither you have. But don't worry about it."

"And I don't feel as though I want to know anyone for a long time."

"Maybe you won't," Millie said to him. "Do you mind if I get into bed? I can drink in bed."

"No. Carry on."

Millie stood up and started to undress.

98

Kinsman could feel little waves of tiredness reaching over him. As he sat there, his body seemed to be sinking and then rising again, as though he was drifting on a slow swell. His eyes wanted to close. He emptied the glass he was holding.

Catching his breath, he said, "You know, Millie, I don't really like whisky."

There was no answer from her, and when he turned to her, he saw her standing there, tall—taller almost than he —with her long arms reaching high above her head, as they held the nightdress which was about to drop over her old, white, naked body. When Millie's face appeared above the nightdress she smoothed her hair and then said, "Why do you drink it, then?"

"I . . . I don't know. I just drink it."

As Millie jumped into bed, Kinsman walked up to the other end of the room. A shiver of beautiful excitement rippled through him, and he suppressed a laugh as he thought of Wakefield. . . . This was better than Wakefield had. This was better than loving Julie or being loved by her. If there was tomorrow, there could be love. But now, before he had to sleep, there was Millie lying there, waiting for him to touch her. He turned and moved to Millie's bed quickly. He kissed her, and then he stood up and pulled back the bedclothes. Millie didn't speak; she just lay there looking at him. In her eyes there was a glazed expression. She looked at him as though she didn't want to see too much of him; as though the film that covered her eyes protected her from the responsibility of knowing who he was or what he was.

"Take that thing off," Kinsman said.

"Let me put out the light."

"No."

Millie took off her nightdress, and as she struggled with the thing, he could see that her thighs were dry and tired-looking. It was better that she was old. Much better.

Before he started to undress he went to the door and switched out the light above them. Then, having taken off his clothes, his knee was on the bed when he remembered something.

"What's wrong?" Millie asked.

Kinsman didn't speak. He reached up to the photograph of her husband which was above the bedside lamp, and turned it to the wall. Millie laughed, and to silence her he kissed her. And when he kissed her, he felt her long teeth hard against his lips.

Wakefield knew that he couldn't stand outside Julie's billet in the middle of the W.A.A.F. site. Someone might see them, and there would be trouble. Trouble for Julie was unthinkable. He laid his hand on her tunic, and then hastily removed it. Julie stood back on to the step, so that her head was not tilted back to look up at him.

"You shouldn't come in," she said.

He said, "No."

"Wakey. . . ."

He looked up from his feet to her eyes, those rich eyes.

"What, Julie?"

"You . . . you're a good boy."

He smiled. His expression was almost shy. He said, "I'll go now." And he turned and had taken about two steps, when she called to him softly again.

Wakefield's long body was sagging in the middle as he leant against the wall behind his bed, and his feet were dropping over to almost touch the floor when the door opened and Kinsman came in. Kinsman switched on the light, looked around the room, switched it out, and then, having realized that his friend was not asleep or even undressed, switched it on again.

Kinsman's eyes avoided Wakefield. He sat on his bed and said, "Aye, aye."

There was a pause before Wakefield spoke. Then he straightened his back and sat straight up on the edge of the bed. He said, "I've got no cigarettes."

Kinsman threw him one.

"Got a match?"

Kinsman threw him some matches.

"Julie's married," Wakefield said then.

"Julie?"

"She's married. She's married to some bloke who's in India. She told me all about it tonight standing outside her billet in the W.A.A.F. site."

Wakefield looked then to Kinsman, and Kinsman's eyes rose to meet his. They were disturbed by the smoke which arose from the cigarette he held, and he rubbed them and coughed.

CHAPTER EIGHT

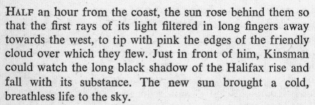

HALF an hour from the coast, the sun rose behind them so that the first rays of its light filtered in long fingers away towards the west, to tip with pink the edges of the friendly cloud over which they flew. Just in front of him, Kinsman could watch the long black shadow of the Halifax rise and fall with its substance. The new sun brought a cold, breathless life to the sky.

It was two hours since they had gone through the target. In an hour they would be home. With the thought, he took his hand from the stick, and allowed the aircraft to fly. It started to fall towards the cloud, and he caught it with trim. The needle of the air-speed indicator steadied, and when the shallow dive was checked, he amused himself by balancing the great thing on the tiny wheel in his right hand. He felt like someone who has been frozen and then gradually allowed to thaw out. The last drop of tension left his finger-tips. He removed his oxygen mask, and smiled to the bomb-aimer when Fred came up from the table below. Fred kissed his big hand to the morning. They didn't speak.

Kinsman looked at the props gleaming healthily on his port side. There was some fabric flapping loosely on that mainplane, as though to remind him where he had been. Fred tapped him on the shoulder. Ahead, a few hundred feet nearer to the cloud, a Halifax was floating across their bows. It was a tired-looking Halifax. From the way it crabbed listlessly across the cloud, it gave the impression of not knowing or caring where exactly it was going.

The sky was fast filling with light as Kinsman massaged his mouth and nose where the mask had been, and looked up. Nature never let you down. You could fly through the night, and feel as though you would never see this again, and then, unless something killed you, it was all there again when the hours had passed.

There was something strange and almost unreal about flying in daylight. The inside of the aircraft looked untidily different. Kinsman felt as though there should be a blind to pull somewhere. He sat there, reflectively holding his chin in a cupped hand, his elbow propped on the arm of his seat. It was good to fly without fear, peaceful. He felt as though he could sit there for ever, without food, or drink, or love, or happiness, or misery: with nothing but the droning of four healthy engines in his ears, a clear sky above and life sealed safely off by the clean white clouds beneath his wings.

Suddenly a feeling of sheer goodness arose in him, and he felt as though he should open his mouth and sing above the roar of the engines. He sat up straight, grabbed the control column tightly, and dropped his port wing. The Halifax fell away towards the cloud-tops below in a long, graceful dive.

Fred turned and laughed to Kinsman. He seemed to share Kinsman's feeling, for he grabbed the front of the cockpit as though trying to make the Halifax dive still faster. Kinsman felt his aircraft scream through the soft valleys, climbing to clear the ridges, and then, having breasted the tops, dropping again down, down to dip his wings in the white, foaming tops of cloud.

Bob came up on the intercom saying that they should be at four thousand feet, and Kinsman turned to Fred. He laughed, and shrugged his shoulders. Fred made a rude sign with his fingers in the general direction of the navigator. Then little Bob came rushing up from his table with a look of bewilderment on his face. He seemed dazed as he saw the edges of the cloud slipping past at a furious speed beneath their wings. The glare of the sun on the white overcast, too, dazzled him. Then he realized that Kinsman was playing, and held up four fingers for the captain to see. Kinsman laughed, and suddenly, almost

103

harshly, dropped a wing and dived the Halifax into the cloud. They emerged two thousand feet lower, still diving, and there, ahead, was the coast.

At the side of the runway on which they were to land, a Halifax was lying with a buckled undercarriage. Kinsman could see, too, as he turned on to the cross-wind leg, that an ambulance was parked beside the thing on the grass. About five minutes after Kinsman had seen the aircraft there, little Chico came piping up from the rear turret with the news.

"Skip," he yelled, "skip, somebody's bought it. There's a prang at the edge of the runway."

Fred, who had been standing beside Kinsman, watching the activity beside the runway, switched on his intercom and said, "Drop off your rear turret, Johnny. The man in there's been sleeping."

Kinsman was fully occupied. He had applied maximum flap, and was turning on to the final approach. The wheels were down, and he had slipped the rev. controls forward to fully fine. He switched his microphone on quickly, and said, "Do you think there's enough room beside him on the grass for us, gunner?"

"Eh?" Chico came back.

"Shut up!" Fred yelled.

Kinsman's eyes were flicking back and forward, between his air-speed indicator and the man wielding the Aldis lamp at the up-wind end of the runway. They had a green. He allowed his speed to fall off from a hundred and thirty miles an hour to a hundred and fifteen, to a hundred and ten. They were over the fence, and now he was gradually allowing his nose to come. They touched. Once.

Chico's microphone came on again, and he chirruped, "We made it."

Kinsman smiled. The aircraft was completely under control, and as he ran past the Halifax crashed on the grass, he looked at the machine to see if it was one of C Flight's. It wasn't. None of the little group of people who were there as he ran past seemed to be particularly sad.

"Doesn't look like there's much blood," Fred said.

Kinsman turned to taxi back to his dispersal. "Just a little boob," he said to Fred, "just a little boob."

Now he could see the disabled aircraft from a different angle. They were carrying something, someone, into the ambulance which stood alongside the crumpled bomber like a fussy little woman. Kinsman wondered who it was who had pranged. He wondered whether the thing had happened because of flak damage, or whether it had happened because of some lack of skill on the part of the pilot. It didn't matter. Whoever it was had had a bad trip. He himself had had a good trip. His aircraft had behaved well. It was still behaving well as he taxied around the curving perimeter track, steering the great machine with little bursts on his outer engines. It had been a good trip, and then, as he was about to park his aircraft, he tried to impress the goodness of his trip on that part of him which remembered. He tried, but he couldn't. He couldn't bring himself to feel that the brightness of that morning was part of the same thing as the heaving darkness of the night he had known over Germany a few hours before. Now he was on his way to breakfast. Then he had been sitting in the sky. Breakfast and the night before somehow didn't go together.

The truck which picked up Kinsman and his crew stopped at the next bay, and when Kinsman looked up at the untidy scramble of aircrew, who were climbing into the back of the vehicle, he saw that the man who climbed aboard last was Wakefield.

With one voice they said, "Good trip?"

They smiled to each other, and Wakefield went on, "as usual I shat myself. That I would say was the most extraordinary thing that happened."

"Extraordinary," Kinsman said. He used the word with some difficulty. It was an Englishman's word.

No one in the truck spoke much. They smoked, and thought of food. The truck had stopped at de-briefing when Wakefield said, "We're standing down for three days. Got any plans?"

"Standing down. Why?"

"I don't know. Group's feeling sorry for us, I suppose."

"You mean we'll get leave?"

"Probably a forty-eight if you want it. You could go home," Wakefield said.

"Why?" Kinsman asked. He spoke without thinking.

"I don't know, Johnny. Why do people usually go home? To see their folks, I suppose."

"Are you going home?" Kinsman asked.

"No."

They were in the de-briefing room, and Kinsman could see Julie Holmes standing at a coffee urn distributing cups of the stuff when Wakefield said, "I've asked Julie to go to York with me."

Kinsman didn't speak. He looked at Julie. She was smiling to the lads who were clustered around the table behind which she stood. Fred of his own crew was there, with little Chico by his side. Kinsman could see that Chico was embarrassed by her beauty. The lad was excited, and as Kinsman drew close, the gunner was making some joke to Julie. But her smile for Chico was just as for the others. There was the same warmth in her expression when she came to look at Wakefield and Kinsman as there was when she was passing cups to the tired boys in front of them.

Julie said to them, "Coffee?"

And if Wakefield expected anything more from her than that, he was disappointed. She passed them the coffee, and then turned to the others who were behind them. Tom Barry came up and asked them if they'd had a good trip.

"What was wrong?" the Squadron Leader asked.

"Wrong, sir?"

"I mean was there anything special about it?" Tom went on. As he was speaking, he never stopped stroking his under-nourished moustache. He told them that three of the squadron's aircraft had still to come in, and that there was no word of them. Bora, the American from C Flight, was one of them.

Bora. Bora was almost finished. Poor old Bora!

Kinsman gathered his crew together and took them from one table to another until they were completely de-briefed. On the last table, that which was presided over by the Intelligence officer, there had been placed a small glassful of cigarettes. All during their interrogation by the Intelligence man, Kinsman had been aware of Chico and Fred staring at these cigarettes, wanting to take one, and yet uncertain as to whether or not that would be the right thing to do. The spare gunner who had taken Geordie's place in the mid-upper turret was a dull youth by the name of Trimble. He couldn't even arouse enthusiasm for the free cigarettes. His eyes wandered around the room as though he was counting how many of his friends were there.

Breakfast was being served in the airmen's dining-hall, for those who returned from the operation, but Kinsman decided to wait and eat in his own mess. The cooking there was better, so with Wakefield, after they had deposited their flying clothes in their respective lockers, he set out to walk there. Wakefield was anxious to see Millie about borrowing her car.

All the squadron seemed to know that there was to be a stand-down, but no one seemed to know where the information had come from originally. Kinsman walked along past the guard-room with Wakefield. They were silent with their thoughts of what should be done with the succeeding two days. It had been a long time since Kinsman was home, for on his last leave he had gone to London with Fred and Geordie. . . . Geordie who was dead. The desire to see Aunt Lizzie was coming to him in little spasms as he walked. He wanted to see her, and then with that thought would come its companion: would going home upset the rhythm of his life? When he came back, would he be afraid? He was living now an existence in which you didn't think. Not at all. You just slept, and drank, and ate, and flew and got tired again. And he liked it. He almost liked being afraid before he took off, because he knew that once he had been there and back he would know the calm of tiredness, and sense again the feeling that he was part of something big, much bigger than he was, which thought for him and guided him and fed him.

There was something almost noble in its simplicity. But it had nothing to do with life back there where Aunt Lizzie was. It was noble because there was striving in it. Everyone dragged out of himself the last ounce of what he had to give. Maybe there was nobility in that. Sometimes Kinsman felt as though he was the servant of some elderly idiot whom he loved. And because Kinsman loved himself he usually hurried away from that thought.

The mess at that time was empty. When they pushed through the swing-doors the smell of the night before was there, still, and hanging heavy in the atmosphere of the hall. There was only one person in the dining-hall, a little middle-aged electrical officer. Wakefield called to the girl waitresses, and then walked noisily down to the serving-hatch. There was no talk in Kinsman so he allowed the door to swing closed, and went into the ante-room. The news on the radio was being read to no one at all. The machine had been left on all night. Yesterday's newspapers were littering the tables and the floor. Kinsman paused when he heard the radio announcer telling him that a force of Lancasters had attacked targets in the Ruhr throughout the previous night. No mention was made of the fact that a force of Halifaxes had also attacked targets in the Ruhr. He felt cheated. That was the kind of thing which would have annoyed Bora. But Bora hadn't come back. Maybe he was dead. Kinsman couldn't imagine Bora dead. He walked out of the room, leaving the radio to talk to no one.

Passing the letter-rack on his way to the lavatory, Kinsman paused. He seldom received mail, but he didn't look at his own rack. He took out those letters filed under B. Bora, Bora, Bora. There was a letter for Bora. Kinsman held the thing in his hand, feeling almost as though he was standing in Bora's bedroom holding something which had belonged intimately to the American. If Bora was dead, was this letter dead too? If he hadn't come back would a letter addressed to him have lost its life at the moment he died? His hand reached out to the bundle of letters filed under K. There was a letter addressed to F-Lt. John Kinsman, and it was written in the loosely rounded hand which he had come to recognize as Aunt Lizzie's.

Aunt Lizzie said:

Dear Johnny,
    You will be surprised to know that your old friend Robby has been killed in Italy. His mother and father are taking it very bad, son, for he was their only son. Robby was a good boy, and you and him were such great pals when you were both wee. It certainly was a great blow to us all here. If I was you, son, I would write to his mother and father for they always looked on you and Robby as great pals.
                    YOUR AUNT LIZZIE, JOHNNY SON.

. . . Since Wakefield had told Kinsman that Julie was married, the subject of Wakefield's being in love with her

108

had not been discussed. There had been little time, for they had flown on three successive nights that week, but between operations, in the moments when they had met in the briefing-room or in their billet or in the mess, Wakefield had never talked of Julie except when he mentioned that he had asked her to go to York. Kinsman had been almost afraid to talk to his friend of Julie. He couldn't think about them clearly.

On that morning, when Wakefield came up from the mess an hour after Kinsman, he found the latter preparing to leave the station.

"Hello, Johnny boy," Wakefield said brightly. "You look like a man with a plan."

Kinsman told him that he had decided to go home.

"Up there?" Wakefield said. "You won't have much time."

"I'll have tomorrow there. I can travel both nights."

"Tomorrow's Sunday."

"It'll be Sunday here too."

"A point, my friend. Indeed, a point," Wakefield said.

Kinsman declined Wakefield's offer of a lift to York. Someone else was leaving right away, and if he went now there was a chance that he would be in time for the afternoon train. He couldn't go to York with Wakefield and Julie.

Squadron Leader Barry took Kinsman to York. Barry was going home to see his wife in Birmingham, and he travelled fast in the little red sports car which he drove, so that Kinsman was in time for the early train.

But he didn't travel on it. He sat in a cinema all afternoon, and then he had something to eat. In the cinema he had told himself again and again that he should have been on that train. If he had gone he could have stayed overnight with Aunt Lizzie, and that would have been the decent thing to do. But it was more than he could do. He couldn't face up to arriving late at night at the house in Clover Road. Aunt Lizzie would be so excited at seeing him when he wasn't expected that she would probably have found it difficult to welcome him. And yet the thought kept coming back to him that it would have been good to have slept again in his own bed.

When the pubs opened he started drinking with the intention of doing so until it was time to get on the train at eleven. In a place called "The Bells" he drank, alone, to his crew, and he wished that his crew, or someone, had been there to drink with him. There were some aircrew people in the place, but they must have come from some other station. He knew none of them.

He emptied the glass he was holding, and then quickly he ordered a whisky and drank to Robby. He tried to remember Robby. He and Robby had grown from the same root, along the same warm, familiar wall. They had been great friends, but now he couldn't remember what it was that had made them that way. Robby had been fair-haired and strong, taller, too, than he was, but Kinsman couldn't remember how exactly his friend had looked when they were last together. Once when they were five he remembered lying with Robby behind the greenhouse. For some reason they were kissing each other, and they had been there a long time when Robby's father had found them. He remembered that.

Across the bar a woman was standing laughing with the barman. At intervals she was glancing across to Kinsman. Once, when he looked back at her, she smiled at him. He tensed, and finished his drink. Then he ordered another one, and when it was safely in his hand he knew a kind of gladness. Suddenly there was purpose in the hour or two that was to follow. He walked around to where the woman was standing.

She smiled, and said, "Hello," as though she had known that he would come to her. He offered to buy her a drink, and she said, "Ta" after accepting a gin and lime.

An hour later she had told Kinsman of her husband, and of her friend. She had come to this place with her friend, but her friend had an appointment. That was why she was alone. She wasn't usually alone. She was young, not more than twenty-seven; and there was a nervousness in the way she told him of how she spent her days, which suggested to him that she was afraid that anything of the excitement of life then should go past her.

Suddenly he wanted to get it over, and he suggested to her that they should go somewhere. She laughed at him and asked him what he thought she was. But when he told her that he had to go on a train at nine, her expression changed. Her face had been attractive, and probably would still have been but for a certain lack of sincerity in

110

the eyes, and the impatient slash of lipstick across her mouth. She looked as though she had dressed with one foot in front of a mirror and the other on the doorstep.

Her name was Martha, and she agreed to go after they had one more drink. He bought the drink, and as he passed it to her she smiled again.

She led him to her home, and when they got there he was surprised to find that she lived in a neat, modern house which was situated in a row of other neat, modern houses. That gate at the entrance crumbled in his hand as he opened it, and even in the darkness he could see that the little front garden was overgrown. This, Kinsman thought, is someone's dream of long ago that they have come back to and pay for whether or not they still want to dream this way.

"The kids," she said as he was removing his coat, "are at his mother's. I always put them there on a Saturday night."

He turned to look at her standing there in the narrow hallway. With her coat and hat off she looked younger than she had done outside. As she spoke she was shaking her head, so that her long, black hair fell backwards. She had a comb in her hand ready to comb the curls which lay on her shoulders.

"Kids?" he said.

She laughed gaily. "Two of them," she said. "Don't I look like the type that would have two kids? They're all right. They're at his mother's. . . . Come on in here. We can go in here."

She prattled on as she led him into a room which was a bedroom, apologizing for the fact that the house was not just as it might be. But she was working all week, and, anyway, she was all for having a good time. Wasn't he?

Kinsman said he was for having a good time.

"I'm sorry I can't offer you a drink. What's the matter?"

She had seen him looking around the room. The bed was rumpled as though it had been used many times without ever having been remade. There was a smell of staleness in the place.

"Nothing. Nothing's the matter."

"Come 'ere," she said. "Come 'ere."

He said impulsively, "Martha, you're a helluva nice little thing." And he meant it at the moment he said it.

She was stale, like the atmosphere. As she looked at him she started to laugh at him, and then, perhaps sensing something of his pity, her lips held back the laughter and quivered.

"I don't do this all the time," she said. "I don't do this with everybody I meet."

Her shoes were off. She was very small, and rather helpless, tired, already old with the tiredness that had come from living, and yet still nervously desperate to satiate the hunger for life that was in her.

He stepped towards her, and kissed her, and they fell on to the grimy bed. They lay there until he became aware that she was weeping. He asked her what was wrong.

"Ah don't know . . . ah don't know . . ." she gasped. She cleared her nose, and held her face up to his. But she was still weeping.

"Look," Kinsman said coldly. "What's the matter? What have I done?"

"Ah don't know. It's just because I'm excited. An' you're so nice. Honest. You're so nice. Ah'll be all right in a minute. Honest ah will."

Kinsman stood up from the bed, and as he stood up he left the desire that had been in him, lying there. He felt dirty, like the curtains hanging limply at the windows and the bed in which this girl lay sobbing. If he didn't go now he would have to be sorry for this woman, and there wasn't time for that.

She straightened her back, and she said. "Don't go . . . don't go. . . . What's your name?"

"Johnny."

"Don't go, Johnny. Ah'll be all right in a minute. Honest ah will."

She started to undress, and he stood there looking down at her until she was completely naked. Then he turned to go. She had been kneeling as though trying to compress her nakedness, but now she jumped to stand up on the bed. She stood there saying, "Don't go, Johnny. . . . Don't go, Johnny! Come back!" until the sagging spring caused her to unbalance, and she fell in a heap back on to her face.

As Kinsman opened the door she was still calling, "Come back, Johnny . . . come back! Ah don't know what's making me do this!"

He didn't go back to "The Bells". Instead he walked the two miles which took him to "Jenny's". It was a different kind of place. Aircrew congregated there when they wanted to talk. When he entered the lounge bar a roar of conversation met his ears, and when he had adjusted his eyes to the atmosphere he saw Wakefield with Julie at the other end of the bar.

But Julie had seen him first, and she called above the noise of the place, "Johnny. . . . Here's Johnny. Come on over here, Johnny."

Kinsman pushed through the crowd to get to where they were standing. They seemed glad to see him, and they said so. Wakefield bought more drinks, and they drank quickly. With one drink inside him, Kinsman felt much better. He looked at Julie standing there, leaning casually with one narrow-sleeved arm on the bar; her smooth, beautiful face smiling from Wakefield to himself and then back to Wakefield: and because he couldn't get the woman Martha, whom he had just left, out of his mind, he found it easy to be with Julie even when Wakefield was there loving her. Wakefield was talking rubbish, and Kinsman stood there protecting his silence by the smile that was fixed on his face.

His eyes stayed on Julie, until, momentarily, the woman Martha came so close that he saw Julie's face on top of that pale, anguished body. He laughed.

"My little tale wasn't that funny," Wakefield said. "He's been up to something. . . ."

"What?" Julie asked.

"The funniest bloody thing happened to me tonight, but I can't tell you."

"Tell us," Julie said.

"I can't. Really, Julie. Maybe later if we have enough to drink."

"Let's have enough to drink," Wakefield said.

Some more people from Liscombe joined their little group. In half an hour the group had become a party. The place was so full of people that it soon became difficult to know who was in their party and who wasn't. But it didn't matter. Kinsman and Wakefield and the squadron bombing leader and another fellow who had recently joined the squadron and whose name Kinsman couldn't remember went on buying drinks, until those who were drinking with them didn't know which drink was theirs.

Julie sat on a little stool so that her head was above the level of those who crowded, laughing around her. Once, Kinsman, turning, almost knocked her from the stool. Quickly he swung back and caught her by the arm. She smiled down to him, and when she smiled her eyes shone, lighting up her whole face.

He said, "Sorry . . . sorry, Julie. You're terribly nice."

Julie's smile seemed to become warmer, and she answered, "I'm glad you think I'm terribly nice, Johnny."

Wakefield's long, hard body leaned across the man who was standing between him and Julie. "What did he say?" he asked.

"Johnny said I was terribly nice."

"He's tight. But you are."

Kinsman caught Wakefield by the arm. "She is, you know, Wakey. She's terribly nice."

Wakefield took Kinsman's hand. "I know, Johnny," he said, "I know."

For a moment their hands were held together as their eyes fixed on each other's face. Then Kinsman caught Wakefield and pulled him past the man who was wobbling between them. He pulled him to the bar, and they turned their backs on Julie.

"I want to weep with you," he said. "You're my friend."

"Weep away," Wakefield told him. "I'll mingle my tears with yours."

"We'll be maudlin," Kinsman went on. "Now is the time for sadness. Call the roll of the dead."

"We could start with Bora: strong, silent Bora."

"He was a good fellow," Kinsman said. "Lift your glass to him."

They raised their glasses.

"And there was Mac. . . ."

"MacKenzie?"

"MacKenzie and Simmons and Arnold and Robinson, and Dacey and Morrison and little Ewing and Rodgers. . . ."

"Ewing?"

"Remember the little pasty-faced fellow in B Flight?"

"No, I . . ."

". . . and Graham and Dillon . . ."

114

"Don't, Wakey, stop! I think I'm going to cry."

They were silent until Kinsman said, "Drink to them all." And they drank.

Kinsman's arm reached around Wakefield's shoulder, and Wakefield placed his on Kinsman's.

"We'll go on living," Kinsman said, "and as long as we go on living they'll be dead. Think of it, Wakey: the image that they had created of themselves at the moment they died will stay that way for the rest of time."

"What makes you think we'll go on living?"

"Well," Kinsman almost shouted, "even if we don't we'll be in good company. What does that sound like? Does it sound maudlin?"

"No."

"But it sounds crazy?"

"Not when it's us who say it."

"You know, Wakey, we've got to be angry. Just a little bit angry sometimes. We've got to, Wakey. For nobody understands like we do. These bloody barmen and postmen and tinkers and tailors and fathers and mothers and sisters and brothers who think they know us, they don't understand, Wakey. Not like we do. You've got to have been there. You've got to have felt the loneliness. Do you feel the loneliness of it, Wakey?"

"All the time."

"Now I feel as though we should go on for ever. When we're out there alone in the darkness we're dead with them, Wakey. We're dead, Wakey. We're dead to all those bookies on trains going to race meetings, and fat women in butchers' shops. The dead are only dead to the living, Wakey. As long as we go on, as long as the war lasts, the dead'll still be with us. It's only when we stop that they'll be alone."

Julie's arms reached around them, and Kinsman could feel her face, cool, between his and Wakefield's. But that was all he felt, just the coolness of her face. There was no anguish in him. He breathed deeply, and thought, "That woman tonight helped me. Julie's just a woman too. That's what Wakey should remember. Julie's just a woman too."

Julie said, "You two have forgotten me. Is this a very private get-together, or can anyone join in?"

They laughed, and Kinsman turned and helped her from the stool. A bell rang, and a woman behind the bar whose dress and finger-nails were striking enough to suggest that she was Jenny herself called in a shrill, affected voice that it was time to go.

Kinsman said that he was going to the station, and Wakefield insisted that he and Julie should see him off. So they walked, the three of them, with Julie between the two men, through the vulgar, beautiful city to the station. Kinsman and Wakefield held one of Julie's arms as though they were helping her, but if the night had not been dark, and if the pavement had not been crowded with hundreds of airmen and officers and Waafs, and the drunken wives of railway workers who were now at the front in Italy, it would have been possible to see that Julie was in fact supporting her escorts.

Wakefield said, "York would become beautiful if it was deserted."

Julie was very happy. She laughed with them and at them, and when they arrived at the station it was she who ascertained the number of the platform from which Kinsman's train would leave, and it was she, too, who found a seat for him when the train finally came in from the South.

That was a long, long platform, and then it was only dimly lit by the tiny lights which were permitted by the blackout regulations. It was a long platform, and after the passengers who were going no farther alighted from the train and dispersed, the only people who were left standing there in the half-darkness were Julie and Wakefield. She stood there, leaning on one hip against his tall, dark body. About them, the two on the platform and Kinsman standing at the door of the carriage, there was a kind of easy, semi-drunken content.

Julie said, "This is like a family farewell."

The train jolted as though warning them that it was about to move. Kinsman grabbed at the frame of the window in mock alarm. "It's really quite mad," he said. "We've never said good-bye before."

"This is different," Wakefield answered. You've never gone off to the wilds of Caledonia before. Usually you've been going to some place like Germany, and then I've mostly been with you. This is quite different."

They laughed, and Kinsman said, "I'll be back on Monday morning. When'll you be there?"

They were smiling as he spoke, and for a moment neither of them answered. Then Wakefield said, "We'll probably go back tomorrow night."

Julie looked up and down the platform as though she was embarrassed. Then the train started to move, and Wakefield and Kinsman called loud good-byes to each other as though there was a chance that they would never see each other again. Julie was laughing, and the laughter seemed to bring tears to her eyes. She said once more, "Good-bye, Johnny. Give my love to your folks."

Wakefield was holding her hand as, with short, skipping bursts of energy, they followed the train along the platform until it started to gather speed. Then they stopped, laughing and breathless, and waved to him. She stood on tip-toe, stretching her body so that her greatcoat was pulled into neat, military lines, and, as Kinsman watched them fading into the bleak darkness of the station, he wondered what she would look like if they allowed Julie to go back to being a woman.

CHAPTER NINE

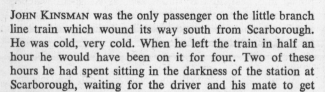

JOHN KINSMAN was the only passenger on the little branch line train which wound its way south from Scarborough. He was cold, very cold. When he left the train in half an hour he would have been on it for four. Two of these hours he had spent sitting in the darkness of the station at Scarborough, waiting for the driver and his mate to get out of bed.

Now, dawn was bringing the green countryside back to life; and the sea, which was visible at intervals between the gently rolling fields on his left, was freshened by a wind from the east that seemed to make it dance against the rough coastline which, occasionally, he could glimpse below.

Kinsman allowed one eye to stay open. He was wedged into the corner of the seat, his head, deep in his greatcoat, rested against the hardness of the window-frame. Any heat which was inside him seemed to escape when he moved his body even slightly. So he remained absolutely still, adjusting himself to the fact that it was morning. He estimated that if daylight was half an hour old he would be at Tupston Magna in half an hour, and the thought filled him with the warmth of pleasure. The muscles of his face almost moved into a smile, but the effort was too great. He relaxed.

It was good to be going back to a life he understood. Yesterday had been awful. Poor Aunt Lizzie, alone and looking old; weeping when she spoke of Robby. And Robby's mother expecting him to explain away Robby's death. He had spoken to them of death as though dying when you were twenty-two was the most sensible thing that a man could do. When he was speaking to them, his words had sounded to himself like a lie, but now, lying there in that wobbling train, he wasn't sure.

He had tried to ease their pain by telling them of all those who had been with him and who had died. He had exaggerated, and told of how on one occasion he had had breakfast at a table where there were eight people seated, and before he went to bed that night he was the only one alive.

He said, "It's those who are left alive who suffer. *They're* all right. Robby's all right."

They had shown him a photograph of Robby which had been taken in the Middle East. He was tanned and healthy, and laughing as though protesting to the photographer. Robby had changed. There was no soft, baby flesh on his face. He said, "Robby was always laughing. He's all right. If he could speak to you that's what he would tell you."

The mother had smiled, and even Kinsman had felt better. Lying in the train, immobile, he smiled again. Now he had given up the fight for sleep. The strange thing was that now he was sure that Robby would agree with him. He hadn't spoken on the day before with any particular conviction. But now he was sure.

Life was best when it made no demands on you. Like now, when he lay half asleep with no part of him moving and no question in his brain. It would be easy now to slip into death. What the hell was all the fuss about?

When the train reached Tupston Magna, Kinsman was asleep, really asleep for the first time since he had left Scarborough. He cursed, and then jumped on to the platform, feeling surprisingly wide awake. There was a truck there to collect mail for Liscombe, so he asked the driver for a lift.

Outside the officers' mess Kinsman jumped from the driver's cabin. He looked at his watch. It was just twenty-four hours since he had arrived home. Walking through the village on the morning of the day before, he had found it hard to believe that there was such a place as Liscombe, that in fact he had ever been away from the village with its grey, worn streets and pavements. The stone-fronted houses of Clover Road hadn't changed. Jessie Brown's little shop in the main street, into which he used to run on the way home from school with a precious halfpenny clutched in a small, grimy hand, was still there. The advertisement for "Boy Blue" toffee was still in the window: the step to the entrance was still sagging in the middle, worn by seventy years of children's feet. Nothing was different.

He could never live again in the village. He didn't know where he could go or how he could get there, but he couldn't go back to the village.

The boiler-house was more pleasing to look at than the tin-roofed officers' mess. All the things that Kinsman loved about Liscombe were of the night. Now the bright morning light shone harshly. He hurried inside.

Aunt Lizzie had been sure that something was wrong when she had seen him. A lifetime crammed with mild disaster had convinced her that every pleasure has its price. She worried about the fact that there was nothing in the house with which to entertain him. She apologized five times for the breakfast she served, and later in the day she insisted on borrowing some tins of food from a neighbor so that she could prepare a meal that was more in keeping with his homecoming.

The old woman—for Aunt Lizzie had become old since her husband's death—seemed unable to believe that there was nothing wrong with him. It was as though the weight of Uncle Willie's helplessness had held her strength within her: with his death she had become suddenly old and tired.

She told him the gossip of the village, but she had wanted him to talk, and she had listened, enraptured, all day, to his stories of life in the Air Force. Before he left, Kinsman was enjoying himself. She had wanted him to visit Xavier Faighley, his former employer, in the evening —not because, from what she heard of that gentleman, she particularly approved of him, but because she felt that by visiting him Kinsman would be protecting his own interests. She said: "The war won't last for ever, son, and you may have to go back to him some day."

But Kinsman decided against the idea.

"Take your face out of that sausage," Wakefield said, "and listen to the words of a man in love."

120

Kinsman looked up to see his friend standing behind him. There was no one else at the table, and only a few people sprinkled here and there in the dining-room.

"Get yourself some breakfast and sit down."

"I don't think I want any breakfast," Wakefield said. He grabbed a cup and poured himself some tea. Then he took some of Kinsman's toast.

He said, "Julie and I are going to get married."

Kinsman emptied his mouth, and said, "That would appear to complicate the issue."

"I'm serious."

"How the hell can you be serious?"

"What do you think we did yesterday afternoon?" Wakefield said eagerly.

"I can imagine that it wasn't very original."

"It was."

"Give me a cigarette," Kinsman said.

He lit the thing, and then refilled his cup slowly.

"Don't you want to hear what I've got to say?" Wakefield asked.

"Yes, I want to hear what you've got to say. Let's get out of here. I'm going up to the billet."

"I've just come from there."

"Well, come back. We'll walk."

As they left the mess they met Squadron Leader Barry. He was with a group of people making their way into breakfast, and he told them to be at Flights early, as there was a possibility that they would be busy.

The winter sunlight was dancing on the road, which was still wet from a shower of early morning rain. It was a beautiful day, and Kinsman wished that he could just have walked. He hesitated to open the conversation with Wakefield, and before he spoke he wished that he didn't care. He said, "What is it?"

"I wrote to her husband yesterday, when we were in York, I told him everything about Julie and me. I told him that we were in love and that we wanted him to give her a divorce so that we could get married as soon as possible."

"You did that?"

"It was the right thing to do."

Kinsman turned to look at Wakefield walking by his side. Wakefield's head was well back, and he seemed to be

121

staring in front with his eyes fixed slightly above the horizon. There was a kind of innocent nobility about the edge of Wakefield's profile.

"The right thing to do." The words rang through Kinsman's brain. He heard them again and again. It wasn't the thing he would have done. Kinsman knew a sudden urge to grasp his friend's arm.

Wakefield, slightly taller than John Kinsman, gave the impression of being unaware of the other's presence. Even when Kinsman said, "And does she love you?" a moment passed before he said in reply, "She loves me."

They had passed the airmen's billets. There was nothing on either side of the road at that particular part. Kinsman's thoughts seemed to come to the boil within him, and he stopped. Wakefield walked on a few paces. Then, aware that Kinsman wasn't by his side, he turned.

"You think I'm a bloody fool," Wakefield said.

"You're all the bloody fools that ever were, rolled into one."

"I love her, Johnny."

"Why the hell couldn't you love her and leave it at that?"

"We love each other. It's got to be all right. There's a chance . . ."

"There's a chance! There's no chance that it'll ever be right. I can't understand you! Julie's a married woman. All right! You love her. You go to bed with her. Isn't that enough for you? You want it for ever. Nothing's for ever. Nothing! What did you say to this poor devil in India?"

One of Wakefield's elegant, dark eyebrows raised itself higher than its neighbour, and his neck looked very thin when he said, "I told him that we were in love, and that we had spent the week-end together, and that we wanted to get married, and that I was sorry."

"You're sorry. Did Julie see this letter?"

"She read it. We felt that we weren't betraying him if we told him."

Kinsman started to speak, then his lips closed in a thin line, cutting off the words. He paused, and said, "Wakey, this is a helluva mess. Why did you have to get all organized? You're a God-awful fool, Wakey."

Wakefield said quietly, "I didn't think you'd feel this way. I thought you'd have been with me."

"What about that other poor bastard?"

Wakefield's eyes dropped to the roadway. Then he raised his shoulders, and started to walk past Kinsman in the direction from which they had just come.

"Wakey . . ." Kinsman said, catching him by the arm.

"I'll see you later, Johnny," Wakefield said. He disengaged his arm, and walked on down the road.

Kinsman stood for a moment looking after Wakefield's tall, slim, battledressed figure. He wanted to run after him and tell him that he was sorry, that he hadn't meant what he had said; but he stood there as though his feet were fixed to the ground, watching Wakefield, until his friend, walking with long strides, and raising himself high on the sole of one foot before reaching out with the other, was gone.

CHAPTER TEN

DUISBURG burned. It burned so that below, the earth writhed in swelling agonies of red and deep yellow flame. The smoke seemed to reach up to twenty thousand feet, for the light of searchlights in the cloudless night sky was dusted with a dirty grey haze.

Kinsman thought he detected shame in Fred's voice when the bomb-aimer said, "Well, I'll be damned."

They were almost over the target they had seen burning for the last hundred miles of their flight. Intelligence had told them that there would be fires, for theirs was the second force to attack the place within twenty-four hours.

This, though, was an inferno. They had never seen anything like it before. When the first of the force were dropping their bombs into the flames, Kinsman could see great bubbling waves of fresh fire rush up as though the sea of flame over which they were about to fly was being stirred into fury.

"Five minutes we should be there," the navigator said.

"Can you see anything, Fred?" Kinsman asked.

"Can ah see anything?" Fred said slowly. "They . . . they should have left the poor bastards alone."

"The poor bastards won't leave us alone. See anything, gunners?" Kinsman asked again.

Chico's voice came up on the intercom, from a distance, as though he was speaking from outside the aircraft. "Two of our blokes look as if they wish they 'adn't come," he said.

The bomb-doors were open, and Kinsman was frozen on the controls as they started into their run. He could hear Fred breathing as the bomb-aimer wriggled on his belly trying to get a sight on the target. Fred had, so far, said nothing. Then quietly, and with great confidence, he said, "Left a little, skip."

Kinsman turned.

"Skip," Fred said.

Kinsman didn't answer. He waited for the instruction, but Fred said, "Skip, I think. . . ."

"What's the matter?" Kinsman asked with anger in his voice.

"There's something . . . there's a black thing below us."

"What do you. . . . ?"

"It's a kite, skip. It's a fighter. There's a Focke-Wulf below us. He's right below us." Fred's voice fell almost to a whisper, as though he was afraid that the pilot of the Focke-Wulf might hear him.

Kinsman could feel warm sweat running down his body. He imagined that the flames were warming him. As they approached, the gunners below seemed to be concentrating their fire in a pattern designed to affect the accuracy of the attack. He couldn't see or think of the burning city below for holding on to his bucking Halifax. But yet his fear was not of the flak which at intervals he could hear rattling against the side of the air-frame. He was afraid that he would drop into the flames below. That was his fear.

"What'll I do, skip?" Fred asked, his voice still low.

"Where is he? Where is he, Fred?" Kinsman asked.

"He's right there. I can almost touch him."

"Drop your bombs on him."

Bob cut in to say, "The aiming point."

Kinsman allowed the used breath to escape from his lungs. Then he said, "Bomb the bastard."

"You mean . . ."

"Drop them!" Kinsman shouted. "Hit him! Hit him, Fred!"

Fred dropped his bombs and yelled.

Kinsman waited, and then he asked. "Did you get him?"

"Yeah . . . yeah, I got him. There was a gun sticking up."

They were still on the bombing run. The doors were

open, and the light on his panel was telling Kinsman that the camera was turning over. His head sunk low on his shoulders, and his eyes half closed, Kinsman sat there holding on. Their bombs were gone, but they were just entering the target area. He couldn't turn off before he had gone through. He held the empty Halifax.

A black shadow above and slightly ahead of them took lines and became a Halifax. Its bomb-doors were open, but there was a look of attack about the machine. It looked as though it still had purpose. All around their aiming point, searchlights were reaching up to them from the flames below.

"In a few minutes," Kinsman thought, "I'll be able to look at this and think about it, but not now." There was a sudden, messy explosion on his port bow, and then just ahead of him something fell off, burning, to starboard.

He was easing his nose down, as the bomb-doors were closing, when the aircraft tilted beneath him. Something happened so close that he didn't hear it. All he knew was a numbness in his ears, and then the instrument panel in front of him dropped. His hand shot out to hit the roof in front, and he was looking down into the flames below.

Calmly Kinsman thought, "I wonder if this is where I'm going to die." There was no fear in him. He didn't think of God, or of the mother he couldn't remember. All he knew was the curious stillness in his ears. The thought of death didn't frighten him, for it left him as soon as his right hand was back on the control column and he had regained something of his balance by leaning back in his seat.

Some instinct told him that his starboard wing was down as he was diving. In his eyes there was the dazzling sadness of a burning city. A faint sickness gathered inside him, and then his ears cleared and the roar of the engines rushed to his brain. He pulled, he pulled at the control column and reached out with his left leg to press the rudder bar as far as it would go. He still dived, but he knew that he was winning. Beneath his mask the line of his lips softened into an inexplicable smile, a soft, silly, embarrassed smile.

Low down, the thing levelled out so that the city fell beneath their belly. Now Kinsman could think clearly enough to be afraid of the bombs that were dropping from above. The aircraft was dragging to starboard. Even when he pushed his throttles open as far as he dared, the thing still dragged.

The engineer was the first to speak. He told Kinsman that it looked as though their starboard inner had gone. That was better. Knowing that he had lost an engine, Kinsman trimmed the Halifax to compensate for the drag on his starboard mainplane. But there was so much noise. For the first time Kinsman realized that a large proportion of the perspex covering his cockpit had gone with the explosion.

His air-speed indicator told him that they were maintaining an air-speed of something like a hundred and sixty miles per hour. There was a fiercely cold air-stream howling through the aircraft. Bob, the navigator, came up the steps from his table, and as his head came in front of the hole at that side of the cockpit he ducked. His little, strong, round hand clutched at Kinsman's knee, and then he pulled himself up until he was level with Kinsman's face. So that the other members of the crew wouldn't hear him speaking, Kinsman pulled off his mask. He laughed, and slapped old Bob on the shoulder. Bob, too, managed to laugh. Bob was yelling in his ear. But Kinsman couldn't hear, and he leant closer to Bob to listen to him telling him that their maps were gone.

Kinsman had a vision of their Halifax flying across the flames of Duisburg low down so that they were throwing a shadow, a long shadow which everyone could see, across the dancing fires. They were out of line, alone, very naked down there, and there was nothing to do except sit there and hope or pray that the Halifax wouldn't fall to pieces. He told himself that they were safer there than at twenty thousand, but he didn't believe himself. There was nothing he could do. He couldn't turn until the gyro compass had settled, and he couldn't climb on three engines.

But the compass did settle, and he had just started to turn towards the south in spite of the fact that his dead engine was on that side when the engineer asked if he had feathered the starboard inner. Kinsman told him he hadn't touched the thing.

"Well, it's feathered," the man said. "It must have done that itself."

Kinsman seemed to remember that when they had been

rocked by the explosion which had sent them down, his hand had shot out to the roof. Could he have feathered an engine by hitting the button accidentally? He started into the unfeathering procedure, and the engine came to life.

Then he was glad. An almost frightening enthusiasm for life arose in him as he felt power coming back to the Halifax. He started to climb, and it climbed. The turn was taking him away from the city, and now Chico came up on the intercom with a report on the carnage they had left behind.

"Are you all right?" Kinsman asked the gunner.

"Can ah say anything about that carry-on back there?"

"No."

"Can't ah even express me displeasure?"

"Are you all right, Fred?" Kinsman asked.

Fred was all right. Kinsman asked them all: the new mid-upper gunner; the wireless operator, young Les, who was hiding below and behind his curtains; the engineer. No one appeared to be hurt.

The glare from the burning city stretched across the Rhine. There was no sharp dividing line between light and darkness. Instead, the awful yellow glow smudged the edge of the night. Kinsman was climbing. Every minute he was climbing five hundred feet. Up and ahead the sky was waiting to cover, but the damned old Halifax wouldn't climb fast enough.

When Kinsman spoke he said, "Searchlights don't seem to be on the ball tonight, Fred."

There was a pause before Fred, still lying in the nose, said, "They've been on the ball. We've taken a bashin'. I reckon we've taken a bashin'."

Kinsman smiled and was silenced. It seemed that Fred's sympathies that night were with the enemy.

"Fred."

"Skip . . .?"

"We've made it."

"Yep, we've made it."

There was some trouble about identifying a beacon on the English coast when they got there, but after some argument with Bob, Kinsman decided that they were almost over Woodbridge. They flew on until they were over the beacon, and then Kinsman turned on to a course of three hundred and forty degrees. He estimated that that should take him across the Humber, and when they were there they would only be about forty miles from home.

Some gunnery crew fired on them when they were close to Hull. They were very late. The main force must have passed that way almost half an hour previously, and Kinsman explained to the crew, when they cursed the anti-aircraft gunners, that the I.F.F. equipment in the aircraft must have been damaged when they were over the target.

They found the marker-beacon on Flamborough Head, and from there it was easy to find Liscombe. The Drem was still lit. Kinsman smiled when he thought of them waiting down there for him to get back. He had forgotten before that moment that there were others who had been there where he was, and who, like him, had been occupied by the business of getting back to Liscombe.

Kinsman circled the airfield twice. Then, having failed to contact them on his R.T., he asked Les to try to get them on W.T. Les still hadn't received a reply or permission to land when, on the second time round, the airfield controller gave him a green as he was on the down-wind leg. He decided to go in without flap, for he wasn't sure as to whether the hydraulics had been damaged, and he didn't want to try and drop some flap, lest they should fall down completely. He turned into a long, low approach. Pitch fully fine, fast, his nose as high as he dared.

Kinsman was travelling at a hundred and five miles an hour when he touched. He wasn't stalled. His brakes were partially on before he touched the ground, so that the nose dipped dangerously as the wheels reached the runway. Brake off, brake on. Off a little more. He couldn't get the tail down. He knew he would never stop the thing before he reached the end of the runway.

The wireless operator, Les, came up on the intercom saying, "Permission to land, skip."

No one answered. Kinsman was praying that the grass at the far end wouldn't be so soft that he would nose up. He switched off the engines to cut down the danger of fire. They reached the end. She ran off and juddered to a stop.

The Halifax was still facing the direction in which it had landed, but Kinsman was conscious of its being down on the starboard side. There was complete silence. The engines were still. No one in the aircraft spoke. Kinsman removed the mask which had been covering his face. His body was very cold, for slipstream had been beating through the damaged perspex all the way from the target. But now he breathed cool air into his lungs. Then he pulled out the pin which held his harness. He allowed his shoulders to sag, and then, when he remembered his crew, he said to himself, "I'm sorry, lads."

At that they appeared from their corners. The gunners came along from their turrets, and Fred and Bob, and Les from below. The engineer, who was shy and laughing, and Fred slapped Kinsman on the shoulders. They were all very happy.

Kinsman lit a cigarette and sat there for a moment trying to believe that the quiet and the stillness outside were real. Then he smiled to himself, and left his seat to get a lift back to de-briefing in the ambulance which had arrived.

The last stragglers from de-briefing were climbing into a bus which would take them to the airmen's dining-hall as Kinsman and his crew arrived at Flights. In the darkness he could recognize no one when he jumped down from the little ambulance. He told Fred to hold the bus for them, otherwise they would have to walk to the dining-hall. But he was too late. The bus was moving off. Fred swore and maintained that it didn't pay to be conscientious in this Air Force.

The long, narrow room in which they went through the process of de-briefing was almost empty. The engineering officer and the bombing and signals leaders were gone with their notes. Only a junior Intelligence man was there to listen to Kinsman. He was a very young man who wore glasses, and when he bumped into Kinsman and his crew as they straggled into the place he said, "Ah, you're back."

"Make it short, will you, old boy?" Kinsman said. "These lads are hungry, and they've got to walk back to their mess."

"Right." The man smoothed some papers which he had placed before him on the first table they came to. "Anything special about the trip?"

The crew waited for Kinsman to speak, and to keep it short he said, "Nothing special. We've had a little trouble. Zebra's bent a little at the end of the runway."

The young Intelligence officer paused piously, and then

130

said, "Nothing special in the way of enemy interference?"

"No."

"That's fine, Johnny. We'll close the book at that."

The N.C.O.s rushed from the place to deposit their kit, leaving Kinsman resting on the edge of the table. Bob sat astride a chair which was turned the wrong way round, facing him.

"Think Zebra will be O.K. for the next one?" Bob asked.

"Don't know. I wonder if there's any coffee left in that thing."

Kinsman raised himself with some effort from the table, and turned towards the coffee urn at the far end of the room. The place was covered with litter, after the passage of the returning crews. A group of three or four people were standing around the coffee urn smoking, and as Kinsman started to walk towards them they seemed to decide to go. They spread apart and came towards him, leaving only one person standing there. It was Julie Holmes.

She saw Kinsman; probably she had seen him before he realized she was there. Perhaps that was why the officer-technicians who nodded and smiled to Kinsman as he met them had walked away. But, as he approached, she stepped back to lean against the wall. And she stayed that way, leaning, tired, her beautiful eyes on him all the time, until he faced her across the table on which stood the big empty metal urn.

"Hello, Julie."

There was a pause before she said, ". . . Johnny."

He dropped his eyes and said, "Coffee?"

"It's empty, I think. There's nothing left."

He took a soiled cup, and turned the tap until some cold coffee dripped into it. Then he raised the stuff to his lips, and as he drank he looked at her. He could see that there were tears in her eyes.

"Not back?"

She said, "No."

"Has it been bad?"

"Pretty bad. Bad, Johnny."

Kinsman replaced the cup on the table. Then he walked around to Julie. He took her hand, and felt her tremble.

"Are you all right, Julie?"

Julie nodded.

"Let's go up to control and wait," he said. "Something may come in."

He took her arm in his, and together they left de-briefing and walked to the control tower. They climbed the outside steps, Kinsman opened the metal door, and they stepped into the darkened interior.

The Group Captain was there, and the Wing Commander; and little Tom Barry along with B Flight Commander. When Tom saw them he came over. Tom looked tired. His moustache seemed to sag with sheer exhaustion, and his cheeks were hollowed so that there was even less of his face than usual.

"Bloody awful," Tom said to them, ". . . bloody awful. I can't understand it. It's crazy."

The control tower was darkened. Some green-shaded lights cast a pale glow over the faces that were there. From a room somewhere out of sight Kinsman could hear a signals man at work. And because little sound except an occasional low jumble of words came from the people standing grouped in pools of interest and authority, in threes and twos and alone: like the control officer on duty, standing at the long desk beneath the board on which was chalked the call letters of the squadron's aircraft . . . because nothing any of them could say would make things better, the clicking of the unseen teleprinter assumed all the real authority that was there.

Kinsman had done some drinking with the control officer, but because the Group Captain and the Wing Commander were there, the man made no signs of recognition. He stood there, looking as though he was completely in command of the situation, his long, thin arms wedged tightly between his shoulders and the desk over which he was leaning.

The Group Captain turned from the Wing Commander and little Tom Barry, and the Commander of B Flight with whom he had been standing. There was an expression of boredom on his face, and when he saw Kinsman, his eyes flashed something which could have been called relief.

The C.O. hesitated, as though he was uncertain of Kinsman's name. He smiled and looked hard at Julie. The smooth, rubbery flesh of his face moved again, so that around the thin, moist line of his lips there gathered on each side of the mouth little question-marks of indecision. He seemed to feel as though he should have known why she was there. But since he didn't, he said nothing which would tell the others that. He said, "Hello, Julie . . . thought you'd be getting your beauty sleep at this time of night."

By the time he had spoken to Julie, and she had said a few polite words in reply, the C.O. remembered Kinsman's name. His smooth black brows came down as he looked at him, and he said, "What kind of trip did you have, er . . . er, Kinsman? You looked for a moment as though you were about to make a mess of my aerodrome out there." And the big man raised one arm in the general direction of the runway on which Kinsman had landed. Then as Kinsman said, "Brakes, sir," Group Captain Savory turned away, dismissing the subject before he had heard the explanation, and smiled to the others who were there.

Something in the way they looked at Kinsman after the Group Captain had spoken, made him feel good. In their eyes as they smiled, there was a knowing, tolerant patronage which he didn't see as smugness. He was far too grateful for their apparent friendship.

Tom Barry said, "Did you want to see me, Johnny?"

"No, sir . . . it was . . ." Kinsman hesitated, looked at Julie standing by his side, and then said, "It was Wakey. We wanted to wait and see."

Squadron Leader Barry was embarrassed. He stepped quickly and rather awkwardly to Julie's side and took her arm to lead her, with Kinsman following, to the balcony outside. Out there in the still darkness they leant on the tubular rail which ran around the balcony. Julie was between Kinsman and the little Squadron Leader. When Barry saw that Julie wouldn't be drawn into talk, he spoke to Kinsman with a nervous rush of words, as though he couldn't bear the girl's silence. He spoke of Kinsman's trip and of other trips, and when he had momentarily exhausted the subject of flying he spoke of a bulldog which belonged to someone at a neighbouring station who was called Parsons. Julie laughed, suddenly.

The Drem system was still lighting the runway in use, and in its light Kinsman could see the whiteness of Julie's teeth as she laughed. Then, as sudden as her laughter, the light went out, and she stopped.

Tom Barry was bewildered. He said, "Did I say something, Julie?"

Julie gave a little sobbing laugh, and for no apparent reason said, "The lights go out all over Europe."

Kinsman put his hand on her arm, and squeezed until he could feel the flesh beneath her tunic tightening. It was the first time he had ever touched Julie consciously, but he didn't realize that until he thought of the incident later, and when he did think about it, he realized that, touching her, he had known quite a different sensation from that which he had imagined he would.

Tom Barry said, "I'm sorry, Julie. Did I upset you in some way?"

"No, sir," Julie said: "you didn't upset me."

"This is a bloody silly night," Tom went on. "They've put the lights out. The old man obviously doesn't expect anyone else now. We didn't expect you, Johnny. When you came in so late the old man decided to keep the lights on in case there were any more stragglers. Seven. . . . Seven out of nineteen. It's bloody. Absolutely bloody. This'll send the month's figures for a complete Burton, old boy."

"I think I'll take Julie in, sir; she's cold."

"No, I'm not. I want to stay out here in the dark. I like the dark from up here."

But Kinsman again took her arm, and turned her in towards the control room. The Group Captain and his party were leaving as they entered, and Barry, who was entering behind Kinsman, as though afraid that he was missing something, said to the Wing Commander who was in the doorway, "What's happening, Peter?"

"Going for a drink, old boy. Er, got room in your car for Julie and . . . eh . . . Johnny Kinsman here?"

When Barry arrived at the mess with Julie and Kinsman, the C.O. had opened the bar and was serving drinks through the hatch to Peter Carr, the Squadron Commander, and the florid Tubby Spiers, who was in charge of B Flight. No one greeted them as they entered. There seemed to be in the atmosphere a conscious avoidance of pleasantry, as though everyone there was determined to impress on his neighbour the fact that this was not a party.

Tom Barry said, "This is a very decent idea, sir."

134

The Group Captain stroked his moustache slowly. "This one," he said, "is on me. All drinks to be paid for. Everything must be strictly regular."

Kinsman saw some stale-looking sandwiches lying on the bar, and started to eat them.

"You haven't eaten, Johnny," Julie said. "You should go down and eat."

"I'd rather drink, Julie."

Kinsman could feel the drink running over the coldness that was inside him. A beautiful light-headed weakness seemed to rise from half-way up his body to reach upwards towards his head: he was light-headed.

There was one man there who hadn't been in the control room. It was the fair-haired Intelligence officer whom Kinsman remembered as having been in this bar on the first evening he had ever come into it. Then the man played the piano for a little middle-aged W.A.A.F. officer whom Kinsman had come to know as Section Officer Ralston. Julie and Millie called her Madge, but no male officer called her anything but Section Officer Ralston. In fact, Kinsman couldn't remember seeing her talking to anyone but this man who was here now. Section Officer Ralston was never in the mess except when the Intelligence officer was there, and then they would be quietly and respectably huddled together in some corner of the ante-room.

Kinsman had only once spoken to the Intelligence man, and that was when he had met him in the corridor of Millie's billet on the one occasion he had been there. The other man had been slipping quietly from Section Officer Ralston's billet to go home to his wife in the village. It had been very embarrassing for the Intelligence man.

The Group Captain seemed to enjoy acting as barman. He stayed there behind the bar, and quickly he consumed three drinks before the others had time to finish one. Julie sat on a high stool, an untouched drink beside her on the bar, talking to Squadron Leader Barry, who, from where Kinsman sat against the wall, looked even smaller than usual, with his head bent back to look up at the girl. Farther along the bar, and facing the Group Captain, sat the Intelligence man, who had hardly moved since Kinsman came in. An empty glass was on the bar before him, waiting for the C.O. to do something about filling it. The Wing Commander and Tubby Spiers held the centre of the

135

meagre floor space. They talked about what it was like in 1941.

Kinsman finished the sandwiches, and at the moment of swallowing the final mouthful came to the conclusion that Tubby Spiers was a dull man. Tubby was insisting that Bomber Command had gone all to hell since it got so big.

"A drink, Kinsman?" the Group Captain asked with efficiency.

"Yes, sir, please. Er . . . one for everybody."

Each of them made their requests to the C.O. except Julie, who didn't want another drink then, and the Intelligence man. Kinsman asked him again, and the man said, "Whisky . . . whisky, thank you."

Kinsman left Julie to talk to Barry. He emptied the glass he was holding, and when he placed it back on the counter, the Group Captain took it without a word and refilled it, in violation of the rules he had laid down before they received their first drink.

The Intelligence man still said nothing. He sipped his drink, but he didn't speak, and Kinsman wondered why he stayed there. If he was uncomfortable at being the only man there who didn't fly, why didn't he go away?

He was a good-looking man, this Intelligence officer. He wore his very fair hair long at the sides, but it was his hands which fascinated Kinsman. They were pink—very dry and pink and long and strong. His age Kinsman guessed as being thirty-seven. Not thirty-six or thirty-eight: thirty-seven. Older than anyone there, and yet not old. Probably in the other world before the war he had been more than anyone there. More, for instance, than the Group Captain, who had once told Kinsman when he was drunk that he had been a dentist's receptionist before he joined the Air Force. Now no one spoke to him. It was as though they felt that because his chest, unlike theirs, was bare, there was nothing of which they could speak to him. Kinsman didn't know that Peter Carr had greeted him politely when he had first entered the room and found the Intelligence man sitting there staring at the bar hatch which was pulled down in defiance of his being there.

Kinsman spoke to him. He said, "What about providing the C.O. here with a Command Performance?"

"A performance of what, old boy?" the man asked.

"The piano."

136

The Group Captain raised his eyebrows, and wiped the flavour of whisky and orange from his lips with a long tongue. He waved an outstretched finger in the direction of the instrument in the corner.

"You play," he said. "Play!"

For a moment the Intelligence man didn't move. His shoulders sagged and rose again as though he was gathering himself together. Then he turned towards Kinsman and fell from the stool. He appeared to be very drunk.

Kinsman helped him to regain his balance, and the Group Captain laughed, and the Winco and Tubby Spiers moved back to avoid spilling their drinks. Julie and little Tom Barry stopped talking. Julie was glad of the interruption, and the Winco was glad to leave 1941 behind. The Intelligence man, with less help than at first would have appeared to be necessary, regained his feet. Then he restrained Kinsman, who was about to help him to the piano.

"Do you know," he said, "what you are?"

"What?" Kinsman asked.

"No. Do you know what all boys like you are?"

"Naughty," Kinsman said, and everyone laughed.

"No, not that. You're half a man trying to discover in whose image you should cast the other half."

"Wimpole's an intellectual," the Group Captain said by way of explanation, "a drunken intellectual, if I may say so. . . . Play, Flight Lieutenant Wimpole!"

The Intelligence man sat at the piano and played quietly, to himself, as though no one else was there; and with the music each of them appeared to forget why they had come there. The Group Captain had opened the two top buttons of his tunic, and was leaning casually on the bar talking to Kinsman, while Peter Carr disentangled himself from Tubby's talk of 1941 and now was talking to Julie, leaving Spiers on the edge of their conversation. Once or twice Kinsman turned to look at Julie, and once when he was looking at her she was looking at him. She was smiling almost happily. It was good for her that these people were with her.

It was good to sit there too. Kinsman felt himself settling into the bar as though there were grooves on the counter where his arms were. This was better than sleep. And when he started to feel himself getting drunk, he spoke to himself for the last time that evening. This was better than sleep, because nothing existed outside himself, and he could still be aware of the warm friendship inside himself for those who were there. Once he turned to the Intelligence officer and said, "Play something sad."

But the Group Captain was against that. He countermanded the request and said, "No, play something gay!" And the pianist ignored them both and went on his way.

"Why doesn't he go home?" Kinsman asked the Group Captain.

"Can't stand his wife, old boy."

The phone rang, and when Tubby Spiers had answered it he came back to the bar to tell the C.O. that Mrs. Savory wanted him home.

Group Captain Savory laughed. "Signal for another drink." And he removed the fern from his mouth which he had been chewing, while he poured a drink for each one of them.

"It's your round, Kinsman," he said.

"Is it, sir? I've no money."

"I'll lend you a pound."

"Thank you, sir."

The Group Captain passed a pound to Kinsman, who passed it back in payment for the drinks.

"I'll expect it in my office tomorrow."

"Quite, sir."

"You bloody Scotsman!"

"Yes, sir."

They laughed, and the C.O. called on each of them to drink up. He was afraid that his wife might come and pull him out of the bar.

Within minutes the phone rang again, and the C.O. was banging his heavy hand on the bar counter and telling them that it was time to go. The bar was closed. Then Peter Carr announced that he, too, was going home to his wife, and Kinsman said that everyone seemed to have wives to whom they could go home, and the Group Captain said that he should marry Julie and thereby solve the problem, and when the big man said that, Kinsman looked at Julie and was sure that on her face was the faint redness of embarrassment.

Tubby Spiers went with the Wing Commander, for he, too, had a wife living on a farm nearby. Of the senior officers only Squadron Leader Barry was left. Little Tom said, "Care for a lift, you two?"

Kinsman didn't answer. He wasn't really aware that the Squadron Leader had spoken. He was wondering why all these people were married. And Julie didn't answer for a moment, so that Tom Barry experienced a kind of intuition which became embarrassment. He said good night, and was gone.

Oblivious to the fact that now he played only to Julie and Kinsman, the Intelligence man played on. He played on, and no one spoke until Kinsman said, "All right, old boy, you can stop now. The party's over. They've all gone home."

But it made no difference. The man acted as though he hadn't heard a word. Kinsman turned to Julie, and they smiled to each other. Then he slipped from the stool, and took her hands in his without awkwardness of any kind, and helped her from the stool on which she was sitting. Standing facing each other, her eyes slightly beneath his and looking steadily into his face so that if he had not contained half a dozen whiskies he might have seen there the faintest suggestion of reproach, she said, "Well, Johnny Kinsman."

He said, "I'm sorry. Were you not in the mood for this kind of thing? I thought it might help. Here . . ."

He turned and took two chairs, and placed them so that they faced each other, and then went on, "Sit down. Sit down here, Julie, and talk to me. Talk to me, Julie."

They sat quite still, facing each other, not speaking: listening to the music of the tired Intelligence man.

"If you want to cry, cry," he said. "He's too drunk to notice."

"He wanted me to marry him," she said. "A few short days ago he wanted me to marry him. We wrote to my husband in India and told him what we were doing and what we wanted to do, and it seemed so right for him, Johnny. And now Wakey's dead and I must have hurt Gerry out there terribly. How bad am I, Johnny? How bad am I?"

"Maybe Wakey's not dead."

"Yes, he's dead," she said steadily. "I feel he's dead."

"If only you hadn't written that letter."

"It was right, Johnny. It was right."

Kinsman looked at the soft black hair which framed the pale, beautiful regularity of her features, and then, as he wanted to reach out and touch her, the blue eyes beneath the smoothly etched lines of her brows melted into the paleness and the darkness, and he was ashamed that now he was slightly drunk.

He said, "I told Wakey that it was wrong. Then, I thought it was wrong, but I was wrong. Julie, I was wrong. Where is the badness in you?"

"He's dead, and I don't feel anything. I feel as though something has hit me on the head, but I don't feel any pain. I should, Johnny, shouldn't I? What's wrong with me?"

"There's nothing wrong with you, Julie. It's this. It's us. He's part of what we are living. As long as we're here he's not . . . not quite dead. Do you see, Julie?"

She didn't answer. She lowered her face, and ran the length of her smooth fingers through her hair. The pianist was still playing quietly, and she smiled slowly at the back of his pink neck. Then she said, "Johnny, you're my friend."

"I'm your friend, and Wakey's friend. Sometimes I feel as though I'm everyone's friend. Life's so bloody silly at times, isn't it?"

"I don't know about life. I thought that there was someone in India with whom I'd once lived for twelve days, and who was my husband. And I thought there was a boy called Wakefield, and now there is no one in India, and there is no Wakefield. Wakefield is just a name which was chalked off a blackboard. . . . Wakefield, Wakefield, Wakefield. It means nothing, Johnny. Neither does Savory or Peter Carr or Tom Barry or Tubby Spiers or . . . Johnny Kinsman."

Then Julie wept.

Kinsman didn't touch her or speak. He just sat there and watched her sobbing. Somehow he wasn't quite aware of her sadness until the pianist stopped, and when the pianist stopped there was a strange loneliness in Julie's sobbing. Kinsman moved towards her, and took her face in his hand and raised it so that she was looking at him. And as she looked at him a kind of wondering came into her face which moved gradually until it came to the verge of a smile.

"I've no right to be here," she said. "This is no place for me."

Kinsman didn't speak, but when the Intelligence man had drawn himself to his full height he spoke. Wimpole was surprisingly tall when he stood up, for he had developed a tendency to thicken and his head he carried low as though it was heavy on his shoulders. "Now," he said, "a woman is weeping."

John Kinsman looked from Julie to the man standing there, and didn't like him, but he didn't move as Wimpole went on to say, "All through the ages women have wept for their men. What quality does a man have to have before a woman weeps for him? I ask you that."

"Don't ask us any questions, old boy," Kinsman said. "We haven't got any answers. Have we, Julie?"

Julie shook her head.

"I envy you," the Intelligence man went on. "Is it you for whom she weeps?"

"You're drunker than I am," Kinsman said, and he stood up. "Why don't you go home, old boy?"

The man spoke in a tobacco-rich cultivated voice. "I can't go home," he said. "I can't go home ever. I can never go home again . . . ever."

"To your wife in the village?"

"To my wife in the village I can never go home. Is it you for whom she weeps?" Wimpole said.

"Your wife?" Kinsman asked.

"This girl Julie. This lovely girl. For whom does she weep?"

"For whom do you weep, Julie?" Kinsman asked.

CHAPTER ELEVEN

THAT night Kinsman had a strange dream. He dreamt that on his left shoulder a dead hand was lying like an empty glove. He could see it very clearly. It was grey, fast decaying, and dappled with dark brown little islands of filth. At its wrist it was ragged, as though it had been torn from the arm to which it had once been attached, and nothing he seemed able to do would shake it loose.

It just lay there, claiming him. In his dream he knew whose hand it was, and, recognizing it, he seemed to see himself smiling. Of course it was a joke. He shook his shoulder, and, when still it wouldn't move, he shook himself again. It became an embarrassing joke. All right, all right! . . . You've had your fun: now take this damned thing away!

But it didn't move. It just lay there letting his eyes examine it. He began to shake himself violently, and, under the hand, the flesh of his shoulder began to shrivel.

As though his whole body was being squeezed by fear, he exuded warm sweat. He didn't seem to be able to move his arms—all he could do was to shake the tainted shoulder in an effort to drop the thing on to the floor beside the bed. Even lying over the side of the bed, so that he was about to fall on to the floor, it stayed there. Vaguely he could hear himself moaning, until over the sound of his own voice came the sound of little Jock the batman saying, "Sur . . . sur . . . what's the matter, sur? Are ye a' right?"

For some moments Kinsman didn't speak. To support himself he had wedged his right arm between his shoulder and the floor, and, when again Jock spoke to him, he still didn't answer. His eyes were wide open, but he didn't appear to be fully awake.

Finally he said, "Yes, Jock. . . . O.K. . . . O.K., Jock." And then, as though uncertain as to whether it would be easier to fall on to the floor or to climb back on to the bed, he paused again before allowing himself to fall. When he had composed himself on the floor, he said, "Give me over my cigarettes, Jock."

Little rock-solid Jock gave him the cigarettes and said, looking hard at Kinsman on the floor, "There's a call on, sur. Youse are all wanted at Flights. . . ."

"When, Jock?"

"Now, sur. . . ."

Kinsman could feel the beat of his heart becoming more normal as he sucked at a cigarette.

"Are you all right down there on the floor, sur?"

"Quite all right, Jock . . . thanks." And he leant back on one elbow. Slowly he was beginning to appreciate the solidity of the floor.

"Have you got a hangover, sur? . . . Ah'll get you some smelling salts."

"Beat it, Jock. Don't fuss around like some damned old schoolmistress. . . ."

"It's a call, sur."

"Right, Jock. . . . Call, call. . . . I'll be on parade."

Julie. Oh, damn you, Julie!

He moved to get up, and it felt as though he was raising something much heavier than himself. As he got to his feet he paused with the memory of Julie's tears when he had held her face in his hands a few hours before.

The thickness of fear and reluctance melted with the thought that he wouldn't have to say anything to Julie that day.

Then, dressed, he met Squadron Leader Barry in the corridor of the billet, and the day before was gone. Barry said, "They're pushing us, eh, Johnny?"

"Better that way, sir. I'm for pressing on," Kinsman said.

"Regardless," the little man said.

"In a way," Kinsman said, laughing.

143

Jock called from his room at the end of the billet. "All right now, sur?"

Kinsman waved to him, and Barry said, looking at him, "Something wrong, Johnny? If you're off colour you don't have to . . ."

"Nonsense, sir. It's only old Jock. I had a bloody awful dream and he woke me up. Apart from a slight thickness between the eyes I'm perfectly O.K."

Barry's car didn't start until Kinsman and Jock had pushed it. On the way to the mess neither of them spoke until the car was parked outside the main entrance. Once or twice Kinsman had turned to look at his Flight Commander, but little Tom had been chewing at his moustache, and in his eyes there was a hard, glaring look. His face, somehow, seemed to bubble with indignation. But it was Tom's indignation. As he got out of the car he said: "Bloody hard luck about Wakey last night." He spoke as though the words embarrassed him, and he wanted to get them out quickly.

Kinsman didn't say anything. He was still unable to speak of his friend.

The day that followed was shattered by successive briefings for an operation which was finally cancelled, and it was almost dark, just after tea, when by Tannoy it was announced that the squadron would reassemble for briefing at eighteen hundred hours.

When, finally, they were airborne again, the sky was very dark, and there was broken cloud up to about eight thousand feet, so that as he turned on to his course over Liscombe, Kinsman could only see less than half a dozen of the squadron's other aircraft.

Now they were heading for Magdeburg, but on the previous four occasions during that day when they had been briefed, the target had been the Kalk marshalling yard at Cologne. Because of weather conditions the operation had been postponed, and in the end cancelled. It had been obvious when they had been briefed for this new target that the met. officer was still uncertain as to the conditions they might meet on the route. And to Kinsman it had looked as though Peter Carr, the Squadron Commander, had not been happy about them taking off when he addressed them on the subject of weather at the end of the briefing.

There had been something of an anticlimax in taking off

that night. In the locker room the crews had waited for another cancellation. Some had been so confident of the whole thing being called off that they were still only half dressed in flying kit when the buses arrived to take them out to their aircraft.

Kinsman didn't want to go. No matter how much he told himself that in the end it would make no difference, he did not want to go that night. The uncertainty of the met. officer's briefing, and the hurried consultations between that gentleman and the Wing Commander, the signals officer, and the man from Intelligence, had irritated the atmosphere until the thought of flying that night had become strange and threatening.

Waiting with his crew, he had said nothing to them of his uncertainty. Fred, at great length, had said that it was all bloody wrong to send you to Magdeburg when your mind had been all made up to go to Cologne. Fred said it again and again, and Chico chirruped perky laughter at him, and Bob agreed that it was wrong. Kinsman merely listened to himself telling them that it didn't matter when the hell you flew, you only had so many to get in, and you may as well get them in as quickly as possible.

They had gone out to dispersal convinced that a red Aldis lamp would arrest their take-off, and even when they were airborne, it still seemed so inconceivable that they would be allowed to go, that Kinsman told Les to keep a listening-out watch on W.T. lest base should send out a recall.

Taxi-ing out to take-off, Kinsman had smiled to himself when he realized how slowly those in front were moving towards the controller's black-and-white box. Rolling around the perimeter track, he himself had felt a strange, sinking loneliness. Because of the reflected light, it was difficult to see through the perspex of his cockpit to the sky, but he could feel that it was very dark and laden with cloud. Until he had turned on to the take-off runway, he had the hope that someone, someone there in that warm flying control tower, or someone pacing up and down a carpeted office at Group, would decide against this injustice and let them go to bed. Then, when all hope was gone, he flurried through his final cockpit check, and as his eyes caught the green of the controller's lamp, he again remembered Julie.

Fred's voice said, "O.K., skip. . . . He's given us the green."

Kinsman looked up and forward, as his right hand, with Fred's following it, reached out to the throttles, and he wondered again why it should be so difficult just to allow himself to love Julie Holmes.

Because he had expected the weather to be bad, he was almost disappointed at first that it wasn't more so. Climbing, he distrusted each cloud. The Wing Commander had spoken of the possibility of oil "coring," and Kinsman found himself glancing again and again at the rev-counters. Normally, he was settled down by the time he had turned on to his first course, but not that night. There was tension, or if there wasn't, he seemed to imagine it in the occasional muttered words that passed between Bob, the navigator, and Fred. Kinsman, and each one of them, was waiting for the signal from base which would tell them to return.

Between the successive layers of cloud through which the Halifax groped its way to altitude, there was no vestige of light. Since shortly after leaving base they had seen nothing of the ground. No aircraft had crossed their path; a thick curtain of cloud was between them and the stars.

It was difficult to feel the aircraft, sitting there at the controls. In cloud Kinsman constantly imagined that it was dropping its port wing, and in spite of the artificial horizon, it was only with a great effort of will that he managed to disregard his instinct.

Gradually he came to accept the fact that there would be no recall from base, and, with that acceptance, came the faint, flickering, then dying fear of groping blindly through the thick cloud that was sweeping past the cockpit.

Until he said to the wireless operator, "Les, are you sure there's been nothing from base?" and Les answered, "Sure, skip . . . there's been nothing," he hadn't fully committed himself to the operation. Until that moment, all he had to do to go back was to turn on to a reciprocal course and fly back to base. But now, going on it, was different. Through all this cloud and thick darkness, he had to find his way. He knew the strange, pathetic fear of a blind man doubting the senses that had been left to him.

There was, too, the possibility that, in spite of what Les

had said, there had been a recall, and that they, alone, were flying on towards Germany, while at that very moment the others were on their way back to the warmth of base.

Kinsman spoke to Bob, and when the navigator answered, his voice was confident. Kinsman said, "How's it going, Bob?" and Bob, quietly, replied, "Not bad, Johnny . . . not bad."

To himself Kinsman said, "I'm tired . . . I must be tired." And he tried to adjust himself to the business of flying when there was nothing with which he could relate his senses.

They had to go on. On, and up, and turning, according to Bob's estimate. At twenty thousand feet they were in cloud which they had entered at eighteen. Kinsman descended to get out of it again, but when he got back to eighteen thousand feet they were still in cloud. The cloud wasn't thick, and as they went on, it showed signs of clearing. Then, when it looked as though they were about to leave it behind, it would thicken again, and once or twice there was the rumbling shock which came when they flew through turbulence.

The mid-upper said, "Ice . . . there's ice, I think, skip, up here." And Kinsman lost some more height.

Deliberately he switched on his intercom, and said to the navigator, "What's the freezing level, Bob?"

"Around . . . around' fifteen thousand. . . ."

Lower, the cloud still thickened. The aircraft itself, possibly because some of the sound of their engines was being thrown back at them, seemed unhappy. Kinsman was unhappy. He peered into the darkening cloud ahead, and watched it rushing over the leading edges of his mainplanes. With the passing of each second, the sky became more threatening.

Instinct was drawing him lower to clear the overcast. It seemed right to get closer to the earth, but when he heard the sound of ice crashing against the fuselage as it broke away from his wings, he gave the engines power, and in spite of his desire to get down, he climbed.

Bob came through, saying: "Johnny, we're supposed to be at twenty thousand!"

It was some seconds before Kinsman answered. No one else spoke, and he knew that each of them was waiting for his words. For that reason he held his breath, so that his voice had a restrained flat quality about it when he said, "I know, Bob. I'm trying to clear this stuff. I'll have to go higher than that. I'm going back up now."

Again the mid-upper said, "There's ice up here, skip. It's all building up on my turret. . . ."

"What kind is it?" Kinsman said quietly. "Is it smooth, or is it like hoar frost?"

"I . . . I don't know what you mean. What do you mean, skip?"

"O.K. . . . OK., gunner. It's all right," Kinsman said.

The thing to do was to get back up there, above the freezing level, as far above it as he could get, where the ice would be less dangerous. But there was the possibility that he had left it too late. He cursed himself for being such a fool in trying to get below that cloud. That night, when the need for decision was so great, he didn't seem to have the strength required to be decisive.

It took a long time to get back up to twenty thousand, for the effect of what ice they had collected on the leading edges hampered their rate of climb. And, when finally the needle of the altimeter was wavering around twenty thousand, they were still in cloud. Kinsman kept the Halifax climbing on until they were at twenty-four thousand feet, and when still they hadn't cleared the overcast, he realized that it was futile to try.

He trimmed the aircraft for level flight, allowing his speed to build up, and, watching the needle move reassuringly towards a hundred and sixty knots, he began to feel more confident. For a long time now they had been in cloud, and, with the realization that the numbness which had been gripping his senses was leaving him, he made a conscious effort to adjust himself physically. He remembered his body.

With one hand he held the control column, while with the other he eased the safety harness where it gripped his shoulders. He compressed his torso inside the parachute harness, allowing the straps to sag loosely and then grip him again with strength. There was a dense pain inside him, and he wanted to belch, but couldn't. He moved his lips inside the mask which covered them, at the same time wriggling his buttocks in response to a tickling sensation he experienced in the region of his bowels.

Kinsman never used the automatic pilot at night because he felt that in an emergency there might be the possibility of delay in disengaging it, and that night, on over Germany in cloud, he sat trimming and retrimming the manual controls of the Halifax until his air-speed was being maintained at a hundred and sixty to a hundred and sixty-five knots, and his altitude, when he had abandoned the attempt to maintain sufficient cruising speed at twenty-four thousand, was never more than a hundred feet on either side of twenty-two thousand.

He asked the navigator if he had any special information on the weather, information that Kinsman himself might have missed at briefing, but all Bob said was, "It's all balled up. It should have been clear from the Channel."

Now that he had overcome immediate fear, Julie kept coming and going from his thoughts. After almost three hours he no longer heard the engines. It was so long since there had been silence in his ears that their drone became a neutral sensation, nothing, no sound. Once, in his imagination, he heard Julie's voice, her lips softly enclosing each word, saying, "I like the darkness. From up here I like the darkness. . . ." But, speaking to him, she didn't use his name. It was Wakefield's name she used. "From up here I like the darkness, Wakey," her voice said.

Julie's words lingered with him for a long time. He leaned on the arm-rest of his seat, and listened to them again and again. And, seeing her as he heard her in his imagination, he saw himself. Not the self he was, sitting there then, being dragged through cloud at twenty-two thousand feet above the earth, but someone confused and afraid on the ground, surrounded by the cluttering accoutrements of life. That was Julie's world: this other dark, waving, swaying, empty, silent world was his, as it had been Wakefield's. And Wakey had only been wrong in Julie's world. A flicker of uncertainty stirred Kinsman, thinking of Julie and her world. He tightened his grip on the control column, and stared once more forward into the murking cloud.

He spoke to the gunners, and had just switched off after speaking to the mid-upper, when Bob came through with a course alteration which would take them on to the last leg to the target. Kinsman started into the turn gently, and turning, he looked around the cockpit. It was a gentle turn of almost forty-five degrees, and, as he waited for the nose to come round, the thought came to him that if she had been there she would have been standing on his right, looking out as he was looking out, and seeing nothing as he saw nothing. If she had thought of him, he wondered, or when she had thought of Wakey or of them both, could she have imagined this?

As he levelled out, he said, "O.K., Bob?"

"O.K., Johnny. What are you on?"

"Zero two seven."

"Make it eight."

Kinsman smiled at Bob's impossible accuracy. "O.K., Bob. Eight it is."

"We should be there in thirty . . . seven minutes," little Bob went on.

"At the target?" one of the gunners asked hurriedly.

"Of course!"

"Hell, I'd forgotten about that."

When the cloud broke up, it did so suddenly. The overcast seemed to become lighter, then, briefly, it darkened and lightened again until it broke, and there above was the deep, rich sky and moonlight.

There was a scattered fluttering of voices on the intercom as each of them had to react to what they were seeing, and they flew on above a smooth, cold, blue-and-grey carpet of cloud which looked to be about three thousand feet below them.

There was nothing consistent in the night. The cloud beneath them split to form gigantic canyons shot by moonlight, and as they flew on and under a thin layer of alto stratus, and then into great streaked caverns of cloud, it was as though they were flying alone into a strange, unexplored world, hanging there suspended in the cold sky between life and death, where nothing stirred except the moonlight dancing on the props.

It was Chico who saw the first of their own aircraft, and, by the time Kinsman had seen P.F.F.'s flares hanging in the sky beneath him at about four thousand feet and still some miles in the distance, there was enough activity around them to destroy the illusion that they were alone. He listened to the gunners reporting the presence of aircraft on every side of them. The sky had so much light that now its secrets were being given up one by one. Around them, converging on the target area, were a dozen black shapes. It was possible to see so much. Beneath, something of a river, and the rolling black earth; above, the purple sky, living with life: the shapes of other aircraft. Once, Kinsman thought, he would have called this a bomber's moon, but there was no moon for bombers. Up until half an hour previously, he had been afraid in cloud. When was the sky his kind of sky?

Because, as far as he could see, there was remarkably little fighter activity around the target area. Kinsman guessed that Command must have been staging a successful diversionary raid that night. When they were through and turning in a wide arc to starboard and the south-west, he looked back and down at the city they had left. The moonlight destroyed the harsh vulgarity of the flames, and the still-twinkling candelabra of the Pathfinders, dangling and dying amidst the searchlight beams, gave it all a kind of sharp beauty.

Now the sky was his. Their bombs were gone, the nose was turning towards home, and, as with revs. high they dived through a couple of thousand feet, the Halifax was fast and light.

Fred said it was the funniest bloody op he'd ever been on, and when he spoke, he did so in a voice labouring with disgust. They seemed to miss the main body of searchlights, which, in any case, had lost much of their ferocity that night. Chico chattered on the intercom, giving a running commentary on the destruction of a Lanc and a Halifax, until he was silenced by the mid-upper crying that he thought he saw something on their port quarter. Kinsman waited into the silence, and, when there was no command from the gunners, he asked what the mid-upper had seen.

"It must have been something else, skip," the gunner said.

"What d'you mean . . . 'something else'? What did you think it was?"

The man said no more, but into the earphones came a voice which sounded like that of Les saying, "He can't see right with his sun-glasses on."

The wireless op's words when he spoke were drowned by the smattering of remarks which came from all of them. No one said anything that meant much. It was as though their words were carried incidentally on the breath which had been building up behind their teeth until that moment of release.

Straight and level, and down and into the west, fast, they flew on with the moon for a time high above them. A thin film of low cloud gradually crept over the earth from the east, and then, when they were little more than an hour from the target, the moon was gone, and they were flying on again, alone, in darkness, between the high cirrus and the low, clinging, misty cloud which rolled over Holland.

Fred said, "You never get it the way you want it. Cloud over the route, and the moon on the target. What a bloody stupid job this is. . . ."

"This is the way they want it," Kinsman said.

"Who? Gerry?"

"No," Kinsman said, ". . . Butch and the boys at Command H.Q."

Fred came back: "It's the way Gerry wants it. Whose side's Butch on?"

"Our side," Kinsman said, and he switched off.

It was all darkening, and it was difficult to see just where the cloud now was, but it seemed to be filling the sky again. At fifteen thousand they scattered occasional wisps of a layer of stratus which must have been forming just beneath them. Then, a little later, they were in it, and Kinsman started to climb gradually until they cleared it again.

"What does the flight plan say, Bob?" he asked the navigator.

There was some hesitation, and then Bob switched on, coughed, and said, "We should stay at fifteen thousand until we cross the coast, and then we go down to twelve."

"If we hit the front again," Kinsman said, more to himself than to Bob, "I'm going back up."

The navigator said: "We're north of our track on the way out."

If the front had moved as it should have done in the two hours that had passed since they crossed the coast on the way in to Germany, there was the possibility that now they would miss the worst of it. But still Kinsman climbed, until, at eighteen thousand feet, he was again in clean sky. Then on, and over the coast. Bob came up with his alteration, and they turned to the north-west. As the edges of a thick layer above smeared the cockpit, Kinsman reduced height, against his will; down, until for a long time they stayed at fifteen thousand.

There was no light, but, now, over the sea again, it all seemed to be breaking. At times the air was excessively turbulent, and the Halifax rocked savagely. He held on tightly when he felt as though some giant hand had plucked them playfully from their course and then dropped them, as though to remind them who was master.

Kinsman didn't think at all. He sat with his head pulled down slightly towards his shoulders, peering into the darkness ahead, and holding on tightly to the control column, as though afraid that it would be taken from him. He didn't think, but every sense in his body was tuned to the frequency of his fear. He had to hope that the lane along which he was flying, between the thick cloud above and that which was broken, wouldn't lead him, in the darkness, into a wall of cloud dense with ice, or a turbulence stronger than he was.

Once or twice little Bob came up to stand beside him. They didn't speak to each other, and Kinsman spoke to no one else. He sensed that each member of the crew was silent because they were uneasy with the night, and he was silent, because to have spoken would have broken the spell of his own concentration.

When it closed in over them, it did so quickly. As though they were in a car which had burst a tyre on some rough country road, the Halifax skidded over a series of bumps, and then, before Kinsman or anyone had realized what was happening, they went up, fiercely for a moment before it changed and everything was going down, down. Not diving, but just down, as though the long column of air between them and the sea had been pulled out from underneath.

Kinsman didn't move his head or any part of himself. A kind of terror was thrusting his eyes at the altimeter, and he saw the needle slipping round, fast, to thirteen to twelve to eleven thousand feet. This was cumulo nimbus. God save him, no! He would be lucky. Someone's microphone was switched on and remembering them, Kinsman's terror was skittered into a panic which ran all through

153

him. He tried to raise his head and his eyes, but there seemed to be such a terrible weight bearing down on him. The altimeter still slipped on down and down from nine to eight thousand feet, and he tried to move in his seat, but he couldn't. His lips wouldn't move. He tried, and a traitorous suggestion of soft tears came to his eyes with the stupid, deliberate thought that he wasn't bad. Every instinct in him cringed, and, without making a sound, he cried in his brain, "I'm not bad! I'm not bad! . . . Not against me . . ."

At seven thousand feet he got his hand to his microphone, and into it he cried, "S.O.S. . . . S.O.S. Les. . . . Can you get out, chaps? Can you . . . ?"

No one answered. Kinsman tried to raise his head again to look up, but he couldn't raise his head or his arms or his legs, and he closed his eyes. And, as he closed them, he left outside of himself all feeling and all thought, except the vague realization that in a minute or two the Halifax would hit the water and he would die.

Kinsman didn't know when it became different, but they didn't hit the water, and, without knowing, it seemed that they were climbing. His head went back, and from him there came a kind of groan as he pressed the nose down. He didn't know why he should be trying to do that, but that's what it seemed best to do. And again, in minutes, it was different. Where before there had simply been that awful pressure, there came a new sensation. Someone cried, "Johnny!" and Kinsman to himself said, "Spin. . . . spin . . . spin." As he said that he moved, and, without realizing it, could move. He had the stick, and he rocked it and rocked. And then he waved the stick, and cried and cursed and pushed and pulled as they went down and around. His brain, alive, swung one hand to the throttle, and he cut off all power before ramming each throttle right forward, so that inside the Halifax in his seat he could feel the painful surge of the engines regaining their grip. He didn't know when they stopped diving, but when in his hands he could feel power in the elevators again, he pulled back and back into his belly.

"Bob," he said, "Bob . . . Bob . . . are we all right? Are we all right, Bob?"

Very low, he saw the sea. His instruments were useless, but when he could see the water, he felt after some moments that they were turning. Kinsman had been thrashed by so many sensations in those minutes that his frightened mind could no longer trust any one of them. He simply sat there, forward, over the stick, holding it and afraid to hold it, lest he was exerting pressure in the wrong direction. But it was turning to port, and his eyes told him that they were losing height from three thousand feet. Feeling the whole thing sighing away and down, he checked its descent and raised the port mainplane until he guessed it might be level. Then he sat, staring ahead with his eyes against the jumbled sea and darkness and broken bubbles of cloud out there, until little Bob staggered on to the steps that led up from his office downstairs, to stand there with such an expression of utter dejection on his face that Kinsman looked at him and laughed. Then he leant forward as far as the straps would allow him to slap the navigator across a shoulder, in expression of his own sheer joy.

CHAPTER TWELVE

THE Station Administration Officer, who was a very important man in the eyes of the two thousand ground-crew at Liscombe, opened the door of the Group Captain's office, and ushered John Kinsman into the presence.

Group Captain Savory was sitting behind a desk which appeared to be too small for him. He sat erect in his chair, his eyes on Kinsman's face as the latter entered the room, and he was wearing a hat, the brim of which was richly embroidered with gold braid. He didn't look at all like the man Kinsman had been drinking with two days before.

The Group Captain's lips parted, and then he said, "You owe me a pound, Kinsman."

Kinsman had saluted at the door, and when the great man spoke, he said, "Yes, sir," took three paces forward to the desk, saluted again, and when he had come to attention, he placed the pound which had been nestling in his left hand on the desk.

"Thank you, Kinsman."

Kinsman waited, uncertain as to his next move. Something of an amused sneer appeared on the Group Captain's lips. On another man's face the expression would have been unpleasant, but now it wasn't. As though he was enjoying Kinsman's discomfiture, the C.O. went on looking into his eyes and saying nothing. Then, when Group Captain Savory had extracted all that he wanted from the moment, and had allowed his eyes to fall to the desk before him, Kinsman saluted, turned about, and, with relief, was gone.

Rain was sweeping across the tarmac outside, so that he hesitated in the entrance of Station Headquarters, uncertain as to whether he should wait until the heavy shower had passed, or whether he should run around to the flight office. It was cold, and he realized that this was the first time he had been conscious of winter.

He jumped down the short flight of steps and ran in the direction of C Flight office. When he got to the Flights, the passage-way outside the office was blocked by N.C.O.s waiting for the Naafi van to arrive. Fred was there, and little Chico. Fred said, "They're making up the leave-roster for Christmas, skip. See what you can do about getting us on."

"You see what you can do about getting me a cup of char and a wad, and I'll see what I can do," Kinsman told him.

"We'll even pay for it, won't we, mate?" Fred said, slapping little Chico on the chest with the back of his hand.

When Kinsman entered the office, Tom Barry said, "Ah, Johnny. . . . You don't care about Christmas leave, do you? You people don't bother about these things. It's a helluva mess, this. I can't. . . . They all want to go away at the same time. It just can't be done. We can't have any more than four crews away."

Kinsman laughed, and sat down at the desk opposite the Flight Commander in order to help straighten out Tom's difficulty.

"Don't give anyone leave," he said. "Then there'll be no difficulty."

"You can't old boy. You simply can't. Christmas is awfully important to everyone."

They were always wanting to scuttle off home, Kinsman thought. Even Fred, who was a man. And when they got home they probably wished they were back here with people who could understand them. It was strange.

"You can take me off the list for a start," Kinsman said.

"What about your crew?" Barry asked.

"My crew will have to put up with the rigors of life at Liscombe over Christmas."

The door opened and Fred's head appeared around it.

157

He omitted to salute Tom Barry, and merely said, "Tea up, skip."

"Oh, tell them to get me a cup, Johnny," the Squadron Leader said.

Kinsman took his tea from Fred, and asked the bomb-aimer to get some for Barry. Fred said, "Sure," and was gone before the Flight Commander said to Kinsman, "That's a helluva man you've got there."

"Fred?" Kinsman said, laughing. "He's wonderful."

"Remember the incident of me and the ditch?" Barry asked.

"You mean, sir," Kinsman said, "that time you shone a torch on the wrong man outside the W.A.A.F. site after the airmen's dance?"

"That's right. It was that blighter who pushed me, you know."

"I can quite believe it," Kinsman laughed. "He's magnificent."

"I knew you thought that," little Barry went on. "That's why I didn't have him locked up."

Fred reappeared then with the Squadron Leader's tea. "Naafi up, sir," he said, before taking the money which Barry had placed on the desk and turning around to make his exit. He was almost outside when Barry said quietly, "You forgot something."

Fred turned, and with nothing of defiance or resentment in his expression, saluted. His attitude was merely that of a man who refuses to give away anything unless it is asked of him, and Kinsman sensed, watching him, that Fred didn't think that Tom Barry was deserving of a salute. He made a mental note to tell the bomb-aimer about Tom Barry.

"See what I mean?" Barry said to Kinsman.

"That's just Fred, sir," Kinsman said. "If you knew him better, you'd like him."

Little Barry looked at Kinsman, and then a fussy expression crossed his face, and he drank some tea and said, "Now then . . . this question of Christmas leave."

Kinsman helped Tom to straighten the matter out, and then went outside to tell his waiting crew that they would not be going home at Christmas.

Chico insisted that they'd been cheated because their captain wasn't an Englishman, so Kinsman apologized for that, and then they were laughing, and Fred was suggesting that Kinsman come with them into Bridsea that night if there was a stand-down.

He didn't want to go with them. All day he had been wandering around the station thinking of Julie and of Wakefield. He had wanted to meet her, and yet, somehow, had been afraid to meet her. He couldn't spend the evening in his billet, for there was too much of Wakey there, and he couldn't stay in the mess, for Julie might be there. His only hope had lain in the weather, and that had let him down. With this rain there was little chance that they would fly that night.

"If you come," Fred said, "Bob'll come, and we can go in his car."

Kinsman laughed. "I thought there must be some ulterior motive behind all this friendliness," he said. "That's it."

"No, skip. No, skip!" they both insisted. "This crew should get together more often. They say it's good for morale. We'll get Les, and then all the old-timers will have a night on the bash. Like the old days at Lossie."

Kinsman told Fred to go back in to the Flight Commander and ask if he knew whether or not they would stand down. He also reminded Fred that he should salute when he entered the office. Fred groaned.

In the mess, at tea, Kinsman saw Bob and suggested that with the navigator's car the crew should go into Bridsea that evening.

Bob was unlike anyone Kinsman had ever known in the Air Force. They had flown together for over a year now, but they had never become friends. Bob was as unlike Kinsman as Chico was unlike Fred. Geordie who was dead had been Fred's friend, and, since Geordie had gone, Fred had drifted awkwardly with little Chico, as though they had both been sucked into the whirlpool of Geordie's death. For when Kinsman had met them, Geordie and Chico were friends—uneasy friends, from gunnery school. Together they had come up to Kinsman when he had been standing with the crowd that was to form the new course, and they had said to him, "We'd like to go with you, sir, if you'll have us."

He had laughed and said, "Of course, of course. I'd love to have you," because he didn't think it mattered much who were his gunners, and these two seemed to be pleasant fellows. Then, standing with them, and still short of a navigator and a bomb-aimer, and a wireless operator, they had seen Fred sitting on the running-board of a parked petrol bowser, unconcernedly smoking, his forage cap pushed far back on his head, and his elbows on his knees. There was something about the man which suggested he would never ask to be in anyone's crew. Kinsman sent little Chico over to ask him if he would like to join them, and he came over and smiled awkwardly, and without saying that he would, became one of them.

The navigator, Bob, Kinsman had met in the mess two days after everyone else had their crews complete. Kinsman had seen that he was a New Zealander, and he saw, too, that he looked like the kind of man whom no one else would have in their crew. But he had asked Bob to join them because he didn't want to be given a navigator, and little Bob had smiled and made an attempt at joviality which, like every similar attempt he had made since, hadn't quite succeeded.

Bob was full of poor jokes which were usually based on an embarrassed sarcasm. He was, at Liscombe, the oldest man operating with the squadron, and sometimes Kinsman felt that if he would have allowed himself to be different from the others, instead of trying so desperately to be like them, he would have been happier.

The New Zealander was an excellent navigator. And, since that occasion on which he had guided them through solid cloud for six and a half hours from the North of Scotland to Leeds and back again, so that, when finally they broke through the overcast, they did so right over base, his skill had been accepted by each one of them. To some extent, too, his irascibility had been forgiven by all except Fred, who regularly told Kinsman that, when they arrived over base on their last operation, he was determined to throw Bob out.

They believed in their captain, each one of them, and he in them. At times Kinsman was afraid of the faith they had in him. He could see it in Fred's face when the bomb-aimer stood beside him on the way back from a target, and it was in Bob's voice when he gave him a course alteration.

In the air they were component parts of a machine,

welded together, dependent on each other. Perhaps for that reason they had scattered on the ground. Young Les no longer slept in the same billet as the rest of the crew. Kinsman, and his fellow N.C.O.s for that matter, seldom saw him on the ground. Someone had told Kinsman that Les drank too much, and it had come to him, when he had been told, that he knew so very little about those of whom he knew so much during those hours they spent in the air. He had asked Fred about young Les, but Fred had shrugged his shoulders and said something about allowing him to drink if he wanted to drink. But even if young Les had given him the opportunity, it would have been difficult for Kinsman to have given the boy a reason for not destroying himself in which he, Kinsman, could have believed.

In the mess, a cup of tea resting on one arm of his chair, and holding in one little round hand a bun, Bob said from the depths of his uneasy comfort, "I didn't think you believed in all this crew get-together stuff." There was in Bob a kind of frontier puritanism which never seemed to allow him to be at ease with pleasure, and now, turning his eyes from the rain which ran down the windows, Kinsman felt that Bob looked as though he was embarrassed at sitting there in public with all those others around him, while the heat from the fire reached out to his legs to warm him.

Kinsman said, "I don't. It was Fred's idea. I think maybe we should show a little willingness."

He had just spoken when Julie came into the room with Millie behind her, and, as he saw her, he felt a sensation near his heart which he hadn't known since, long ago, he had loved someone else. He moved uneasily in his seat, and told himself that he was a bloody fool. He placed the tea he had been drinking on the floor and lit a cigarette. Then he said to Bob, in an attempt to quieten the near-panic that was inside him, "All right, Bob. Are you on? If we leave in about three-quarters of an hour, the pubs'll be open when we get there. O.K.?"

"I suppose so," Bob said.

Julie and Millie were helping themselves to tea at the table by the door. He couldn't leave now, or he would have to walk right past them. He turned to Bob, but there was nothing, apparently, that Bob wanted to say. The navigator just sat there with his brows wrinkled.

"What's the matter? What are you thinking about?" Kinsman asked.

"I was just thinking. . . . If I sell that car now I might get eighty or ninety quid for it, but if I wait until we've finished, and they know I'm in a hurry to get rid of it, I might get as little as fifty."

"That would be awful," Kinsman said. "And if you go for a Burton before we finish, you won't get anything for it. Just think of all that good money gone to waste."

Bob turned to him and smiled, and waved his head from side to side, as though uncertain as to whether or not he should be amused. "Well . . ." he said, ". . . well."

Bob and himself mixed as badly as Chico did with Fred. How awful it would be if, because of Wakey's death, he found the need of someone's company or sympathy, or whatever it was that other people gave you, to such an extent that, as Fred in spite of himself seemed to drift with the little gunner from Bradford, he had to drift together with this little, sensible man who had been a builder—a master-builder—and who appeared to be devoid of any human attachments whatsoever; whose one saving grace was that he had journeyed half-way around the world to become an airman when he was old enough to have known better.

Kinsman arose from his chair, and said, "I'll 'phone them at their mess. See you here. Outside. Half an hour. O.K."

Bob nodded, and there was now eagerness in his gesture, so that Kinsman was a little ashamed.

"Right, Bob," he said. And to make amends for what he had been thinking, he ran his fingers through the few lonely wisps of hair which decorated the top of the navigator's head.

Julie was there. There near the door she was sitting with Millie. If there had been some man with them, he could have waved to them and continued on his way, but they were alone. He felt Millie's eyes on him as he walked across the centre of the floor. He looked up, towards them, and smiled as he turned in their direction.

Millie, when she smiled to him in reply, gave the impression of merely being in the process of uncovering her long teeth. Then she said, as though her words were substitute for something better unsaid, "Hello, stranger."

Kinsman looked at Julie. When she spoke to him her first word was inaudible so that her greeting sounded like, ". . . Johnny."

"Rotten day," he said.

"Yes."

Millie's eyes never left him. She didn't speak again, but on her face there was an expression of amusement. She turned from him to Julie and then back again, as though waiting for one of them to speak, but no one spoke until Kinsman said, "I'll have to get cracking. The boys have got something on tonight."

Fred's favorite pub was the White Swan, and they had been drinking there for perhaps an hour when Kinsman saw Millie come in. She came in and walked with confidence up to the bar, so that he saw her being served with her usual large whisky.

When Fred saw her, he moved the pint glass he was holding so quickly that when it landed on the bar some of the beer was spilled. The ageing barmaid created some little fuss, so that Fred was unable for the moment to say what he had intended to say. When he had pacified the woman, though, he said to Kinsman, "There's big Millie. Now, that's my kind of woman, skip."

Kinsman laughed, and continued drinking while Fred nudged little Bob. "Eh, Bob," he went on, "how would you like a little piece of that?"

"Too old," Bob said.

"Heh, listen to what's talkin' . . . listen to what's talkin' . . . Too old, he says! That's just the age when they appreciate it most . . . eh, skip? . . . eh, skip?" Fred's hand reached out to Kinsman.

John Kinsman stirred himself and laughed. He was annoyed with himself because he wasn't enjoying their company. There was a time when there was nothing he liked better than to be with them like this in a pub with a pint in his hand, but on that evening their laughter, for him, had lost its life.

Fred's insistent "eh . . . eh?" went on until Kinsman raised the glass to his lips. He wondered if the way he felt meant that he was weakening. Could it be that Liscombe was eating into him? He had known men before, maybe not men like Wakey, but he had known men well who had been killed or hadn't come back; he had seen people killed and he'd got drunk and forgotten about it. But not now. Why not now?

Wavering in the background of Kinsman's thought was a fragile vision of Julie. It was there, and would for a moment take shape to become the loveliness of her face, and then would fade, until the fact of Wakefield's absence was there with him again. But Julie kept coming back. He didn't want her. If she became important, more important (could she?); if she broke the shell of indifference that he had worn like a suit of armour for so long, what else would come flooding in in her wake? There was no room for anyone or anything but himself. He had no strength left for love or ideals or anything except hope—the faint whispering hope that if he didn't make too much noise he might yet creep stealthily past.

"Have a gander at our Mr. Kinsman," Fred said.

Kinsman was emptying his glass with one long draught, and when it was emptied he placed the glass heavily on the counter and called, "Millie!"

"What?" she called back.

"Have a drink?"

"I've got one."

"Come on over here."

"You can come over here."

Fred said, "Aye, aye . . . what's this?" And little Chico echoed him, and Bob laughed. Kinsman left them and walked over to Millie.

"You'll get me court-martialled," she said, "calling my name like that in a public bar."

"What would I call you?"

"I don't know . . . Flight Officer Sefton, I suppose."

"I never think of you as that."

"What do you think of me as, Johnny?"

"I think of you as a noblewoman of ancient Greece."

"Really . . . ?" Millie laughed.

"Medea, maybe . . . not Millie."

"I don't know whether that's flattering or not, but it's a little odd. Why do you think that?"

"Never mind. Have a drink. Here's Les with mine. Do you know Les, Millie? . . . Les, this is Flight Officer Sefton. She's a friend of mine. Say 'how do you do,' Les. . . ."

Les mumbled something, placed the drink which Fred had bought for Kinsman on the counter, turned awkwardly, and fled back to the crew.

"He looks too young to be away from his mother," Millie said.

"He is."

Millie paused, and then said directly, "Is the boy afraid?"

"I think he is," Kinsman said.

"He's drinking whisky."

"Yes," Kinsman went on; "they say he's overdoing it."

"Why don't you stop him?"

"It's his business, and I haven't time."

Millie dropped her voice to say, "Someone should stop him. Look how he gets rid of that drink."

"He'll be all right in a month or two. We'll be finished in a month or two."

"Then what?"

He didn't answer.

Millie said, "Will you go away?"

"Yes, I'll go away. But it's a long time. It's a long, long, time, Millie."

Kinsman looked over to his crew, and saw them standing there in their own group, apart from everyone else in the place.

"Would you know they were a crew?" he asked Millie. "Is there something about each one of them which gives him a common identity with the others?"

"Do you think there is?"

"Looking at them now," he said, "I think there is."

"Do you love them?" she asked.

"When I'm drinking I love them, and when I'm flying I love them. Sometimes I hate them. I hate the need I have for them."

Millie was finishing her drink as Kinsman said, "Come on over and meet them," but her hand restrained him.

"Don't you know," she said, "that Julie needs you?"

Kinsman's eyes flashed to her face and then to the woman behind the bar, to his crew.

"She doesn't need me, Johnny," Millie went on. "She needs someone. She needs you."

"I . . . Julie's . . . I think Julie's . . . He was my friend. Wakey was my best friend. He was going to marry her. . . . Why does she need me?"

"She needs someone. Who is there but you?"

Kinsman looked at her. "Julie's good," he said. "She's sane and beautiful and good, but I'd love her, Millie. I'd love her. I don't want to love anyone. Not even myself. I don't want to ask too much or expect too much. I want to take what each moment gives, and nothing more. I don't want to love Julie. Not now. Not here in this place now. I sometimes get the feeling that it's not real, that we'll all wake up some morning and find ourselves back where we started from a long time ago. It's not real, Millie, and I don't want to love her."

"You've loved her for a long time," Millie said.

"Why the hell do I talk this way?" Kinsman went on. "Let's . . ." he laughed by way of punctuation . . . "let's laugh, for God's sake."

Fred was behind them, and he said, "That's a good idea, Mr. Kinsman. This is supposed to be a crew outing, a real rollickin' thrash in the big city."

They joined the others, and Millie, when Kinsman had introduced them to her, appeared to enjoy their company. She was strangely out of place there, taller than any of them, standing with Chico and young Les and Bob grouped around her in a tight semi-circle as they looked up at her long, cold face with its amused smile. Kinsman stood on one side of her, and Fred on the other. Fred appeared to be particularly interested in Millie. She talked to him, and he acted as a kind of interpreter between her and the rest of the crew. Each of them was overawed by Millie except Fred, and Kinsman sensed, watching him, that, with growing confidence, Fred was thinking of Millie in much the same way as he had himself when he first met her.

Kinsman drank without taking much part in their conversation. Once or twice Millie turned to him and said something like "Save me from this man of yours. He's a terror. He frightens me." And Kinsman laughed and retreated into his thoughts.

Perhaps half an hour had passed when Kinsman turned to Bob, and said, "Bob, I've got to go back to Liscombe. Let me take your car."

Little Bob, his eyes slightly glazed, and looking at Millie before he spoke, said, "How do we get back?"

"Take a taxi. I'll pay for it."

"When?" Bob asked.

"Tomorrow!"

Bob's protests were joined by the others. Half serious, they complained of having a skipper who had gone round the bend. Little Chico said, "I think he's lovesick. He's got some woman hidden away up there that we don't know about. That's what he's got there."

Kinsman laughed. "Millie's my woman. Isn't that true, Millie?"

Millie smiled. Although, when he looked at her, Kinsman felt that her eyes weren't smiling. There was a kind of preoccupied wondering in them. Then he added, "Don't you forget that, Fred." And they laughed while Bob gave him the keys of the car, and he was gone.

He had no idea what he would say to Julie when he saw her. All he knew was that he shouldn't be going back to her. What had been wrong for Wakefield was wrong for him. The thought that someone needed him was frightening. Driving along the long, straight road which led south to Liscombe, with the rain beating down on the canvas roof of the little car, and one plaintive little yellow light reaching out vainly into the darkness ahead, Kinsman felt as though he was being drawn towards the centre of the vacuum that had existed between them since the moment they had both known that Wakefield wasn't coming back. And yet it wasn't Julie who was wrong. It was he who was wrong, and Wakefield had been wrong. They were wrong because they were standing with one foot on either side of the chasm of death while she lay luxuriant in the soft green grass of life, laughing and bright-eyed, free and willing to love, and sure of the rightness of living.

She wasn't in the mess. He looked in the bar, and in the empty writing-room, and in the long, bare ante-room where three people were listening to jazz records. He didn't know them, and, as he opened the door, each of them looked at him from where they were sitting sprawled by the wide fireplace. There was annoyance on their faces at the interruption. He closed the door and went to the bar.

Paddy, the barman, said, "To be sure I haven't," when

Kinsman asked him if he had seen Section Officer Holmes; and, when he had received the drink that Paddy had poured for him, Kinsman said by way of politeness, "You'll be able to catch up on your reading tonight, Paddy."

"That pal of yours was sweet on her, wasn't he? That big, good-lookin' fella what-do-you-call-him that didn't come back the other night."

"Wakefield," Kinsman said.

"That's right," Paddy said, "There was somethin' goin' on all right. I could tell by the way he used to look at her when the two of them would be in here. He was a fine-lookin' big fella, too."

Kinsman toyed with his drink, saying nothing.

"They tell me he was a great pilot, too."

Kinsman muttered agreement.

"Aye, they say he was a good one all right. Funny how it's always the good ones that go first. It's a funny game, isn't it?"

Kinsman smiled.

"Old Paddy's seen a few come and go, I can tell you. Seen more come than go . . . home, that is, on their two feet."

"How long have you been here, Paddy?"

"Sure, ah came here when the station was opened. Four years. They were on Whitleys at first, and then them old Halies . . . them that was death-traps."

"Do you like it here?"

"Sure it's a grand place. Ah've seen a few come and go, ah can tell you."

Kinsman replaced his glass on the counter.

"Are you off now?"

Kinsman said he was.

"The trouble with you fellas is you're always rushing about. You don't know how to enjoy yourselves, you don't. You're either rushing off to bed or Brid . . . or breakin' up my bar or somethin'. The whole lot of youse is mad. Youse is mad. Where are you goin' now?"

"I don't know," Kinsman said, and went out to the 'phone-box in the entrance-hall. He had to wait some time before the girl in the W.A.A.F. site came back to tell him whether or not Julie was available, and then he heard the receiver being lifted, and a voice said, "Hello."

"Is she there?" Kinsman asked.

"Hello," the voice said.

"Hello, is Section Officer Holmes there?" Kinsman asked.

"Johnny . . ."

Kinsman lowered his voice to say again, "Hello."

"Where are you?"

"In the mess, Julie."

"Will I come there?"

"It's raining. I'll meet you on the road. I've got a car."

"A car, Johnny. . . ."

"I'll meet you in five minutes."

"All right, Johnny."

There was a tiredness in Julie's voice, as though she spoke with some effort, and when she had gone, Kinsman was a little afraid, now that he had spoken, to meet her. The words Paddy the barman had used about Wakefield and Julie were coming back to him. Was she still Wakefield's? Was he betraying his friend? Was he helping her? He stood staring at the scribbled telephone numbers and Christian names and messages like "Bill. Phone Betty at Esk. 1920" without seeing any of them, until the operator in the exchange did something to the 'phone which made a noise. Startled, he realized that he hadn't replaced the receiver on the rack. He did so, then his eyes focused on the crazy pattern scribbled on the wall, and he saw the letters W, W . . . WAKE as though someone had been scraping his name absent-mindedly there while speaking on the telephone, It was part of Wakefield's name.

She was there standing by the gate, half sheltered by a dripping tree. Julie, coming into the car, came in neatly, as no one else he knew would have. She seemed to fold herself without hesitation in to the seat in sympathy with the age of the vehicle. Close to him in the tiny cabin it was difficult to see her clearly, or even to realize that she was Julie.

Kinsman waited for her to ask why he had called her, but she didn't. Julie said, "Don't let's go to the mess."

"We'll go where this infernal thing will take us. It's a peculiar car. It's old Bob's."

"Good old Bob," Julie said. "Who's he?"

"My navigator."

"Go to Beauford, Johnny."

"It's a dirty pub."

"Let's go to a dirty pub."

"You don't sound sad. Millie said you were sad."

"Millie worries about me," she said.

With some difficulty he engaged the gears of the little car. It jolted, and then almost stalled before it started to run forward quite seriously. Julie laughed clearly, and then she said, ". . . And I worry about your driving!"

The pub at Beauford gave the impression of continuing to exist long after there was any real reason for its being there. Even the presence of an airfield three miles away had failed to give it life again, so that when Julie and Kinsman entered the low-roofed bar they found themselves sharing the place with a trio of agricultural laborers who sat staring bovinely at two airmen playing darts. They were young airmen whose bodies looked as though they had grown out of their cheap uniforms long after their faces had ceased to have growth. There was nothing quaint about the Beauford. It had all the unbeautiful age of an insanitary old man.

They drank sitting behind a rough wooden table on a bench next to the bar, out of range of the flying darts, and at the opposite end of the room from the ploughmen. They drank beer, because neither of them really wanted to drink.

There was a grey quietness about the place, punctuated at intervals by the thud-thudding of darts into the cork board, and the "ohs" and occasional "ahs" of appreciation which came from the players and spectators. The landlord, a thick man tending to fat who wore an extremely ill-fitting tweed jacket which looked as though it had once belonged to someone else, stood leaning on the bar as though anxious not to invade their privacy.

They both sat for what seemed a long time watching the dart-players, until Kinsman said, "I've got no cigarettes." His hand reached to a pocket as Julie reached to hers. They touched, and withdrew quickly, as though there was pain in their touching.

Julie said, "It was miserable tonight with the rain."

He lit the cigarette she gave him, but didn't speak. He wanted to speak.

She said, "It was good of you to come for me, Johnny."

170

He sipped his beer, and said, "I feel as though I'm out of character."

When he turned on the bench to look at her their knees touched briefly. Kinsman expelled his breath, and said weakly, "Are you all right?"

"I'm all right."

"I can't be your friend, Julie. I can't help you by being your friend. I should, but I can't. I can only love you."

He turned his eyes away from her face at that, and looked at the two laughing, toothful airmen throwing their darts. There was something restful in the rhythm of the sharp little darts sinking into the cork.

Julie's hands were wedged deeply in the pockets of her greatcoat. With Kinsman she stared at the airmen without seeing either of them until she said, "I don't know, Johnny. I don't know anything. Just days ago I was listening to Wakey telling me that he loved me, and I was telling my husband that because Wakey loved me I couldn't go on being his wife. Now Wakey doesn't exist, and I feel that I'm forgetting him. Already I'm forgetting him, just as Gerry out there doesn't exist. And you're here, and I know you like I knew Wakey, and against the background of knowing you I feel I love you. I can touch you because you're here, and I can hear your voice by my side, and I can feel myself trembling because you're by my side, and I wonder whether I love you . . . I love you. I want to love you. I think I love you; and I think I loved Wakey because he was such a boy. More than you are a boy. And I think I loved Gerry because he was the first man to love me. I loved him for loving me. I don't know whether I have the right to go loving anyone, Johnny. Myself or anyone."

As she spoke Kinsman didn't look at her. He sat by her side listening to her voice. It was a gentle voice, each word pausing for a moment in her throat before coming to him. His eyes were fixed somewhere on the dirty yellow wall of plaster at the other side of the dimly lit room, and he left them there because it was easier to talk when he wasn't looking at her.

"You remind me that love exists," he said. "I don't want to love you or anyone. But there's something in you that makes all this seem wrong. And yet in that other world I couldn't have had you."

171

"What other world?" she said.

"I was a boy in the other world."

Julie turned to him and took his hand. Oblivious to the staring yokels, she took his hand from his knee and placed it on the table. He looked from the hand to her face, one dark eyebrow raised higher than its neighbour in a way that he had, and he smiled as she said, "Was that where you were a boy? . . . Let's go away from this place, Johnny."

"I like this place," he protested. "We're alone, and there are people here. That's better sometimes than being alone, too alone."

They laughed so that one of the dart players missed the board, and the yokels and the airman and the landlord stared at Kinsman and Julie. They went outside and there they could hear a different kind of laughter so that Kinsman said to Julie, "They're laughing at us."

"You said it was a dirty pub."

"That's right," he answered. "It's a dirty pub."

Bob's car started with some difficulty. In fact, by any normal method the thing refused to come to life at all, so that in the end Kinsman had to push it from the entrance of the Beauford to the main road, which, in the direction of Liscombe, dropped towards the coast in a long gentle slope. When he had manoeuvred it to the road he climbed behind the wheel.

"Push!" he called to Julie.

"All right!" And she pushed until, overcome by her own laughter, she had to allow the thing to roll forward, propelled by no power other than gravity. Kinsman kicked it into gear until, reluctantly, it spluttered into action. Then, with the engine running, he stopped the car so that Julie could get in. She ran up to him, and leaped in excitedly before the engine could stall again. Kinsman laughed at her, and they started off. He was glad of this old car. In spite of its obstinacy, he was regarding it affectionately. It had made Julie laugh, and somehow had brought them together in trying to start it. It was the first thing they had ever done together.

But their triumph was short-lived. They were little more than half-way back to Liscombe when the engine stopped again. Kinsman got out, and was about to raise the bonnet when he changed his mind and suddenly became conscious

172

of one of his own limitations. Nothing he saw in the engine would tell him anything about its troubles, so leaning back into the tiny cabin, he suggested to Julie that they walk the remaining distance.

"But you're a pilot," she said. "You should know all about these things."

He shook his head slowly and smiled. "Not me. Not a thing."

"What would you do if one of the engines of your aeroplane stopped?"

"I'd jump out. That's what we're doing now."

"But what'll old what-do-you-call-him say about leaving his car here?"

"We'll push it on to the verge and get it tomorrow."

"Do we push again?"

"We push again," he said.

With much more noise from both of them than was strictly necessary, they moved the little car on to the grass, and then, when Kinsman had done everything he could to make it secure, they both patted its bonnet and left it there. There was a new gaiety in them, so as they left the car, Julie started to run and Kinsman followed her. From behind he reached out and caught her arm. They stopped suddenly, and Julie looked at him. She said, "We hadn't noticed. It's stopped raining."

The sky above them was beginning to show through the ragged edges of cloud drifting apart as though all the anger had gone from it. As they stood there looking up, a handful of stars became visible. The wetness of the roadway reflected light. "We can see our way home now," Julie said, "Come on, Johnny Kinsman—let's go home."

She ran again, and he caught her. "Where is home?" he asked.

"It's just around the corner, I think." And she laughed.

They walked on, he with one hand on her arm; high up on her arm, so that the deep warmth that was there between the arm and her body he could feel in his hand.

After some time he said, "I've been fighting something that wasn't there. All this time I've been trying to keep myself strong. I was afraid of you, Julie. I was wrong."

She looked at him, but didn't speak. Then after some little time she said, "I don't know, Johnny. I don't know."

Walking with her, Kinsman knew a completeness he

had never known before. They spoke little. Once, he raised her cold, uncovered hand to his lips, and she said, "Johnny." Only that. All other words stayed deep within her where her fear lay: deep, as the strange new desire to give lay within him.

They had passed the entrance to number three site, on which Kinsman was billeted. Soon, on the right, they would reach the gate through which Julie would pass. His hand on her arm moved down until her hand was in his. Their fingers interlaced. He stopped walking.

"Julie," he said, "don't go away, Julie."

"I don't know, Johnny. I've stopped knowing anything."

"My place is there." And he looked over her shoulder.

"There . . ." she said quietly, without turning her eyes from his face.

Kinsman looked at her, at her eyes, and beyond her eyes. "If it's right," he said, "it's now it's right. I think it's right, Julie."

Neither of them could have said who turned first, but they turned and walked along the cinder path, past the concrete block in which the batman lived, quietly, to enter Kinsman's room.

He switched on the light, and leant back against the closed door, as though relieved that they had reached the place in safety. Julie's back was to him before she turned to look at the uncovered spring of the bed which had been Wakefield's; the picture of his sister on the wall which they had forgotten to take away; its companion into which the knife still stuck viciously; the beer-stained blanket on the table, the scattering of shirts and socks and underwear on the floor, the pile of dusty ashes by the stove, the mangled blankets on Kinsman's unmade bed; Kinsman's face; Kinsman. She smiled.

He moved to her hesitantly. Her hand reached out to him, and, taking it in his own, he stopped.

"This is my place," he said.

"It's awful." She spoke slowly, smiling.

"Julie."

"What?"

"I love you . . . I've heard those words so often that even when I say them myself they don't have any meaning . . . as words. I love you."

"I know, Johnny Kinsman."

He took both her hands in his, and slowly raised them to his lips. Then he moved to her, so that she was as close to him as she could be. When he kissed her, he fell back against the light-switch at the door, so that, once, when he moved, the light went out. For a long time they stood there in the darkness, quietly, with only the sound of their own sighing in their ears until they sank to the soft, warm confusion of his bed; and there, their whispering broke before the sharp cry of Julie's breath when he touched her, and again when his flesh touched the smoothness of hers, and again, although he heard nothing but the dull pounding of his own blood, when, in answer to the frightening rhythm of their young bodies, she gave herself to him.

CHAPTER THIRTEEN

LITTLE Chico, from the swivelling glass cage in which he was enclosed back at the tail of the aircraft, communicated to Kinsman by the shiver in his voice of the fear he had known when he saw the dangling black shape of what he had been sure was an enemy intruder.

Kinsman said, "Why didn't you fire?"

"I . . . I wasn't sure. It might have been a Mossie."

At that Kinsman snarled something about shutting up unless he was sure, and then, having spoken that way, immediately tried to calm them by saying quietly, "Just keep your eyes open, gunners. There might be something about."

They had been to a place called Opladen, which to them was a name on a map of the Ruhr valley. In less than half an hour they would have touched the ground. There would be food to eat, and they could talk of what they had done. Now, the echo of Chico's word, "intruder", rang in Kinsman's brain.

For months intelligence had been warning them to expect intruder activity on their part of the coast. Two squadrons of German long-range fighters had been in training on the Baltic with the specific idea of attacking the Bomber airfields of Yorkshire. But nothing had ever happened. They had been told at countless briefings of what Flying Control would do if Liscombe was attacked when the squadron was landing. The procedure had been repeated again and again. It had become as much a part of each briefing as the Group Captain's expressed desire to go with them, and almost as much of a joke.

Kinsman was tired. All of them were tired. They had been in the air for almost seven hours. There was nothing left in any one of them that could have been called fight. Kinsman didn't so much fear the thought of being attacked, as he disliked the thought of having to stir his sagging senses.

Where Molston should have been, there was nothing to disturb the darkness, and Molston was only eight miles from Liscombe. Kinsman could see the aircraft circling down there with their navigation lights on. Then a Drem system was switched on. From somewhere a single searchlight scanned the sky, only to be suddenly extinguished. There was a nervousness in the darkened landscape beneath. Fred came up from below to stand beside Kinsman. They looked at each other briefly, and Kinsman could see that on the bomb-aimer's face there was a troubled frown.

Below, on the port, Kinsman could see a Halifax dragging in low to Molston. It looked as though they had decided to take their aircraft in, and if they were landing their squadron everything must be all right. Fred was looking up through the perspex to the sky above, until he was aware of Kinsman's eyes on him. Then he leant over, and when Kinsman had pulled back the flaps of his helmet, said, "It's a funny night, skip."

There was no airfield between Molston and Liscombe. In minutes they should have seen something of their base, but now the only light that was visible was that of the marker-beacon ahead.

Kinsman turned to Fred, and said, "There's something queer going on." And then, without waiting for Fred to speak, he adjusted his microphone, and said to the gunners with some urgency in his voice, "See anything, gunners?"

The mid-upper, in a thick Lancashire accent which Kinsman found difficult to understand, was the first to speak. He said, "There's some kites with their lights on over on the port, skip. They look as if they're goin' the same way as us."

Chico said nothing. He was offended that the other man, who was not really a member of the crew, should have spoken first. Kinsman asked him again, and was told that there was nothing behind them which looked unusual.

"I think I'll put the lights out," Kinsman said to Fred, and as he spoke he switched off the navigation lights which had been on since they crossed the English coast.

Fred laughed into his mike, and said, "I hope they don't all get the same idea."

"I've switched off our navigation lights, gunners. So remember that we're not visible to other aircraft!" Kinsman called to the gunners.

Someone who sounded like Chico said, "You hope," and then there was silence in the big Halifax except for the lazy droning of the engines, and the occasional metallic shiver of its fuselage.

The past few minutes had brought Kinsman to the surface of his tiredness. He had pulled himself up from the depths of a satisfaction which had allowed him to sit slumped in his seat with each arm resting so that his fingers could just reach the control column, while his aircraft sank smoothly to two thousand feet; until now he was sitting erect, staring into the darkness ahead, the muscles of his face alive again, his mask dangling by one cheek, the side window by his head open slightly so that the fresh air could come to him. He moved his feet lightly on the rudder bars as though testing the response of his controls. He waved the control column gently from side to side in answer to the uneasiness which trickled through him.

Bob said curtly, "We should be there."

There was nothing below. Kinsman felt lost. This time they didn't seem to have approached their base. There had been no long descending drag to the familiar circuit. He felt as though he had been taking part in some game in which he had been whirled around blindfold in a familiar room, and then asked to find the door. Suddenly, looking down, he thought he saw a suggestion of the coast-line. Stumbling in the dark, he momentarily mistrusted his sense of balance.

Chico called, "It's right beneath us, skip. Right beneath us. You're just passing it. They've put the lights on."

Almost at the same instant Kinsman dipped his port wing to turn tightly, and switched on his microphone.

"Zebra to Mulberry Bush," he called. "Zebra to Mulberry Bush. . . . May I pancake?"

There was a confused jumble of words in his earphones, nothing of which he could decipher.

"Did you get it?" he asked the crew.

No one had understood Control's message. So Kinsman repeated his request for permission to land. His turn had placed him on a slightly tight down-wind leg. He decided to go straight in. He released some flap and cut his throttles back in an attempt to lose some speed quickly. Then he dropped his wheels, in spite of the fact that his speed was still too high. Chico, from the rear turret, came up saying that there were some others in the circuit.

"Your lights, skip," Fred said.

Kinsman thought quickly, and decided to switch his lights on, and then extinguish them on the final approach. He turned steeply on to the cross-wind leg. They were close, very close, and losing height every second.

He called angrily, "Zebra to Mulberry Bush. . . . May I pancake? Shake a leg down there, for God's sake!"

Control came back: "Mulberry Bush to aircraft approaching. . . . Repeat your call-sign!"

Kinsman dropped his flaps fully, and moved his pitch control to "Fully Fine." He was now approaching the end of the runway in use, fast. Again he switched on his microphone.

"Zebra's my call-sign. Zebra! Zebra! Zebra! I'm making my final."

The airfield controller towards whom he was dropping, suddenly flashed a red Aldis lamp at Kinsman from his perch at the end of the runway. Still Kinsman descended. Control came back on R.T. as though the question of his landing had been discussed fully. "Mulberry Bush to Zebra. Mulberry Bush to Zebra. . . . You may not pancake. Repeat. You may not pancake. Orbit West Light. Bandits. Repeat. . . ."

Kinsman switched off his microphone, and was about to attempt to go round again when the controller's lamp on the runway changed to green. No one down there seemed to know what was going on. At that he remembered his navigation lights. He switched them off and dropped to the runway. He touched badly, and was about to sink on to the tarmac for the second time when suddenly there was darkness. The long line of lights on the runway ahead of him disappeared to leave him staring into blackness, fighting to keep control of his aircraft.

As, instinctively, Kinsman fought to keep the Halifax

running straight—he couldn't see whether or not he was heading for the grass at the side of the runway—he was aware of Fred standing beside him and reaching up to the escape hatch above. Then he ducked, as beside and above and ahead the darkness was ripped open. In his ears, above the frightening violence of exploding bombs there was a cry, close by, of someone afraid, and then he knew the horror of sitting in a machine with which he had been familiar and which he no longer knew, like a child no longer knowing a mother gone mad.

Kinsman didn't try to hold the Halifax. He didn't know which way to hold it. Instead he leapt for the throttles and closed them, while with his other hand he groped wildly for the ignition switches. He was still trying to find them when, after spinning around for some long moments like a catherine wheel, they stopped. Fred was sitting on top of him. It was frightening to be there, tied to a seat so that he couldn't move his shoulders while Fred struggled on top of him. Fred gasped something about, "We've stopped. We've stopped, I think, skip."

Kinsman tried to undo his safety harness. Fred was standing on him now, about to climb out of the escape hatch on to the roof.

"Get out, Fred!" Kinsman said. "Get out!"

The very silence in the big machine, broken only by the sound of Fred's scramble to reach the roof, was threatening. There was no thought in Kinsman for the others. He had forgotten about them all, until the wireless operator, Les, appeared from beneath and grabbed at Fred's legs. The bomb-aimer cursed loudly, and swung his knee at young Les's face so that the boy cried with the pain of the blow.

Then Fred was out, and Les, recovering from the blow he had received, jumped on to the pilot's seat and kicked wildly as he reached up with his arms in an attempt to pull himself on to the roof. With each jerking movement of his body the boy's breath was expelled in a tight little cry of fear. Then Bob appeared, and grabbed the wireless operator's legs to push him out.

The split-pin which secured Kinsman's safety harness had been damaged, so that he was finding it difficult to release the thing. Bob saw him struggling with it, and the frown on the navigator's face changed to a kind of smile.

There was not the strength in Kinsman's hands to release the thing, but Bob took it in his. Kinsman watched fascinated, as Bob's thick, deeply weathered hands pulled the flattened pin free.

"Thanks, Bob," Kinsman gasped, and as he spoke there flashed through him a kind of regret that he had failed to know Bob before that moment.

"Get out, Bob."

"I can't reach that high."

"Stand on me. Hurry. This bloody thing might go up at any moment."

"If it was going to burn, it would be burning now," Bob said slowly.

"Maybe it is. Get out, Bob!"

It was difficult for Kinsman to find a secure footing owing to the angle at which the aircraft had settled. But he wedged one foot against his seat, and the other against the side of the Halifax. Then little Bob climbed on to his shoulders from the seat, and was out.

Kinsman reached the roof easily, and as he did so he saw the mid-upper gunner climbing out of a hatch further back on the tilted fuselage. He waited for the gunner to jump, and was about to do so himself when he saw little Chico trying to draw himself up. Chico was having difficulty. His head appeared, and then disappeared, and with each disappearance there came from Chico a jumbled collection of boyish curses.

From below, Fred was telling Kinsman to jump, but the bomb-aimer's words were lost in the roaring sound of aircraft engines which spread then in thick waves over the whole airfield. A Halifax appeared to be trying to land as they had landed. Kinsman looked up from where he was sitting, to see the big black shape waving in towards the ground. Its guns appeared to be firing. One of its engines was starting to burn, and above and behind it something else was there. Something sure and controlled which knew its way in the darkness. It was a Messerschmitt. And as the Halifax hit the ground with an ugly, grinding crunch to slither away across the airfield in the direction of the administration building, hopelessly out of control, the Messerschmitt pulled up and over the heads of Kinsman and his crew, its guns still spraying long streams of fire uselessly into the darkness above.

181

Kinsman started to crawl along the roof of his aircraft to get to little Chico.

"Give me your hand, Chico."

Chico reached up, and Kinsman pulled him towards the hatch until the gunner was high enough to reach the roof with the hand that was still free. Kinsman could see then that the rear-gunner's lips were puckered as a little boy's are when trying to control tears, and he said, "It's all right, Chico. It's all right."

He waited until Chico had jumped to the ground, and then he followed. He was confused and afraid. The others were there waiting for him, and they were crouching as though they felt that it was better to be close to the earth.

In the sky around them there appeared to be almost a dozen aircraft. None of them was using lights, but it was possible to tell that some were the hunter and some the hunted, for the plaintive droning of the Halifaxes was interlaced by the high-pitched, angry whine of the Messerschmitts. There was revenge in the cry of those German engines. It was an ugly sound.

Before they could move, a stick of bombs, the first of which appeared to land on the cluster of buildings behind Control, was planted across the airfield. Kinsman, lying with his face on the grass about twenty yards from where his aircraft lay crippled, remembered that Julie would be somewhere around where that bomb had landed. He opened his eyes, and looked into the grass beneath him so that for a moment all existence was there in that six square inches of dark green grass. "Now," he thought, "I should be wanting to get to her, but I don't. I'm afraid."

"Let's run," Kinsman said. He waited for them. No one moved. Then Fred spoke.

"It's better here," Fred said.

Kinsman raised his head to see an aircraft falling two or three miles to the north of Liscombe. There was a streak of flame downwards from about two and a half thousand feet. Then when it hit, he ducked instinctively in answer to the roar of the impact, and the trailing series of echoing explosions.

Thoughtfully, stupidly, big Fred said, "I wonder who that was."

"Come on, Fred. Let's run. I want to go over there."

John Kinsman stood up, and automatically Fred followed. They were gone before the others had time to think of following. Kinsman ran without any very definite idea of why he was running or where he was going to. But he was facing in the general direction of the de-briefing room where he thought Julie should have been.

They had covered some distance over the grass, stumbling occasionally in the rutted earth, when Fred called to him from behind. Kinsman couldn't hear what the bomb-aimer was saying, but he looked in the direction in which Fred was pointing, and there he could see in the light that came from the half-hearted flames which were trying to consume it, the aircraft which someone had tried to land just after they themselves had landed. Kinsman changed course, and started to run towards it.

Around the great black shape three or four figures appeared to be running without purpose. From behind, Fred was shouting, saying that he wondered who it was. And that, even as he ran, Kinsman thought of as strange. How could it matter who it was?

Before they reached the burning Halifax which they could now see was on its belly and bent half-way down the fuselage, a fussy little ambulance arrived. Kinsman stopped as the ambulance stopped. Then Fred came up, breathing heavily, by his side.

"What's wrong?" Fred asked.

There was something intensely violent in the vision of that aircraft lying there, slowly burning. Flames were dancing grotesquely from the engines of its starboard wing, and the darkness around the thing was moving back as though in deference to its agonies.

"That's how it looks," Kinsman said.

Almost as he spoke there was a whine from the sky on their left, and then they were on their faces again as a Messerschmitt ripped a final burst of fire across Liscombe. The fighter flew over their heads, low, and as it passed, Kinsman jumped once more to his feet, and started to run.

When he reached the Halifax, he realized that the men he had seen running around the aircraft before the little ambulance arrived were those of the crew who had managed to escape. The doctor, when Kinsman arrived, was trying to get one of them to lie down, but whoever it was,

was resisting with violence, so that as Kinsman came up Doc Kenway was trying to land a blow on the man's chin. Suddenly the man was quiet, and fell down as though exhausted.

When he recognized Kinsman, the doctor asked, "Who's the captain of this thing?"

It was Squadron Leader Barry's aircraft, and Kinsman told the medical man. It appeared that no one had seen Barry yet. None of the crew was able to say whether or not their captain had come out. Kinsman started to move quickly around the Halifax, and with each moment he was there he became more afraid. There was a hideous kind of threat in the impatient flames. There may have been bombs still aboard. There was ammunition still to explode, and petrol-tanks.

The doctor came up to Kinsman, who was trying to decide whether it would be possible to reach the cockpit by way of the gaping hole in the fuselage. But it looked as though the main spar, damaged, would be in the way.

Behind Kinsman the doctor's voice rolled on angrily. He talked as though this whole thing had been caused by some kind of inefficiency.

"Why did he try to come in? . . . This would never have happened if he hadn't tried to come in. It would never have happened," the doctor said again and again.

Kinsman turned quickly, almost colliding with the other's face. "It happened," he said, "because someone shot him down. That's why it happened."

The doctor, who had a black moustache which was more violently operational than that of any aircrew man in the squadron, said, "I know . . . I know," in a way which suggested that in fact he did not know, and made way for Kinsman so that the latter could go on around to the nose of the Halifax.

They were trying to get those members of Barry's crew who were out of the burning Halifax into the ambulance.

"They're all out," Fred said to Kinsman, "except the Flight Commander."

"I thought I only saw four."

"That was the ones that could walk," Fred said.

Kinsman got Fred to help him up until he could get a footing on the port mainplane, which, because of the buckled undercarriage, was not very far from the ground. Then he climbed close to the cockpit until the heat from the burning engines on the other mainplane was as much as he could bear.

His face was blackening, and the sweat which ran down his forehead and into his eyes was making it difficult.

"I wouldn't, skip," Fred shouted.

The doctor and some others were standing with Fred, below, and Kinsman, as he was pulling down his helmet, and fastening the mask over the exposed part of his face, shouted, "Come on up here and give me a hand, someone."

Fred started to obey, but the doctor held him back, and it was he who climbed on to Fred's shoulder in order to follow Kinsman.

Someone shouted that the fire-wagon was on its way. If little Tom, Kinsman thought, could hold on until they arrived with their foam, everything might be all right for him.

The window by the side of the pilot's seat was open, and there was some loose fabric just behind that so that it was possible for Kinsman to hold with one hand on to the damaged side of the fuselage and reach the window with the other.

He reached the window, and then he saw little Tom Barry. Tom must have been hit by the same burst of fire that had damaged the fabric by which Kinsman was now holding. The top of his head had been blown off, and what had been his inoffensive little face was now steeped by the deep redness of his own blood. The control column had been thrust back into Tom, and from the way the head was forward on the narrow chest, yet tilted back to display the terrible ugliness of its death, Kinsman, without real knowledge, knew that Tom's neck was broken. So much blood, streaked with the greyness of secret tissue and what was probably brain, ran down to cover the flying-suit in which little Tom was lost. The still arms by his side gave Tom's body a peculiar quality of restfulness which, alive, it never had.

As Kinsman's arms weakened and he fell sick to the ground, the fire-wagon arrived, but too late. For then the first of the tanks in the starboard mainplane exploded, throwing the doctor from where he had been standing on the other wing to the ground, so that, along with Kinsman, Fred had to help him to crawl clear of the now blazing aircraft.

The ambulance had moved off with its cargo, and the others who had been there had started to run. Behind Fred and Kinsman and the doctor, crawling until they could get up and run, the sharp explosions of bursting tanks blew Tom Barry's Halifax in every direction. The flames reached up to fifty feet in the air, so that the crew of the fire-wagon gave up hope. When Fred and Kinsman started running, forcing, as they moved, the doctor to run with them, they ran until they met the Group Captain's car on the perimeter track.

"Who's that?" the Group Captain shouted. "Where are you from? Where have you come from?"

Kinsman, when he reached the little car, started speaking before he remembered that he was still wearing his mask. He unfastened the thing, and said, "Kinsman, sir."

He could see that the Wing Commander was with the C.O. Carr shouted, "Were you in that thing?"

"No, sir. Squadron Leader Barry. He was dead before it went up."

Neither of the two officers in the car said anything then. The Group Captain engaged the little car in gear noisily, and shot off, leaving Kinsman standing there supporting the M.O.

"Can you walk, Doc?"

"I think a little. It's my leg. When I came off that wing."

Slowly they started to move in the direction of the building clustered around the control tower. It appeared now to be over. The perimeter track on which they walked was lit by the flames from behind. The Station was quiet except for the distant sound of a car engine. There was nothing in the sky. Then suddenly, as though Liscombe realized what had happened to it, there was activity. Kinsman could hear the shouting of men's voices, and again the cry of revving motors as fire-engines and ambulances started into life. Headlights were approaching them.

It was the little ambulance which had taken Barry's crew away, and when the driver saw them he stopped with much screeching of brakes. Kinsman and Fred helped the doctor into the back before following him, and in minutes they were outside the debriefing room, leaving the doctor to go on up to sick quarters.

"You look bloody awful, skip," Fred said when they were inside.

Kinsman laughed, and insisted that he was all right.

There was no sign of other aircrews. It appeared that only two aircraft had landed, his own and Barry's. His crew, excepting Fred, was still somewhere in the middle of the aerodrome, and Barry's was in sick quarters. He and Fred were all of the squadron that were there. When they had made their way through the ante-room which was used by Intelligence, a crowd of assorted people gathered around them: electrical officers and engineers; radio people; the navigation staff. They were congratulating him and saying things like "Good old Johnny. Glad you made it," when the group was dispersed by the reappearance of the Group Captain with the Wing Commander by his side.

"You're down, Kinsman, and there was Barry. The others appear to be scattered all over the group. . . ." The Group Captain turned from Kinsman when he had spoken, and as though unaware that there was anyone else there, went on to say, "That makes four, Carr. Including Barry, five. They've caught us with our pants down, and kicked our backside soundly. Druffield say they got one. Seems they had some kind of a gun at the end of the runway in use. . . ."

Without waiting for comment, the C.O. turned sharply and headed through the door. But the Winco paused, and smiled to Kinsman. "You all right?" he asked.

Kinsman nodded, smiling.

"Aircraft bent?" the Winco asked.

"A little, sir."

"You kept them alive," Wing Commander Carr said. Then he turned to follow his senior officer, and Kinsman sat down. He was lighting a cigarette from Fred's when, turning only his eyes, he saw Julie in the doorway. She stood there for a moment, smiling as though embarrassed at having to move to him in front of all these people. Then when she did move it was with a little skipping run, and when she reached him she took his hand, instinctively, as he started to stand up.

First she laughed nervously, and she said, "Johnny."

Kinsman pulled deeply on his cigarette, still holding her hand, even after he pulled her down to a chair which was beside that on which he had been sitting. In order to do something, he pulled off his helmet with the hand which was free, and ran his fingers through his hair.

"Where have you been?" Kinsman asked. "Did you find yourself a place to hide?"

"I crawled miserably into a shelter outside."

Fred hadn't moved. He stood there, quite relaxed, looking from Kinsman to Julie and then back again, until Kinsman said, "This is Fred, Julie."

Julie looked up and smiled. "Did you look after him, Fred?"

Fred merely said, "Hello."

"Fred never knows when he's not wanted. That's his greatest quality," Kinsman said. "Fred, go and see if they need anything from me."

"Aye, aye." The bomb-aimer looked again at Julie, and then turned on his heel.

"That was Tom out there," Julie said then.

"It was."

"He was a nice little man."

"I liked Tom," Kinsman said slowly.

Neither of them spoke then. He took her hand again and squeezed it gently.

"Someone said it was you, Johnny. I wept. That's why I wasn't here. I was weeping in a corner of the shelter. Then I met the Groupie outside, and he told me it was Tom Barry, and even then I couldn't stop crying. I'm silly, aren't I?"

"Completely. The nicest, sweetest little silly thing I've ever known."

"I should have known that it couldn't be you."

He turned to look at her face, and she smiled, but even as she smiled he could see the redness in her eyes. "Of course you should," he said. "I'm fireproof."

"That's right. I forgot."

"Do you want a cigarette?"

"No. . . . You're holding my hand, Johnny."

"The most sensible thing I've done all evening."

Julie moved slightly, but Kinsman wouldn't allow her to take her hand away from his. She sensed that he didn't want her to speak until he was ready, so she waited for

188

him to say, "I'm coming back to life. Now I can feel your hand in mine. I'll want to put my arms around you soon."

"It was awful tonight," she said then.

"Not as awful as the things we do. Maybe not as awful as we deserve."

"I've never thought of the things you do," she said.

"No one does. I don't. No one does. When we leave the ground we leave reality. What we drop our bombs on doesn't exist for us. Tom Barry isn't dead to the fellow who blew off the top of his head tonight."

Julie's voice softened. She said, "Poor old Tom! He wanted to go home for Christmas."

"What the hell does Christmas matter, Julie? Before Christmas . . . after Christmas. Christmas doesn't matter. It's getting killed that's important."

"You're angry, Johnny."

"No I'm not, Julie. I don't want to be angry, Julie."

For the third time, John Kinsman brushed the tunic which he referred to as his "number one blue", and placed it carefully, for the third time, over the back of a chair. Then, again, he stood back to look at it, or rather at the sleeves on which Jock, the batman, had just sewn the braid of a squadron leader.

As well as Tom Barry's rank, Kinsman had taken his room in the same block as that which he had shared with Wakefield. Unlike the other, though, it had furnishings.

In his shirtsleeves he went to the door and called along the corridor for the batman.

"All right, sur?" Jock asked when he came.

"Fine, Jock. No phone call for me?"

"No, sur."

"Jock . . . phone the W.A.A.F. site, and see if you can get Section Officer Holmes for me. . . . No, it's Assistant Section Officer. . . . If you get her, give me a shout."

"Right, sur. That's no' bad, eh?" Jock nodded in the direction of Kinsman's tunic.

"As good as Savile Row could do."

"Aye," Jock said. He hadn't understood Kinsman, and after thinking for a moment he went on, "How's the room, sur?"

"Much too grand for me, Jock. I can't get used to all this luxury."

Jock was quite serious. He said, "You'll get used to it," and was gone.

When he put on his tunic, Kinsman turned to the mirror and looked at himself with pleasure. The extra ring on his sleeve seemed to make him look heavier . . . Squadron Leader John Kinsman.

"Formerly," he said aloud, "of the *Western District News*. Late of Clover Road, Millingraving."

For the reflection in the mirror he said, "Your age, Squadron Leader Kinsman?"

"Twenty-two," he said to it.

"Is that all?"

Solemnly he told himself, "I was twelve years old when I was born."

He pulled himself to his full height, then bowed slightly to the mirror before adding, "If you like, I'm as old as time itself."

Three times he said quietly to himself, "Squadron Leader John Kinsman," and the words were carried to his ears on waves of music that only he could hear. Then he leant forward to the dressing-table, and brought his face close to the mirror. He pulled back his lips, examined his teeth, and smiled to himself. He thought of his aunt, and his home. It was pleasant to think of going there now.

Before Jock came in, he took some paper and started to write to his Aunt Lizzie. He told her of his promotion, and of his intention to write to Faighley as she had suggested he should in case he might have to go back to the *Western District News* when the war was over. At that he put down the pen, and to appease the tiny itch of fear that had started up in him with the thought of the war's ending, he smoothed again the braid that Jock had sewn.

There was no knock when the batman opened the door. Jock's head appeared, and he said, "She's no' there, sur."

"Oh . . . right, Jock. Thanks."

"Are you goin' to the dance?" Jock asked.

"Yes."

"Ah'm on the bar, sur. Ah'll see ye all right. Ah'm on the bar at every dance, sur . . . to help Paddy."

"As long as you're not under the bar, Jock."

"That's where ah'll be before the night's out. See you there, sur."

"Right, sur. Maybe she's away out to buy you a Christmas present, eh . . . ?"

Kinsman laughed, and went back to his letter.

"A Squadron Leader," he wrote, "is a rank equivalent to that of a Major in the Army. It's quite a step up, Aunt Lizzie, but I'll tell you about it when I see you after the New Year. By the way—is Dawson at home? Let me know in your next letter. I must write to him. I suppose everything is much the same in the village. Looking forward . . ."

There was a knock on the door.

"Come in, Jock." Kinsman turned, and when he did, he saw Julie.

"It's not Jock," she said. "It's me."

He stood up. "You look pale, Julie," he said. "Is something wrong?"

Julie moved into the room, and then, before she reached him, she sat down on the bed.

"What made you come here, Julie? I've been phoning . . ."

"I had to come here."

He tried to laugh. "You're, eh—you're not exactly behaving according to regulations."

"Oh, Johnny, it doesn't matter."

"Julie . . ."

He moved close to her, and took her face in his hands, and then the door opened, and Jock's awful face appeared in the entrance. "Oh!" he said. "She's here, sur. . . ."

"Outside, Jock," Kinsman said. "See you in the bar."

"Aye." And Jock was gone.

Kinsman pulled a chair over, so that he sat close to Julie. He looked up at her.

"What's the matter, Julie darling? Are you ill?" he asked.

As she answered him, after looking into his eyes and then away and back again as though there might be something there which would make it easier for her to speak, Julie appeared to crumble up. Her hat was in her hand, and as her head fell forward, her beautifully loose black hair tumbled towards her face. Kinsman took her hand.

"Where've you been, darling? Where've you come from?"

"York."

"Jock said you'd be out buying me a Christmas present." Kinsman tried to make her smile. "Is that why you were in York?"

"I did that, but that's not why. I saw a doctor, Johnny."

"What's wrong with the Doc here?"

"I couldn't see him, Johnny."

"Why, Julie? . . . Tell me."

Then his hand tightened on hers, and he said quickly, "You're going to have a baby."

She nodded, and all the time her head was down so that he couldn't see her face. Finally she said, "I'm going to have a baby."

Kinsman knew that he couldn't trust the words that might be in him, so, instinctively, he took her in his arms and felt the warmth of her face and the most intimacy of the tears that were there. He kissed her so that she raised her face to his, and then, after holding her tightly with his own face against the sweetness of her neck, he said, "That's all right, Julie. It's all right. There's nothing wrong with that. It's good, Julie. It's good."

"Now I know that I love you," she said.

"I know, Julie. I know that you do."

She looked up at him, and as she was about to speak again a little shiver of fear appeared at the corners of her mouth. She breathed deeply, and then coughed as though the breath was choking her. He took her hand again, and she said, "This could be Wakey's child, Johnny."

Kinsman's legs straightened, and he stood up. He wanted to move away, but he checked himself, and lied. He said, "I know that too."

Quietly, Julie said, "I don't understand anything any more. I don't understand myself or anything. I don't feel like a woman who would have had to say that. But I am, Johnny. I am, and I don't know whether it's bad or good or right or wrong. I don't feel bad, Johnny. But it's wrong. I think it's wrong."

As she was speaking, Kinsman was hating the memory of Wakefield. And then a kind of anger at himself arose in him. There was a hard edge on his voice as he said, "Wakey's child, my child. What the hell does it matter, Julie? I was responsible for Wakey's loving you. It was I who allowed you to love him. I stood by and watched him when I hadn't the guts to love you myself."

192

"You're angry, Johnny."

"Of course I'm angry!" And then his voice slid down, and he said, "I'm angry because I love you, and I'm angry because things have been so bad for you. Julie, if Wakey and I loved you—there's nothing wrong in that. The only one of us three who was wrong was me when I didn't admit to myself that I loved you."

He knelt down in front of her then, and, for a moment before looking up into her face where the tears ran slowly down, he watched his own hand stroking hers. Then he said, "Are you afraid, Julie?"

"It's you, Johnny. It's you."

Kinsman stood up and walked across the room. After four paces he could walk no further. He turned as she was saying, "Your uniform's changed, and I didn't congratulate you. You look very handsome."

"Julie, we'll get married. Right away. As soon as possible."

She wiped the tears from her eyes, and, tired, she attempted to laugh. "Oh, Johnny. We can't. That's all part of the muddle. I haven't heard from Gerry since Wakey wrote to him. I don't know what I'll say or do. I don't know what I can do. . . ."

He almost ran across the room, and she stood up to go into his arms. "To us," he said—and the words were stifled as his lips met hers until he went on— ". . . to us we'll be married. You'll get out of the Service, and we can live together some place. . . ."

"The R.A.F. might object . . "

"To hell with the R.A.F. We'll live together and we'll have your child . . . and then you'll get your divorce, and we'll get married. We'll be happy, Julie. We'll love each other . . ."

"Johnny. . . ."

He kissed her again, and then laid her on the bed gently. She was lying there looking up into his eyes when he said. "Do you feel all right? I don't know anything about babies, Julie. Are you going to be ill or anything?"

"No . . . no, Johnny." And for the first time since she had come into his room Julie laughed; and as he felt her laughing, he looked at the freshness of her lying there in his arms and was aware of a kind of reason for being young. He kissed each of her eyelids.

"Johnny," she breathed.

"I feel like dancing, and drinking and laughing, because I love you, and we're going to have a baby. Wakey and you and I are going to have a baby . . ." he said.

"Johnny, don't. . . ."

He laughed. "That's all right, Julie. Wakey and you and I are the kind of people who should have babies and babies. If this is . . . is unorthodox, so is everything else. Julie, let's go and dance and laugh because we love each other, and because tomorrow's Christmas Eve."

She put her arms around his neck, and pulled him down until he was close enough for her to whisper again into his ear that she loved him. Then she pushed him away and rose from the bed. She was smiling and Kinsman could see that she was happy as she pushed back her dark hair. "Let's go and dance and be happy because we love each other. . . "

". . . and because tomorrow's Christmas Eve!"

"That's right," she said.

"Do you feel all right, Julie? Are you sure?"

Julie laughed at his concern, and then freshened herself with the water which was in his room. Kinsman had a utility van outside, and in that they made their way to the mess, and as he drove along the road they laughed. Each of them was happy—Julie because she was no longer afraid of life; Kinsman because he was somehow less afraid to live.

As they parked the car outside the mess they could hear music coming from the ante-room, intermingled with the shouts and laughter of those inside. Julie ran up the steps, and he caught her as she reached the top. Then together, his arm in hers, they entered the gaily decorated entrance-hall.

"First stop—the bar," said Kinsman.

Julie glanced at him, and there was gaiety in her eyes as she repeated, ". . . The bar!"

The bar had been moved into what was normally the writing-room, and as they swept into that large room with the long table running along one side, laden with drinks, and labouring under the weight of suckling pigs ridiculously perched with their tiny dead white legs pointing towards the ceiling, beside and surrounded by ham and chicken, goose and turkey, a moving little crowd of aircrew officers, drinking, already slightly drunken, parted, and there in their midst, laughing, darkly handsome as ever, if now somewhat gaunt, but certainly alive, was Wakefield.

CHAPTER FOURTEEN

"THE only man, sir," Kinsman said to the Wing Commander in the latter's office, "who could go would be Wakefield. He only got back to the squadron last night. As far as I know, he hasn't flown for weeks. I'd rather leave him off for a day or two."

Wing Commander Carr blew a cloud of smoke across his desk, and then raised his eyes to Kinsman standing there with the other two Flight Officers, and said, "I'm sorry, Johnny. They're asking for everything we've got. With so many chaps sick and on leave, a situation has arisen where we've got aircraft and no crews. He'll have to go. . . . After all, he did practically walk back to us from somewhere near Strasbourg. He won't mind. . . . Make up the lists, chaps. We'll brief in an hour and a half."

Kinsman asked Fred, and someone else who was sitting there, to leave when Wakefield came into the flight office. He watched them go, and then fidgeted in his pockets for cigarettes before looking at Wakefield's face. It was Wakefield who spoke first, and Kinsman was glad when he said, "How is the Squadron Leader feeling this morning? Intelligence tells me that he tried to empty the bar last night. . . ."

Kinsman attempted to smile as he threw a cigarette to his friend. Then, as he spoke, he expelled his breath quickly. "I feel bloody, Wakey. God knows what I drank last night. Wakey, I'm sorry about having to put you on.

196

I've got to . . . the old man. . . . Wakey, this is a bloody silly job."

Wakefield didn't appear to hear him. When he laughed there was in his voice that charm which Kinsman had always envied. He said, "The last thing I remember seeing of you was when you were standing singing "The Ball of Kirriemuir" with that batman of yours. You were trying to hold him up."

"I was very drunk," Kinsman said.

They laughed together, and then there was a pause when each of them appeared to be looking for something to say. Kinsman spoke first. He said, "What happened to er . . . er . . . ?"

". . . Julie?" Wakefield said. "I don't know. I seemed to lose her half-way through the evening. I think I must have been very drunk too."

"Wakey . . ."

"Don't worry about putting me on, old boy. That's what I'm here for . . . fool that I am."

They laughed at that, and Kinsman held his head as though laughter was painful. Then he raised his face to his friend and said in a voice laden with effort, "I don't even think I said I was glad to see you back. . . . I'm glad you're back, Wakey."

"Thanks, Johnny. What aircraft are you giving me, chum?"

"I don't know. . . ." Kinsman busied himself with the availability list, and soon Wakefield was helping him by phoning the mess and the billeting sites in order to find people whom Kinsman wanted to fly. There were phone calls from the armament and engineering officers. Aircraft were substituted in place of some that Kinsman had already listed. There was considerable confusion, so that, until it was time to go over to the briefing-room, Kinsman forgot his desire to get in touch with Julie. The real need to ask her had gone since Wakefield had told him that she had disappeared half-way through the previous evening, but he still wanted to speak to her. Since the moment they had seen Wakefield standing there in the bar, there had been no opportunity to say anything to her.

Wakefield never left him. They were about to leave the office when Kinsman said, "You go on over, Wakey, and I'll follow you. I've got a couple of things to do."

But Wakefield didn't go. He said, "That's all right, chum. I'll wait for you." So Kinsman, without explanation, left the office, then, and they started to walk over to briefing.

Perhaps there would be a chance to phone Julie before he went off. She might even be around the briefing-room, and he could be with her, just to speak to her . . . a word or two. He had to know that everything was still the same, although he didn't know how it could be. Something like a land-mine had exploded in the straight road along which he and Julie had been walking. Right in front of them. He hadn't started to think about it yet. Last night he had got drunk, in order to allow himself to mark time, and this morning when Jock, the batman, had pulled him from his bed with the information that there was an "ops" call, he would have called out with joy, if the horrible sickness inside him would have allowed him to open his mouth.

"The responsibility of your exalted rank appears to have saddened you, Johnny," Wakefield said, walking by his side.

"A hangover has saddened me. Nothing more exalted than that." Kinsman laughed quietly. "I don't have your irrepressibility."

"That third ring appears to have improved your vocabulary too. I always had a feeling that you'd get on in this world."

"Oh, shut up, Wakey!" Kinsman said, laughing.

"Any special gen on these daylights?" Wakefield said. "I feel as though there's something slightly indecent about flying in daylight."

Kinsman explained that three aircraft would fly in a V formation, and that the rest of the squadron would stay as close by them as possible. When he had finished speaking he paused, and then apologized again for sending Wakefield on this operation.

Wakefield laughed. "If they get me again," he said, "I'll walk back again. Maybe next time I'll walk slower, and perhaps the war'll be over before I get here. . . . The damnable thing is, there's Julie to consider."

"Julie?" Kinsman said without thinking. And when he had spoken, the dregs of the previous evening's alcohol seemed to bubble and stir within him.

When Wakefield was serious he seemed to be unable to look directly at the person to whom he was speaking, as though there was something in people which to him was always funny. Now he looked straight ahead when he said, "It was really bloody awful, Johnny. I don't think I could have done it if I hadn't been walking back to her."

Kinsman emitted a non-committal "Mm . . ."

"You wouldn't understand that, Johnny," Wakefield went on. "I think I envy you."

Kinsman couldn't speak of Julie to Wakefield. Now he looked ahead, praying that the thirty yards between them and the briefing-room would suddenly close. They turned the corner around the side of the paint-shop, and he was saved when they met Bob, his navigator. Bob was carrying maps and instruments, and as he saw Kinsman he asked if they would be leading the squadron, and Kinsman said that he didn't yet know. If they were, there would be a special briefing for them after the main briefing. Would Bob tell the rest of the crew?

When Kinsman walked between the crews in the briefing-room with Wakefield by his side, something of a cheer started up. Then the crews were laughing and someone shouted, "Down with the Flight Commanders!" and, with the same enthusiasm as they had cheered, they booed. He was introducing Wakefield to the crew which had been gathered together for him, when the Wing Commander entered the room and they cheered again. It was the mood they were in. Something of a holiday spirit had crept into the proceedings. Or perhaps they felt that way because it was morning, and outside the sun was shining with a hard, winter brilliance. They appeared to think that a daylight operation was easier than one which took place at night.

The Wing Commander announced that Squadron Leader Kinsman would lead them, and when Kinsman heard that, he decided to ask the C.O. to allow Wakefield to fly with him as one of the leaders. He would know then where Wakey was. He might even be able to see him occasionally.

Kinsman heard practically nothing of what was said at briefing as he sat with his crew looking at the backs of all their heads, and Wakefield's. Wakefield's neck, thin, his elegant hair swept behind his ears. . . . It was wrong to send Wakey. And it was he who was sending him. Why couldn't he have stayed away, another day—two days, until some of the others had come back?

"How do you feel, skip?" Fred asked.

"I'm recovering . . . slowly, Fred. I'll be all right."

When he had recovered, what then? When this op was over, and they were back: Wakefield and himself, and Julie. All three of them, in a way, loving each other. And Julie going to have a child which, also in a way, belonged to all three of them. What then?

Behind Kinsman's eyes a stale, numb stillness lingered like old tobacco smoke in an empty room. Experiencing little flashes of improvement in the progress of his hangover, he felt as though someone was intermittently opening and closing a window, so that through the dullness of his brain there shot cool flashes when it was possible to experience the closeness, almost the interchangeability, of those around him with himself. They moved and shuffled, and occasionally there was a low murmur of amusement; a cough, a gasp expressing their attitude to what was being asked of them. The room was warm from the steam which ran through the pipes stretching around the walls. Each one of them in blue, almost without personality; component parts of a body of men: a madman's body where they beat as the heart, and along the flaying arms and legs of which they raced as the life-blood to get back from where they had started. Yesterday Kinsman had felt as though he was going to live his way, but all that had changed again. There was nothing he could do now. Perhaps he had to go with it all, and wait to see where it would take each one of them.

Fred said, "O.K., skip?" and Kinsman became aware that the main briefing was over. He saw the Wing Commander, and arranged that Wakefield should fly as number two in the formation which was to lead the squadron. Since it was a very experienced navigator who was flying with Wakey, the Wing Commander agreed to that. He smiled to Kinsman when he said it was all right, too, in a way that made the latter wonder how well he knew him.

With Wakey, and Tubby Spiers, the Commander of B Flight, who was to fly on his left, Kinsman was briefed again by the Winco. Then they left to dress and get out to the aircraft. It was then that he tried to 'phone Julie from the parachute room, but she wasn't at her mess or her office. He was standing there, vacantly staring at nothing with the telephone receiver in his hand, when Fred saw him from the counter, and called to him that the bus was waiting.

"What's the matter, skip? You look worried," Fred said.

Kinsman forced a smile. "Nothing," he said. "Let's go."

When they were airborne, through the slight ground fog which had risen in response to the sun, and into a clear, blue sky, they climbed to seven thousand feet above the Head, there to wait for Wakefield and Spiers to form up on either wing, and then to fly for thirty miles due east over the North Sea. The idea was that before they arrived back at Flamborough Head the squadron should have found the leaders, and have settled down in a tight gaggle behind.

Circling there, waiting at seven thousand feet, Kinsman felt good. The crew chattered on the intercom as though they didn't think that the operation was yet to be taken seriously. The sun, almost as high as it would be that day, shone with a brilliance which danced, dazzling on the perspex of the cockpit, so that each time the Halifax turned slowly into the south he had to shut his eyes until the nose came around to the east. He borrowed Fred's sunglasses, but before he put them on he looked down to the sea below, where it was dashing itself in long, torn ribbons of white foam against the placid rocks.

"It doesn't look like Christmas Eve," he shouted.

Bob came up to see, and stood there blinking beside Kinsman until he had accustomed himself to the brilliance of the cockpit. A smile spread across the navigator's round, fat face, and, looking at him, Kinsman felt that he wanted to say something which would express his feelings towards the gaiety of the morning. But Bob winked, and that was all. He had been slapped on the back by Kinsman, and was trying to save himself from falling down the three steps, when Chico came up on the intercom shouting, "Here's somebody coming up, skip. What's Wakefield in?"

Kinsman looked around hurriedly, but because they were turning to port he could only see on that side. His

201

hand grabbed at his mask, missed the switch of the microphone and then found it. "Wakey's in Tommy," he said to Chico.

"He's just coming up your starboard, then."

Kinsman levelled out, and called, "Where is he now?"

Two of them at once, the mid-upper and rear-gunners, answered. "He's coming right up now."

"All right."

Before he settled down and discovered at what speed Kinsman was flying, Wakefield flew past once, and as he did so, Kinsman laughed and waved to him. It wasn't possible to recognize his friend, and somehow the figure sitting there at the controls of that other aircraft didn't look like Wakey. He sat straight up in his seat, and there was none of the easy casualness about him which Kinsman knew on the ground. He sensed that Wakefield wasn't happy, for he didn't come in close enough for a man who was thoroughly at ease with what he was doing.

A few minutes later Tubby Spiers came up on the other side, and then Bob was telling Kinsman that it was time to set course over the North Sea. They were to fly a compass course which was practically due east.

"Anyone else around, Chico?"

"Not up here. I can see some away down below who look as if they're lookin' for us."

"On course . . . now!" Bob called, and Kinsman turned out towards the sea, slowly so that the other two would find it easy to turn their big Halifaxes with him. He levelled and knew a curiously satisfying sensation when he had done so.

There was no one in front of him, only the sea below stretching away to the east as far as he could see, and the sky like a great grey-blue curtain reaching up from where the cold greenness shivered and broke. Flying straight and level, as accurately as he could, Wakefield on his right, Tubby Spiers in Orange on his left, he was leading.

"How far do we go, Bob?"

"Ten minutes out: ten minutes back. Keep your airspeed bang on, Johnny."

"I'm doing that!"

Before he turned to steer a reciprocal course which would take them back to Flamborough Head, about eight aircraft were trailing behind Kinsman and the other two. As he turned, he saw them, below; settled heavily in the sky, loosely bunched, one after the other, above and below each other, turning, with the sun glinting on their cockpits, in a plaintive attempt to get to their leader. They looked strong, and to Kinsman, looking down at them, strangely beautiful.

He couldn't remember having known before such life as there was in his aircraft that morning. The power which shuddered through the airframe from the four Hercules engines, he could feel in his arms and fingers, and, because it was daylight, he could see the Halifax vibrating here and there. He became busy in a way that night-flying would not allow. On either side of him there was Wakefield and Spiers to look at, each of them rising and falling as they rode on great unseen, swelling streams of air, appearing in front of his wing-tip and then disappearing.

"How are they, Chico?" Kinsman asked.

"They're coming up now. I think I would slow down a bit, Johnny. There's one . . . two . . . three. There's seven of them with us. No, eight. Somebody else has just come up. Whoo! Look out," Chico laughed. "Somebody nearly hit somebody!"

Suddenly out of the west, Kinsman saw the rest of the squadron coming towards him. They reached across the sky in a long, uneven line. He counted. Eight tiny dots which in a minute took on the grace of aircraft.

"Here they come," Fred said.

"If we don't get out of the way we'll go right through them. Think they can see us?" Kinsman asked.

Fred laughed when he said, "Let's wait and find out," and almost as he spoke the line of aircraft approaching them parted to the left.

"Fire a red Very, Fred."

The bomb-aimer came up from the nose to fire his signal, and when it shot up from the roof the aircraft approaching started to turn in towards them, climbing. There seemed to be more noise in his ears than there ever was at night, but perhaps that was because, knowing those others were there around him, he imagined he could hear them.

"How are they now, Chico?"

"It looks great, skip. They're all coming in. It looks great!"

In his imagination Kinsman saw what only Chico in the rear turret could see with his eyes. He saw himself at the head of a heavy spear of aircraft. As he felt his own Halifax throbbing, swaying occasionally, the nose slightly down as it cut through the air towards the coast which was now becoming visible, he felt as though he was controlling something much bigger than this one aircraft.

Chico was on the intercom giving something of a running commentary on what was happening behind. Occasionally the mid-upper came in, and then Fred, until Kinsman, feeling that the operation was started now in earnest, said, "All right, chaps, let's all shut up."

Bob said, "Let me know when you cross the coast, Johnny."

"I'm going to turn south over Liscombe when we get there."

"That's not in the flight plan," Bob said by way of protest.

"The old man'll get a kick out of it," Kinsman said quietly.

So far everything had gone well. Kinsman was happy. The entire squadron was now in the gaggle before they had reached the coast. Now all he had to do was to ensure that they arrived at the Humber in time for the rest of the Group to fall in behind. For that day Liscombe's squadron were leading their base, and the Druffield base were in turn leading the Group.

Kinsman heard someone switch on his microphone, and then Chico said, "Where are we going, skip?"

"Mulheim. . . ."

"Ah, that's right. I forgot."

"Essen Mulheim," Kinsman elaborated.

"Essen Mulheim! Ah didn't know there was any Essen about it. If ah'd 'ave known that ah wouldn't have come."

"All right . . . all right. It's an airfield."

Kinsman thought of their target. It was a good target. They were trying to bomb an airfield on which fighters were based which were supporting Rundstedt in his Ardennes offensive. When it was a factory you were going to, or a rail yard, there were always other buildings or other rails to hit. He did what he was supposed to do, but only Fred could see how effective was their bombing, and Kins-

204

man's understanding of the bomb-aimer's job was so slight that he never really could accept the fact that it was possible to hit a target from twenty thousand feet. But this time it was important. They were trying to hit something for a reason he could understand.

Flamborough Head was now almost underneath their nose, and Kinsman said to Bob, "I'm just about to turn, Bob."

"Tell me when you start."

He was trying to keep his air-speed absolutely constant, for Bob was navigating for all the squadron. His Halifax was trimmed. He sat upright in his seat, feeling as though he was sitting on the axis of a see-saw, ready to counteract the slightest tendency to sway one way or the other. The engines were as finely synchronized as he could make them.

"Fred! Ready with a Very."

Fred came up, and inserted a cartridge in the gun fixed in the roof. "Ready, skip."

"Fire it now."

Very gradually he dipped his port wing and started into a gentle turn to the left. He could see Spiers, a good pilot, sinking back and slightly beneath. He leant forward to look for Wakefield, and Wakey was there, above, not far enough back; a little too high, so that Kinsman could see the great underbelly of his friend's aircraft rising and falling, a little too close for comfort, just above him on his right, as though it was being dangled on the end of a string. He smiled into his mask at the thought of Wakefield having trouble when making the turn.

Bob gave him the course, and Kinsman leant forward to fix it on his gyro compass before he had come out of the slow turn, when the gyro compass started to spin round. For a moment Kinsman wondered if it should do that. Then he said, "Bob, I think something's wrong."

"What?"

"This compass . . ."

"Aw, J . . . J . . . Jonah!" Bob exclaimed, and then he cursed obscenely.

"Wait a minute. Maybe it'll settle down."

Hurriedly he selected the new course on the moving magnetic compass. He could only guess when he should check the turn, and he did that, coming out slowly, so that it would be easy for those on the other side to stay with him. Spiers was with him. His aircraft was steady, but Wakey's wasn't there. Then Wakefield came up. Too much. To slow down, he pulled his nose up slightly so that he was high again. Little Chico seemed to sense that Kinsman was thinking, for, without being asked, he came up with, "He's coming in now, skip." And then, as though afraid that Kinsman would tell him that it was none of his business, he switched off.

Wakefield hung there, just above on the starboard, threateningly close.

"It's no good, Bob. It's still going round."

"Well, I can't navigate if you haven't got that thing, Johnny."

When the navigator spoke there was a break in his voice which sounded almost tearful.

"I could use the magnetic compass."

"It's no good, Johnny. We've got to be bang-on accurate. It's no bloody use, Johnny."

"All right. All right, Bob. I'll have to think something out."

Kinsman looked at the magnetic compass, still spinning stupidly around. He swore at the thing into his mask. Then he closed his eyes with the vain hope that when he opened them the thing would be all right. But it wasn't. Wakefield was his number two, and if he was going to hand over the lead to someone, it should be to him. But Tubby Spiers was a senior officer, and a better pilot. A dozen thoughts and wishes came into Kinsman's mind, and he cursed when he thought of how well everything had gone. It was when something like this happened, some stupid little thing, that the whole thing could go wrong. There was no prearranged signal which would tell Wakey to take over. Wakey might do something bloody silly when he was trying to change positions with him. But, Kinsman thought again and again, if he went over on top of Tubby Spiers to port, that would leave Wakefield out on the right so that he wouldn't be able to see him. He decided, finally, to try to change positions with Wakefield.

Now the whole squadron had turned with them, and they were flying steadily, with Liscombe slightly behind to the north. Wakefield had settled down, so that Kinsman could see the nose of his aircraft without actually seeing Wakefield himself, there, just beyond his starboard wingtip. He looked again and again from right to left, making sure that each of them was there.

"Fred, fire three Verys. White ones."

"Now?"

"Yes, now."

Fred fired, and when he had done so, Kinsman could see Tubby Spiers leaning forward in his seat as though asking what was wrong. Wakefield came up so that he was visible, and Kinsman tried to indicate with his hand that he was intending to change places with him. Wakey took off his mask and smiled, shaking his head in a way which suggested that he didn't understand.

"I'm going to move now, Bob."

Kinsman moved violently. He cut his throttles right back, and pushed his nose down so that they dropped. Then down beneath them he pulled over to starboard as he increased his boost to take the Halifax well out in front. The whole thing was done violently and decisively, in order that the others would not think that he intended them to follow him.

"Where are they, Chico?"

"They're away back. . . . Above . . . on the port."

"What are they doing?"

"Nothing."

"I'm going to fall back in on Wakefield's right."

"O.K., skip. I'll tell you when we hit them," Chico said.

Kinsman climbed gradually again, and when he was at the same height as the rest of the squadron, he throttled back until he saw Wakefield's aircraft with Spiers on the other side, both of them perhaps fifty yards away. Then, gradually, he crabbed in until he was just behind Wakefield's starboard wing.

They were approaching the Humber, and Fred, standing by Kinsman's side, pointed out a great black cloud of bombers drawing over from the west to converge on their track.

"That'll be the Group," Kinsman said to Fred, and Fred nodded knowingly.

A light started flashing from the astrodome of Wakefield's Halifax. Someone was using an Aldis lamp.

207

"Les," Kinsman called on the intercom, "come on up here and read this."

With considerable difficulty Les read the message.

"They're asking us what's wrong," he said, finally.

"Tell them our compass is u.s."

Kinsman heard his wireless operator muttering curses before he switched off his microphone and went below for his lamp. Then Les reappeared, frowning fiercely to Kinsman as he made his way up to their own astrodome. Kinsman unfastened his mask and shouted after young Les, asking what was wrong. He laughed as the operator held up the lamp in his hand and cursed angrily, but inaudibly beneath the roar of the engines on either side.

South over England the weather held. It was a beautiful morning: a morning for flying, and, tucked closely in behind Wakefield's starboard wing, Kinsman enjoyed himself as he tried to keep his own aircraft positioned just where it should be. He was occupied in a way that was impossible on a normal operation. It was good to work as he was now, to feel the big bomber respond beneath the touch of his fingers on the throttles; to smell the sweet smell of sweating rubber in his mask, and yet still be able to see outside the cockpit.

Over France there was some low cloud, so that it was only possible to glimpse the earth occasionally. There was snow in places on the ground, and as a layer of alto-stratus gradually built up between them and the sun, a coldness came into the atmosphere which removed some of the unreality of the morning.

Bob, who had little to do other than to check the work of the navigator in the leading aircraft, stood beside Kinsman looking at the cloud building up above them. After a long time he said into his microphone, "Looks more like Christmas now."

Chico, always anxious to talk, for it was lonely back there in that glass cage on the tail of the Halifax, took a cue from Bob and said, "I wonder what they're going to give us for a Christmas present when we get to what-do-you-call-it. . . ."

"How's it look back there, Chico?" Kinsman asked.

"Looks fine. Nobody's hit anybody yet."

Because he was occupied with formating on Wakefield,

Kinsman was surprised when Bob announced quietly that they were about to make the turn on to the last leg. They were in Germany, and, with that realization, he began to feel something of the coldness that until then he had only seen.

Kinsman felt himself tensing. He was close in to Wakefield—too close, so that once his own port wing dipped viciously as it caught in the slipstream of the leading aircraft. When he could, he moved out, and he had just done so when Wakefield started in a slow turn to port, so that Kinsman was left far out and feeling rather silly.

There is a certain suggestion of weakness in the word "silly," and just then Kinsman was weak. The kind of joy he had known was gone with the appearance of a grey, misty sky, and the strange coldness of the earth below. A faint tinge of fear had come to him, too, with the realization that they were so close to the target. As he opened the throttles slightly and started to move in close again to Wakefield, he said, "Gunners!"

"Skip . . ."

"Skip . . ."

"See anything of the escort?"

Chico answered. "I think I saw some Spits a while back. I think they were Spits."

Kinsman had the feeling that Wakefield's nose was down slightly, and when he looked at his own air-speed indicator he saw that in fact they had increased speed. Wakey's mid-upper was moving his guns from side to side. Then a flash of sunlight caught the moving turret, and Kinsman looked up to the thin cloud breaking above. He was behind Wakefield now, close behind, but not so close that he couldn't take his eyes from him.

Bob said, "We're late."

"We must be," Kinsman answered. "Wakey's going like hell."

Wakefield appeared to be losing height very gradually in his bid to make up time. Their air-speed was almost two hundred knots, and Kinsman felt as though they were flying *at* something. Below, the low cloud was gradually dispersing, and from beneath it, Germany was shining up at them. With increased boost and increased revs., they still hadn't caught up with Wakefield. From where he was, Kinsman suddenly saw something beautiful in the two aircraft ahead, glistening where the sun caught them, diving slightly, and he with them, helter-skelter into a target with their engines revving high. A kind of song suddenly came into the cry of the engines, and, hearing it in his imagination, he felt himself become warm again, so that the fear he had known minutes before was gone.

The wireless op. said, "Window, skip. . . ."

"Is it time? Is it time for window, Bob?"

Bob came over the intercom. "Yes. Yes, it's time now."

"O.K., Les," Kinsman called, "get cracking."

Fred announced that he had gone into the nose, but Kinsman couldn't answer immediately, for he had just drawn level with Wakefield, and he was trying to ease off power so that he would fall back. For a moment, before he fell back, he saw Wakefield sitting straight up in his seat, his eyes apparently fixed on the horizon ahead.

"Ten minutes," Bob said.

The window started falling from the other two aircraft, and Kinsman could see the silver strips of tinfoil glistening in the sunlight. The thought came to him then that the only aircraft in all those four hundred which was unprotected was Wakey's.

"How are they behind, Chico?"

"O.K. . . . O.K., Johnny. You should see our mob. It's marvellous. They're all strung out like an arrow on each side."

It was a strange excitement which Kinsman knew then, quite different from anything he had known at night, for now he felt that he was sharing something with those behind him and beside him. A gunner in Wakefield's aircraft waved to him, and Kinsman smiled into his mask as though trying to reassure that man that he was with him.

In his imagination he saw the arrow of aircraft of which Chico had spoken. The thought came to him that there should have been a great mass of people perched on the remnants of white cloud on either side seeing this, and then, just as the first of the black flak burst over on the port beside Tubby Spiers, he wondered how his imaginary audience would have reacted.

A string of flak followed the first burst over on the port, and then, a little later, half a dozen bursts ripped along the sky on Kinsman's starboard, so that the Halifax bucked angrily. Instinctively Kinsman edged closer, a little closer to Wakefield.

Fred said, "Bomb-doors, skip."

Kinsman switched on the microphone and left it that way so that he wouldn't have to take his hands from the stick again. He opened the bomb-doors, and expelling his breath as he spoke, said, "Bomb-doors open."

"They're showing us the way in," Fred said.

"Yes."

Kinsman's eyes were on Wakefield's Halifax until an untidy pattern of flak burst ahead and amidst them and behind. With both hands he held on. His eyes were closed, and when he opened them, a little frightened, he looked to Wakefield. Wakefield was still there, nose down and charging in.

"Somebody . . ." little Chico said—"somebody's bought it, skip. I think somebody's bought it."

"All right!"

Kinsman could hear himself breathing heavily into his microphone, but he was afraid to take his hand from the control column in order to switch the thing off.

"Close," Fred said quietly.

"Yes."

"He's burning on the port, skip. I think he's goin' to hit. . . . No, he's not. . . . !"

"All right, Chico . . . all right."

Right ahead, across their bows, another series of black explosions swept over their path, so that in seconds they flew through the smoke, and the smell of it crept into the cockpit. Kinsman looked to Wakefield, half expecting, without realizing that he was, his friend to turn off. But Wakey was still there, heading on and on. All around them, ahead and behind, the sky was smudged with the black smoke of shells exploding and exploded.

Kinsman was so afraid that he could think of nothing or sense nothing. All the parts of his body and his brain seemed to have run together like some melting jelly, and he could just sit there, waiting and waiting, not even hoping or caring or knowing anything.

Even when the Halifax on his left and a little ahead—Wakefield's Halifax—was hit, so that it reared upwards, staggering and clutching at the air before casting both its wings, spinning, to either side and then plunging down in a long, winding, utterly helpless dive to the earth, he could only sit there and watch the useless fuselage go down and down while he went on and on.

CHAPTER FIFTEEN

JULIE said, "But, Johnny, what about poor Les?"

"I don't know. He went kind of mad when Wakey went down. He must have seen him. Fred hit him over the head. Make some tea, darling. . . . There's an idea, Julie. Make some tea."

"Tea?"

"I'd like some. I need some."

"Johnny!"

". . . and I think the baby needs some. Get the baby some tea, Julie." As he spoke Kinsman was rubbing Julie's middle gently.

"Johnny, stop it darling."

"You like that, Julie Holmes. I know you do."

"No I don't!" She was about to laugh, and to stifle her laughter she rolled over to bury her face in the pillows. For a moment there was silence, and then Julie went on to roll right over, so that again she could look at him lying there by her side.

"What's going to happen to him?" she said then.

"I don't know. I suppose they'll send him away. I'll have to get another wop."

"The poor boy must have been ill. You sound as if you don't care."

"I do, Julie. I care as much as I can. I've known him a long time."

"It's awful. Did he know Wakey?"

"No, I don't think so."

"I thought maybe seeing Wakey . . ."

"No it was just seeing Wakey's aircraft getting hit that way."

"Was it awful, Johnny? They shouldn't have put Wakey on when he had just got back."

"He had to go, Julie."

"I don't see that."

Kinsman moved to sit up on the bed, and said, "I'll make some tea. Where's the thing?"

"No darling." She reached up to him with one long, white arm, took his neck in her hand, and then pulled him slowly, because he did not resist, back to the pillow. They lay still for some time until he kissed her again.

"Johnny, I'm glad you came here. . . ."

Kinsman kissed her neck, and stayed with his face buried there in the softness of her skin until he said, "Sweet's a word I didn't like until now. You're sweet, Julie. You smell sweet."

"You are too, Johnny. I like to smell you."

He laughed, so that alarm came into her eyes, and she silenced him by placing her hand, quickly, over his mouth.

"Darling, be quiet. Someone'll hear you. . . . You mustn't . . ."

". . . I was going to say 'Stick around, babe'."

"Johnny Kinsman, you're awful."

". . . I'll make some tea. I think I'll have a cigarette. . . ."

"What's wrong, Johnny?"

"Nothing, Julie. Why?"

"You're so restless. You seem to be always going."

"I'm not really, darling. I'm all right."

He sat on the edge of the bed, wondering for a moment where he had left the coat which he intended to wear in place of a dressing-gown.

"You've got a good back, Johnny."

"How do you know? You can't see it," he said.

"I can touch it. I can feel it."

Kinsman found his greatcoat on the chair by the window. The lining was cold against his skin when he slipped it on, so that a tingling shiver ran down his spine.

"God, it's cold. I should have stayed where I was."

As he lit a cigarette Julie insisted that she had told him so. He pulled the curtain back to look outside.

"It wasn't right to run off and leave poor old Millie like that," Julie said then.

Kinsman laughed quietly. "It was quite right. If Millie had been acquainted with the facts, I'm sure she'd have approved. She loves parties. She'll probably still be there. . . . It's very dark, Julie. Out there it looks like what I imagine a prison camp must look. It's all mud and wooden huts."

"But it's nice here," she said.

"Wonderful. Can I put on the light?"

"Wait till I get up. I'm coming up, Johnny."

Julie jumped from the bed then, and in the darkness found her dressing-gown. She switched on the light, and when she had done so she smiled, and said, "For a man wearing only a greatcoat, you look remarkably good."

"Thank you." There was a mock embarrassment in his voice as he smiled to her, and ran his fingers through his hair, smoothing it.

They lit the little electric ring, and Kinsman filled a pot with water from the container which had been left by Julie's batwoman. Julie busied herself with the business of finding cups and biscuits which she was sure were somewhere, while Kinsman knelt by the little stove watching the water slowly approaching boiling point.

From behind she placed her hands on his face, and then she knelt down, slipped her arms around his neck and rested her face against his. "Do you know what I wish, Johnny?"

"What?"

"I wish I could capture the gladness. I feel because you're here."

"That's funny. . . ." He turned quickly so that he almost knocked over the pot containing the water. But he caught the thing, and went on, ". . . I was thinking just that. This is all so real, Julie, that now I can't imagine there's anything else."

"I'm afraid, Johnny. Don't be angry."

He tightened his grip on her hand, and then, without really thinking of what he was doing, raised it, naturally, to his lips.

"Oh, Johnny! I'm afraid. Yesterday Wakey spoke to me in the morning before you went off, and I had to listen to him telling me that he loved me. And all the time I was

215

thinking of how I loved you, and of what was happening inside me. He sounded so real that I never thought of him not coming back again. I had to talk to him as though I was still going to marry him. I had to try to laugh when he laughed. I couldn't tell him then, Johnny. But it was when he went away, and then when you told me that he wasn't coming back, that I started to be afraid. Somehow I felt as though we were all wanting something from each other, and . . . and the thing, the thing we were wanting wasn't the other's to give. I'm afraid now, Johnny. . . ."

She moved over to throw herself on the bed, and he stood up to follow. When he reached her, and was leaning over the bed to hold her shoulders, she turned around quickly and said, "I'm sorry, Johnny. I know I shouldn't talk this way. . . ."

"That's all right, darling. It would be no good if you didn't say what you believed."

"It's just, Johnny, that there's something so sinister about it all. As though we were all puppets dancing on the end of a string. I feel so weak. Talking in whispers here in this . . . this little cage. . . . Only these thin wooden walls to protect us. I want there to be sunlight for us, Johnny. I want to shout out about us."

Kinsman stood up and cupped her chin in his hand.

"When you weren't thinking, you were happy," he said.

"Yes, it's just . . . it's just . . . ."

"Well, don't think, Julie. Not yet."

Julie said, "The water's boiling," and Kinsman went over and finished the making of the tea. Then he brought her some, and they sat on the edge of the bed to eat biscuits, and when the stuff had warmed her Julie felt better, so that when he said, "When we're married I'm going to insist that tea made after two o'clock in the morning will be made by you," she laughed: quietly, when she remembered where they were, and said, "I'd love to; only when we're married you won't want tea at two in the morning."

"That's the thing about me. I will. I'll keep waking you up all night to make love to you."

"No, you won't. You'll probably be like Millie's husband, and never make love to me at all, and I'll have to get someone else."

"You underestimate me, Julie Holmes."

216

"Darling," she said impulsively, "you make wonderful tea."

Kinsman took their cups and placed them carefully on the table, before going back to the bed on which Julie now sat with her legs curled up beneath her.

"Feel better now?" he asked, and when she smiled to him he thought again of how beautiful she was, her body wrapped in the deep wine-coloured dressing-gown, her hair dark, almost black, and swept back loosely away from the blue of her eyes. He turned his eyes from her then, to where he rubbed his hands against the warmth of the rough blanket.

Julie moved and said, "What's wrong?"

"I'll put out the light, in case Millie sees it and wants to come in. I'll open the fire. We'll get some light from that."

The soft darkness, broken only by the glow from the fire, somehow enhanced the beauty of Julie when she sat above him, leaning against the wall at the head of the bed. As though the thought had suddenly come to him, he said, "I'm not afraid, Julie."

"I know," she said softly.

"I mean I'm afraid when I'm there—like yesterday with Wakey, but I'm not afraid for us. . . ."

He caught the edge of her gown, and as he did so she leant forward to place her hand on his.

"We're right, Julie," he went on. "What we're doing is right. The child inside you. You . . . us . . . it's good, Julie. Before there was you, I didn't think I needed a reason for all this. Now I don't know what it would be like if there was no reason. It's not just that because I love you I think I have a right to live when Wakey died, and all those other died. But I believe in life, Julie. Loving you has made me that way, I feel as though you've made me discover a lot of life in me that I didn't know was there before, and it's got to be used up. It's a kind of faith I have. Like some people believe in God."

"I want to believe in God, Johnny," she said.

"And I believe in you and that child inside you," Kinsman said. "Maybe that makes me a believer once removed."

Julie smiled to him and reached out to him, so that, without thinking, he moved closer to her. She leant forward to him as he raised her face, and their cheeks touched gently.

Kinsman said, "You'd get on well with my Aunt Lizzie. She believes in God."

He felt Julie smiling then as she said, "If she's your Aunt Lizzie, I'll love her, Johnny."

"No you wouldn't. I don't think you would. You belong to the new life we're going to live. . . . There's fresh air where we're going to."

"I'll love her and I'll love you and I'll love the life we're going to live, Johnny," she said slowly.

When Kinsman's arms went around her Julie slipped down until she was looking up into his face. She started to say something, but the words wouldn't come. Her eyes moved over him as though trying to take in every part of his face at once, and her lips moved, then quivered hesitantly, to be stilled only when he kissed them. Once he breathed, "This is enough to believe in, Julie," and then there was silence, a long, warm silence broken only by the occasional tiny crash of crumbling coal in the fire, the moving springs on which they lay, the sobbing breath of Julie.

The dull glow which had reached the far wall from the fire faded to the bed and past them, until they were lying there in the cold darkness. Kinsman stirred, and his voice was dry when he said, "I'll have to go now and sleep, Julie. There's something on in the morning."

"Sleep here, Johnny," she said.

He laughed. "I can't sleep here. Someday, when I know you well enough, I'll sleep with you. Now I can only love you."

And then they both laughed, quietly, when they remembered that they might be overheard.

In the morning, as Kinsman had expected, there was an ops call. The ten o'clock Command broadcast requested a maximum effort. The target was Hanover. Briefing, the Wing Commander announced at the conference in his office, would take place at 14.00 hours, but before the crews assembled it was postponed, on instructions from Group, by one hour. At 14.30 briefing was again postponed by an hour. There was some curtailment, too, of the bomb-load in order to allow more fuel to be carried.

Kinsman was in his office, surrounded by the captains of most of the C Flight crews detailed to take part in the operation, when Tubby Spiers popped his head around the corner of the door to give them the news. There was a muddled sound of protest and relief at Tubby's announcement, and Spiers laughed, half-heartedly saluted Kinsman as the pilots started to get to their feet, and was gone. Although he didn't like him, Kinsman thought of Tubby Spiers as the perfect type of operational officer. No one would have said he was unemotional: there was violence in him, but with it went a heavy-handed kind of practicality which the job seemed to demand.

Fred, sitting there oblivious to the fact that he was the only N.C.O. present, stayed seated. While the officers scrambled to get through the door in order to get to the mess for an early tea, he looked at Kinsman, who was seated behind the desk, raised his almost hairless eyebrows, lowered them, and then again raised them before saying solemnly, "I don't like it, skip."

"Carruthers!" Kinsman shouted. Then to Fred, "Get that Carruthers bloke, Fred."

Carruthers had joined the flight a few days previously, and this would be his first night operation. He was an Australian. His hair was a very decided brown, its colour probably accentuated by the deep dark blue of his uniform, and while his face was boyish it was not so in the normal English way. There was something about the nose and the mould of the jaw which suggested strength, and the faded tan of the boy's complexion, sprinkled with freckles, suggested something more: a kind of clean, colonial strength. Carruthers looked as though he had been to a school at which cold baths and cricket were the most important features of the curriculum.

"Carruthers," Kinsman said when Fred reappeared with the Australian, "I want to see you and your crew after briefing. How do you feel about going on this night op?"

"Fine, sir," Carruthers answered in his flat voice.

"You know we're on seven tanks? You know what that means?"

"Yes, sir."

Kinsman looked down at the papers which were on the desk before him, and then back to the boy's face. The Australian showed no signs of anything which could have

219

been called apprehension, and Kinsman wondered how he would have felt if he was about to take off for Hanover on his first night operation. But of course Hanover meant nothing to this lad. Nothing at all. It was just a name on the map, and of no more significance than Essen or Bochum or Bremen or Gelsenkirchen or Dusseldorf. To Kinsman these names were not of places. They were descriptions of experiences. Then, of course, this boy did not know that the target for that night was Hanover. No one had yet told him. All he knew was that they would be using seven tanks, and that meant they were going a long way. Hanover was Kinsman's problem.

"I would have liked to have sent you on a pansy one for the first time. Have you done your night circuits here?"

"Yes, sir."

"Well, don't do anything bloody silly, Carruthers, or I'll get a rocket. . . . I'll see you after briefing."

When the Australian had gone, Fred said again, "I don't like it, skip . . . seven bloody tanks, and us on yesterday, an' a new wop an' all that."

"After this one we'll be off for a month, Fred. I'll have to spread my tour out a bit."

"Seven tanks," Fred repeated slowly, and then he looked at Kinsman in a way which suggested that he expected him to announce the name of the target, but all Kinsman said was, "Go and have some tea, Fred, and I'll see you in the briefing-room."

When the squadron was finally assembled for briefing, and Kinsman had entered the long briefing-room behind the Group Captain and the Wing Commander, he found Fred seated at the end of the bench at the back of the room which had come to be looked upon almost as their private property. Bob and Chico and the three others who were making up the crew were sitting alongside him. The little navigator was busily engaged in working out some calculation on his knee, so that there was considerable confusion when he had to move along the bench to make room for Kinsman. As Fred gathered up some of the maps and instruments which had fallen, he said, "What do you make of these bastards, Johnny?"

"Which particular bastards?" Kinsman asked, sitting down.

Fred nodded in the direction of the crew in front. It

was Carruthers' crew. "Tried to take our bloody seat they did."

The member of the Australian's crew who had been arguing with Fred as to the tenancy of the bench turned to make some remark, and seeing that Kinsman was a squadron leader, the newcomer's face was covered with confusion. It reddened, and the man turned so quickly to face the front that he almost fell from his seat. Carruthers himself then, sensing the man's embarrassment, turned to see who had arrived, and, seeing Kinsman, was about to make some kind of explanation when Kinsman smiled to him and said, "Don't pay any attention to Fred. He's flak happy."

They laughed, and Fred's muttering was drowned by the stirring of the crews as the senior Intelligence officer mounted the platform.

"You didn't tell me it was bloody Hanover," Fred said to Kinsman.

"It was a secret. You didn't ask me."

"They keep trying to send us there," Fred said warmly. "How many times is this?"

"This is the third time," Kinsman said. "Maybe we'll get there this time."

"Third time bloody lucky," the bomb-aimer said slowly. "It's not the gettin' there. It's the gettin' back. Ah don't fancy the bastard, if you ask me."

The crews were becoming silent as the Intelligence man started to speak, so Kinsman almost whispered when he said, "Never question the workings of Providence, Fred."

Fred smiled then, and Kinsman slapped his knee. They smiled to each other, and then turned to listen to the Intelligence man as the squadron murmured loudly at something which the ageing Squadron Leader had told them.

Kinsman missed what he had said, and, because of that, he tried to concentrate on what followed, but as was usual for him at briefings, his mind wandered. The Intelligence officer was stepping down from the platform to make way for the Wing Commander when Kinsman came back to the present. Hurriedly, with a little flutter of panic, he tried to think of what had been said, and then, when he couldn't, of what he had been thinking. He had been thinking of Julie, and of how ordinary had been their meetings in the mess for tea. It was difficult to realize that

221

he had been with her at all, and yet he felt as though he could reach back to the previous night and touch her as she had lain there on the bed, so real was his memory of her then.

While the Wing Commander was explaining the complicated flight plan, Kinsman busied himself with the drawing of a line between Hanover and base on the simple pilot's map he carried. It wasn't a straight line, but it was as straight as he could make it without a ruler.

Carruthers, sitting in front of him, looked like a good proposition. The Australian sat still, and was apparently confident. Kinsman could see him allowing his eyes to occasionally wander over the heads in front. He didn't appear, either, to be too interested in detail, and that was good.

When the Group Captain mounted the platform, the squadron stirred as though glad that briefing was almost over. The postponements of that day had been hard on them, and there was an impatient energy in the atmosphere, as though each of them was anxious to be airborne before the whole thing was postponed again.

At every briefing Kinsman could remember, the Group Captain's little speech had run on almost exactly the same lines. The old man never said anything, anything at all, which was important, but he seemed to feel that, as the Station Commander, it was his duty to add something to the proceedings. He talked to the crews as though they should be appreciative of the fact that he and the Wing Commander, and some other nice gentlemen at Group, had spent a great deal of time and effort in laying on a new kind of game for them; and he gave the impression that the only thing which would disappoint him would be their failure to appreciate what had been done for them.

Group Captain Savory was a relic of another Air Force which had ceased to exist about three years before, and, sitting there then, looking at him, Kinsman sensed that he knew something to be wrong without knowing quite what it was. When he spoke of "high adventure," and "looking like a jolly interesting trip," they didn't understand him, and old-young Group Captain Savory, Royal Air Force, likewise didn't understand their lack of interest in hunting.

The Group Captain always concluded his address by expressing the wish that he could come with them, which of course in those days he never did. But on that occasion the words were stolen from his mouth. He was just about to use them when some gunner, hidden in the body of the squadron, shouted, "Wish I was staying with you!"

Everyone laughed, including the Group Captain, who waved to them with good humour, and briefing was over. As they stood up, the first of the crews rushing from the room in order to get to the locker room, Kinsman remembered that he had asked Carruthers to wait. He allowed his own crew to file past him, then he sat again on the now empty bench and said to the Australian, "Any questions?"

"No, sir."

"Do you know anything about coring?"

"They told us at conversion unit to use high revs. . . . They said that was the best way to avoid it."

"That's what we do here," Kinsman said.

The Australian's navigator looked enough like the pilot to be his brother. As well as looking like each other, there was about them both the same clean awareness. There was an eagerness in all the crew, in fact, which suggested that their optimism was untinged by any doubt, and as Kinsman spoke to them he began to wonder if his concern for them was the product of some shortcoming of his own.

"If anything," he said finally to Carruthers, "anything at all goes wrong, for God's sake turn back. If you have to turn back, don't forget to drop your bombs in the sea. Remember you don't want to be any heavier than fifty-five thousand pounds on landing . . . O.K.?"

"O.K., sir."

"Remember your cockpit drill . . . and don't be proud. Whatever you do, don't be too damned proud. It's your first trip, and"—Kinsman laughed—"I'm on your side."

Carruthers was flying in Yorker that night, which meant that on the way out to dispersal he and his crew shared the bus with Kinsman and his. The weather which had caused the postponements of that day had finally passed on their south to sweep on towards the east, so that the low cloud which had obscured the sky was gone. As the bus made its way around the perimeter track there was still enough light to see Liscombe through the window in the side of the cabin. The airfield lay there, neat and green and swollen proudly in its middle.

"Do you like this place?" Kinsman asked Carruthers.

"Yes, sir. I like it. It's the cleanest aerodrome I've ever been on. And easy to find, too." The Australian leant forward in his seat in order to see better through the window. "See how it rises in the middle. I didn't realize there was a hill out there."

"It'll be dark when you take off. Just take it easy, Carruthers. We're taking off towards the sea. You shouldn't have any difficulty. You have taken off here at night, haven't you?"

"Yes, sir."

Bob and Fred and Chico sat opposite Kinsman. From the way in which they sat there, not speaking to each other or to the three spare men who were flying with them, or to the Australian crew, Kinsman felt there was something like aloofness in their attitude. But perhaps it wasn't that. Perhaps they were bored. They had done this so often. Once or twice he spoke to them without raising much by way of reply, and once to make Fred laugh he joked about the non-appearance of the bomb-aimer in town recently. Fred hesitated, and then he did laugh as he said, "Tomorrow night, Johnny . . . what about you and me both going in? Young Les was tryin' his best to help me out, but he wasn't so good. You'd be just the thing!"

"What about me?" Chico asked.

"Who told you you were any good as a lover?" Fred said. And at that they all laughed.

The bus had stopped for the Australians, and they were standing up, making their way to the doors at the back, when Fred had spoken to Chico, so that they laughed too. As though still unwilling to forgive them for having taken his bench in the briefing-room, Fred was quiet immediately, but little Chico said to them as the first of them dropped to the tarmac, "Have a good trip, lads," and the Australian boys laughed and wished them the same. The Australians had excited the atmosphere of the bus so that when all of them except their captain had gone, there was an uneasy stillness left with Kinsman's crew which wasn't quite comfortable.

As Carruthers, having waited until all his crew had gone, stood up from beside Kinsman to follow them, Kinsman placed his hand on the other's arm, and said, "Have a good trip, lad."

224

"Thanks, sir," the Australian said as though embarrassed.

"Remember all the things I told you."

"I'll remember."

Carruthers jumped down then, and before the driver slammed the doors closed, Kinsman saw him smiling happily up to the Halifax which stood there towering over him in the bay.

The doors slammed shut and Kinsman said, "Good lads, those Aussies."

But no one answered him, so he introduced the three newcomers to Fred and Chico and Bob. Only Chico displayed anything which could have been called friendliness, so Kinsman talked to the strangers until the bus stopped alongside Zebra.

Each of them seemed to feel something like relief when they had arrived at the aircraft. The ground-crew greeted Fred and the other two with great shouts of welcome, and then the three hurried into the aircraft to attend to their preparations, leaving the spare men to follow in their wake. Little Chico, especially, was proudly familiar with his job.

The corporal in charge came up to Kinsman, carrying something in his hand. Kinsman said, "Hello, Johnny."

"I've got it, sir," the corporal said, holding up what Kinsman saw to be a model in a wood of a Halifax.

The corporal passed the thing to Kinsman. "Like it?" he asked.

"It's beautiful, Johnny. Beautiful. . . . It's got the wrong numbers on it."

"It's the old one, sir. I painted the old numbers on it because you'd done more on the old one. . . ."

"Yes . . ." Kinsman breathed. He looked at the thing closely from all angles. It was a beautiful model. Then he said, "Is it finished? Can I take it with me?"

"Not quite. I've got to paint the Zombie on the nose. I'll do that when you've gone off. I'll have to. I'm off on leave in the morning."

"Can you leave it for me?" Kinsman said.

"I'll leave it in the mess for you," the corporal said.

Kinsman said, "Yes." And then, "No, don't . . . don't do that. Someone'll whip it. . . ."

"I can't leave it in my billet or here," the corporal said.

"No. . . . I tell you what," Kinsman said then. "Do you know the Code and Cypher room?"

"I can find it."

"In Headquarters," Kinsman said.

"Yes, sir."

"Take it there tonight on your way from here. There'll be someone there. If she isn't there, tell them to give it to Section Officer Holmes. She'll give it to me."

"Section Officer Holmes," the man repeated.

". . . or Assistant Section Officer. I can never remember which. Give it to her, and I'll collect it. O.K., Johnny?"

"Sure, sir." He made a gesture in the direction of the aircraft spreading above them. "Looks good, doesn't she?"

"I can't see much difference in this light," Kinsman said. "I'll take your word for it."

"She's a beauty all right. She's got that new paint for searchlights."

"Yes," Kinsman said, "I noticed there was something different about her when I saw her yesterday. Is the paint to help the searchlights or us, Johnny?"

"Us," the corporal said, laughing.

As he moved to the Halifax, Kinsman called to the corporal. ". . . Holmes is her name, Johnny."

Fred reappeared from the entrance hatch just as Kinsman was about to go in to start his run-up.

"Where are you going, Fred? We're late," Kinsman said.

"Two draws, Johnny, an' me duty against the wheel."

Kinsman stepped back and took a cigarette when the bomb-aimer offered him one. Then he followed him the few steps to the wheel.

"What's wrong, Fred?" Kinsman asked.

"Wrong, Johnny?"

"You're not your usual gay self today."

Fred turned to him, and then he smiled. "Ah," he said, "there's too many sprogs around this place now. Things are not the same as they used to be."

Kinsman laughed at that. "Things are never the same as they used to be," he said, "Let's go, chum. Cheer up!"

"Ah'll cheer up when we get airborne," Fred said then.

"Let's go, then." And as he turned, Kinsman playfully smacked Fred on the stomach before jumping quickly in

226

the direction of the hatch and then raising himself up with some agility.

By the time the warming-up process was completed, it was quite dark. The gunners had tested their turrets, the wireless operator who had taken the place of young Les had reported that his equipment was working satisfactorily; the engines were running smoothly and quietly now that Kinsman had throttled back to wait until it was time to taxi out. Young Carruthers, in the next bay, should have started to move by now, but he appeared to be having some trouble with one engine. It had started, and then Kinsman had seen the thing stopped. A service van had arrived some minutes before, but now when it was time for Yorker to move off, nothing had so far happened.

Fred leant over to say, "It'll be a nice dark take-off, Johnny."

Kinsman nodded. He was thinking of Carruthers in Yorker. But Fred went on, "Just like ah said. Nothin's the same here any more. Not even the bloody aircraft."

"Cheer up, Uncle Fred," Kinsman shouted back, "it might only be a heat spot."

Fred laughed at that and swung his arm playfully in Kinsman's direction so that the pilot ducked.

Then, in the fast-darkening gloom Kinsman saw flames shooting from the exhaust of Carruthers' starboard outer engine. It looked as though they had got the thing started, but it was now too dark for him to see much from that distance.

Over the intercom Bob said, "Time now, Johnny."

Without thinking Kinsman said, "Right." He had been waiting in the hope that Carruthers would have moved before him as he should have done, but now it was too late. He told Fred to wave the chocks away on his side, while he himself waved to the ground-crew who had been waiting beneath him on the port for his signal.

Slowly, they started to move toward the perimeter track. Kinsman applied brake in order to slow down as he was passing Yorker's bay. There was some activity there, he could see that, but it was impossible to tell what was happening. Fred pointed and raised Kinsman's earflap to say, "Looks like our Aussie friend's havin' some trouble."

Kinsman only nodded. He was wishing again that he

227

hadn't decided to send Carruthers. He should have told the Wing Commander that the boy didn't have enough experience to go on a trip like this. It was all wrong. How could Carruthers be expected to decide—if something was wrong with that engine—whether or not to take the thing off?

If, for some stupid reason, the boy decided not go to off after Kinsman had impressed on him the importance of not doing so if he was in any doubt, there would be a row in the morning. He, Kinsman, would be responsible. And if Carruthers went off, and there was something wrong with that engine and he pranged on take-off, he would still be responsible. Responsible to Carruthers.

Kinsman taxied on, revving up his engines occasionally with sharp little bursts in order to keep them warm. He moved quite fast until he was right behind the Halifax which should have been ahead of Carruthers, and all the time on his right the squadron was taking off down the runway which headed for the cliffs and the east.

Because they were taking off towards the east, C Flight's dispersal was nearest to the point of take-off. Only two aircraft were still in front of Kinsman when he was close to the end of the runway. He steadied the Halifax delicately on its brakes as he stopped it, and then started in to his first cockpit check.

"Trim," he said to himself, "Mixture, Pitch, Fuel . . . Flaps." And when he had checked them all and had started to fasten the mask across his face, Chico switched on his intercom and said, "Here's what-do-you-call-him, skip! . . ."

"Carruthers?"

"Yes. . . . He's comin' up behind us. . . . Like hell! He's goin' too fast. . . . No, he's not . . . no, he's not! He's stopped it. He's got plenty room. He's about three inches from me nose. . . ."

"All right, Chico. . . ."

Fred turned to Kinsman, and raised his eyebrows. Then he said, "He's made it."

Kinsman, without expecting an answer which would make any sense, asked Chico, "What does he look like, Chico?"

"He looks fine. Smashin'."

It was completely dark now, so that Kinsman could

228

only see the aircraft in front reflected in the light that came from the flare-path. The yellow light glinted on the turrets as the Halifax moved from side to side, and occasionally when the man moved, Kinsman could see a gunner there.

He checked his controls again, took off his gloves, and then put them on again. There was only one Halifax now between him and the runway. Kinsman switched on his microphone for the take-off.

"Ready, engineer?"

"Ready, skip."

"Gunners. . . ."

"O.K. . . . O.K., Johnny."

"All O.K., Bob?"

"Right!"

Light danced from the propellers of the Halifax which was running up against its brakes on the runway. Kinsman looked at it as he waited for it to move forward. There were no half-lights there. It was all deep black and highlight: strong, inhuman and ugly, and yet where there was light on it, living with a bright life. When Zebra was there in a minute it would look just like that, and Zebra was full of Fred and Bob and Chico and the rest; and himself. And when Carruthers was standing there the minute after they had gone, in Yorker, Yorker would look just like that; and it would be full of Carruthers and his Australians and all the things they didn't know.

He turned to Fred, and Fred nodded, indicating that he was ready. There was the wrinkle of a smile around Fred's eyes and above his mask as he looked at Kinsman. Then they moved forward as the Halifax which had been in front of them started to roll. As they turned on, all that was visible of the machine in front as it was leaving the ground was the flame from its exhausts.

"Carruthers still there, Chico?"

"He's followin' us, skip."

"Here we go!"

The light from the flare-path was filling the cockpit when they turned on. It was almost embarrassingly splendid, and Kinsman, for a moment, felt as though he had walked on to a variety stage as the guest of some magician. Ahead, the flare-path was arranged in two long, beautifully exciting lines that danced their way far out into the darkness. In the centre of the runway Kinsman halted with decision when he was headed correctly. Then he slowly increased revs. until he could feel the raging engines straining against the brakes. For some reason then he looked up through the perspex, and, above, he could see that the sky was clearing, so that just a few early stars were visible. He thought of something Julie had once said. Or had he said it himself? He couldn't remember.

"We've got a green," Fred said.

Kinsman nodded. "Chico," he said, "keep an eye on that bloke when he's taking off."

"O.K., skip." The little gunner's voice came from far away back in the tail.

Without hearing himself, Kinsman said slowly, "Ready, Fred?"

"Ready," Fred answered. There was something ludicrously, terribly serious in the bomb-aimer's voice, so that Kinsman laughed quietly at Fred before he said, "O.K., lads, Let's go!"

As he released the brakes he increased the power in the engines so that they moved forward, slowly at first, and then with still more power forward, fast; tail up, towards the darkness.

CHAPTER SIXTEEN

THEY fell from the great arc of the night sky over Hanover, which is a pleasant city. They fell, at first slowly, as though airborne only on the little bubbles of their own surprise, disbelief, rejection which stayed with each one of them for some moments when the Halifax shuddered, staggering under the sudden strange violence of three successive explosions.

Like a breath arrested on the verge of a quivering lip, it held there, the shattered fuselage conceding height gradually, inevitably, reluctantly as it caught the startled jets of fury which sprang from each of the men there, only to fall back on them and disintegrate, to become the fear which was all that they could clutch at.

An avalanche of cold sound swept through the Halifax, drowning the cry of each one of them who was still alive; the futile cursing of Fred, the trapped whimpering of little Chico, the grating of the still turning mid-upper turret which joggled the dead body of the gunner there from side to side; the untidy reactive slapping of Kinsman's gloved hands against the arms of his seat, the sound of Julie's name rising from his throat against the alien violence of it all.

Zebra slipped on away down in the dark sky, burning. Like a torch once held high, but descending in spite of his will in the arm of a tired man, it measured their detachment from those still living at twenty thousand feet until the flames ate through its main spar so that, grotesquely, at the end, it curtsied to port, sickened, and went down steeply to the earth, leaving nothing there in the immensity of the sky but its black smoke, to wither, overwhelmed as little Chico's voice had been, and Fred's and John Kinsman's when he cried out, "Julie . . . Julie . . . Julie."

Julie said, "Hello, Sam," quietly, in keeping with the mood of the place, when she entered the de-briefing room. Squadron Leader Wilkinson, who was the engineering officer, was the only person present when she walked into the long, low room. He was a friendly man who loved the Air Force, and, when he saw her, he raised one of his very large hands to wave to her in silent salutation.

When she was seated opposite him, Sam sat, speaking only occasionally in a voice which seemed to ooze from the contented, immobile assurance of his fat, pleasant-looking man's body, looking at her as she sat waiting, without moving any part of himself except the hand which clicked an empty cigarette-holder against the desk before him.

It was relaxing to sit there lobbing occasional words back to Sam, and gradually she began to feel that she was allowing herself to be tired without there being any purpose in her presence, until Sam stopped speaking, so that the only sound in the place was the tiny click-clicking of his faded white cigarette-holder against the desk.

Julie looked at Sam. There was something in the ruddy healthiness of his thoroughly used body which made it possible for her just to sit there looking at him while he, without speaking, occasionally glanced back at her without embarrassment.

All that Sam was: unquestioning, grateful, good, top-of-the-world, man, Squadron Leader Wilkinson reached across to her, to hold her there like a strong dry hand silently clasping another, until her nerves lost their grip on the sound that his voice had made, as though the cable which had taken the smooth flow of their energy had lost its contact and was now dangling out in the space between them where there was nothing except, eventually, the unsatisfactory little sound of an old cigarette-holder beating rhythmically against a desk. . . . A trickle of irritation reached down through Julie. She stood up quickly, and said, "Sam . . . Sam, stop that damned thing!"

Sam stopped, and the swing-doors opened when two airmen brought in the urn from which Julie would serve coffee to the crews. She said to the old engineer, "I'm sorry, Sam," and hurried away from him to supervise rather pointlessly the installation of the thing they were bringing in.

When the airmen were gone, and before the others had come in to take up their places in the room, Sam said, "What's wrong, lass? You're upset. . . ."

"Nothing, Sam . . . nothing. I suppose I must be tired." She was standing against his desk looking away from him, but close to him, as though in atonement for having spoken to him as she had.

From behind she heard him say quietly, and in a voice which made her feel him smiling, "Are you in love? . . . Is that it?" She made no answer. On her left, the doors opened through which the crews would pass when they had been interrogated, and half a dozen officers entered.

These men represented the various sections of the squadron, and they were arriving to await the crews. The sound of their voices caused Julie to turn towards them. One of them, seeing her, waved to her, and then out of the sky above there came the low, purposeful droning of a Halifax's engines. Behind her Sam said, "Here they come." They listened, and their ears were drenched by the noise of another aircraft crossing Liscombe at not more than five hundred feet. One of the officers filtering into the room must have said something which was funny, for their voices were raised in laughter as they approached Julie and Sam, so that the sound of other aircraft coming into the circuit was smudged against the sound there in that room, and Julie lost count of how many she had heard.

She turned quickly to Sam and said, "How many did you make it?"

"Don't know," the old Squadron Leader said. "Four or five . . . or six maybe. They can come back so close together."

Julie waited for the sound of more engines above. After the first few had come in to encircle Liscombe, there was nothing for some minutes. There was still so much empty space up there, that it was possible to hear them separately circling one and one and one and one over headquarters.

Listening for them was like eating against a hunger still unsatisfied. The interrogating officers moved to take some coffee, but she stood there looking only towards them, smoking, half sitting against Sam's desk, until the sound of engines above grew to such intensity that it was impossible to tell how many aircraft there might be up there, and the sky seemed almost to weigh down on her with a kind of lush fulfilment.

From behind her, Sam said, "Let's go out and watch the first of them landing, Julie. They should be touching down now."

With Sam she went outside, and across the grass to where it was possible to see the end of the runway on which they were landing that night. The first of them was down, and turning off at the far end on the perimeter track. With Sam standing solidly by her side, Julie watched the great black shapes weaving down out of the darkness to drop suddenly into the glare of the flare-path, and then hang there, a few feet from the runway, their wheels reaching out tentatively, until, tail down, they sank, finally, with throttles completely closed, so that back through all exhausts came little burbling explosions of utter exhaustion.

Sam cleared his throat, and after a pause said, "You know, Julie, this hasn't got much to do with you and me . . . has it?"

A Halifax, snorting flame, having bounced once and then again, held her eyes until it settled. She turned to the old Squadron Leader. "You mean we only look at them?" she said.

"Aye."

"I was feeling that."

"Do you want to go back inside, lass?"

She said nothing as she stood there staring at the brilliantly lit runway.

"Are you cold, lass?"

"No, Sam. I'm all right."

She was cold. But the chill of the night air reaching deep inside her, hardening, held the fear in her and

234

seemed to fill the emptiness she had felt; to bring a kind of life to the lifelessness she had known standing there with old Sam who no longer could really understand, or feel or fear as she could fear; whose very oldness seemed to claim her from them out there.

They could hear the first of the buses approaching, its tyres whirring across the tarmac of the perimeter track. Sam turned to look towards it, but Julie stayed with her eyes on an approaching aircraft. He looked at her as though he was on the point of suggesting that they go back inside, but when she didn't respond, he turned his eyes away from her face to look again at the landing aircraft.

Because the possibility that he might not be in the first bus had to be faced, and faced with calmness, she stayed with the stillness of herself. But the approaching bus carried with it the idea of him, and the idea of him became a vision of him which brought with it a quick flurry of pleasure, delightful, real, suddenly sensual, so that in reflex she breathed deeply and pulled back her shoulders and her back, until she could feel her clothes tightly gripping the deep recesses of her body. As the bus whined close in low gear to stop, she slowly allowed the breath she had gathered to go, as though now that he was all around her, covering her, holding her, caressing her brain, she had no need or desire for anything which gave her life except him, the thought of him, the nearness of him. For he could be there in that bus. She lowered her eyes towards her feet which she had parted slightly, and allowed herself to sink deeply into her hips; heavily, pregnantly, secretly from Sam.

"We'd better get in lass."

She had to turn quickly with him. She did, and she hurried ahead of him to meet them, and the rubbery smell of them, in the entrance of the de-briefing room. From them, there seemed to radiate something unseen which halted her. They made a great deal of noise, but it wasn't that. She was stopped by the thick barrier of nervous animal excitement which, moving clumsily together, they seemed to generate. Now, forgetting Sam, their kind of excitement was hers. Her eyes flicked from face to face. He wasn't there. Of course he wasn't there. It was too early, much

235

too early. Only occasionally was Johnny first back. Not on this occasion.

Some minutes passed before the next bus spilled its contents into the long room. Not yet. It was too early. As well as the sound of them and their voices, there was the sound of aircraft still landing. The night had become so full of life. It was all around her. Sam Wilkinson, at the table opposite, was talking now with deep interest to a pilot and an engineer. She was pouring coffee, rinsing cups, smiling to them, laughing with them when they laughed.

They were all spreading away down towards the exit at the far end, past Navigation and Bombing and Signals to where Intelligence was. And, behind them, the buses came, and filled the room with more of them and then went back, and back for more of them; until they packed the room, so that when there came to her the strange little idea that because there were so many there, all around her, filling the room like thick steam, there might not be a place for him, her Johnny, her eyes, with each careless opening of the doors, fled there, and in their flight raised in her the delicious expectancy which swung back and forth, more and less, and less on the dwindling power of those creaking hinges.

Not yet, or yet, or yet when she saw the Wing Commander, moving amidst them, look up and across to the Group Captain, whose lips were drawn down at the corners. She asked them nothing. They would have told her nothing.

Carr said something to her as she passed him, pushing through all of them there to the door and then outside, alone, against the vigour of the night air.

Oh, Johnny, damn you, Johnny, for doing this. Come quickly. Come quickly. To me. To me, come quickly. She ran across the grass towards nowhere until a movement away out in the darkness, two points of light, a truck, another bus perhaps, stopped her, stumbling on her knees. Johnny'll laugh. Johnny'll laugh when I tell him. And in a way she laughed to herself.

The truck, the bus, came closer and then turned towards someone else, leaving her there alone, her knees on the cold wet grass, her fingers thoughtlessly rubbing the temples of her head, her head bent back with effort to look up towards the tremendous depths of the black sky. She listened to the mechanized fretting of an airfield settling down. But there was no Halifax left airborne in the circuit, or moving now on the ground; no life except back there in the de-briefing room from which she had come; and he wasn't there.

Julie's head gave a peculiar little wiggle of decision. She inhaled cool, sweet air deep into her lungs, and then, strengthening, she wavered, seeing herself there alone against the limitless range of all existence; she held herself away from the edge of panic until she found a sprinkling of possibility, just enough, so that, on her feet and turning back, possibility produced a pinpoint of reason. There must be a reason, a good reason. The thing she had to do was to go back, ignoring the strange feeling of inadequacy that had come to her, controlling the yearning that was inside her, holding, checking her impatience to find a way to him. . . . He would come to her.

She turned to face the new, frightening knowledge of what a woman was, and, walking, her limbs, strong and still lovely, moved as all her body moved, with an aimless, easy flexibility which somehow, then, had not the discipline of grace. The slow writhe of her shoulders rising to allow her hands up and into the pockets of her raincoat; the exaggerated, over-long sweep of her legs from the hip, her face taking her eyes upwards and then from side to side, as though she was unable to believe that only she had been there, betrayed the extent of her retreat from what she had been. Half a creature beating the now vapid air, away from itself, in search of the other half: afraid that it might die before it found the lost department of its own being.

Peter Carr, who commanded the squadron, was standing near the door of de-briefing. As she approached, he came towards her, bent solicitously forward, one shoulder lower than the other. He said, "Julie . . . Julie, it might not be so bad." He took her arm and walked by her side into the room where now only a few remnant knots of people stood here and there, past Sam Wilkinson gathering up his papers, to where Group Captain Savory was standing at the far end.

The Group Captain looked only briefly at her eyes be-

237

fore saying, "We'll go upstairs, Julie, and see what's coming through." She said nothing and followed them out of the building and around to the tower.

Up there she sat back in the shadows looking into the rush of clear light which fell on the board above the platform on which stood the controller. Three, it appeared, were missing: Hoskins, Barclay and Kinsman. Johnny. Johnny Kinsman. Behind her were the gentle memorable sounds of the signals room. Peter Carr sat in a chair by her side, so deeply in it and so still that he could have been asleep. The Group Captain walked slowly, between her and the board, from the wall on her right to the high windows which looked out over Liscombe. Occasionally he stopped, and for a moment would look through the glass before turning back. Once or twice he spoke to Carr in a way which commanded no answer, and he received none.

Someone brought tea and placed it on the floor by Julie's side, but she left it there to allow her hands to stay against the rounded middle of her body as though, holding herself through each separate, silent moment, she could keep inside herself all the knowledge of him. When perhaps two hours had passed, and her head fallen forward, was held against her finger-tips, Peter Carr stirred beside her and said: "Feel like a drink, Julie?"

The three of them—the Group Captain, and Carr, and Julie—went to the mess, and when they entered the little bar, Wimpole, the Intelligence officer whom Julie knew to be the friend of Section Officer Ralston, was lying asleep in an armchair. His long fair hair was disarranged and the slackness of his body suggested that he had been very drunk when he fell asleep. The Group Captain said, "This bloody man's always tight. I think I'll have him posted."

Wing Commander Carr made no comment until the C.O. had gone behind the bar to pour drinks. Then when he had swallowed the last of his whisky and coughed, he said, "I think he's got some kind of domestic trouble. He's all right really."

"Everyone has domestic trouble," the Group Captain said. And then hurriedly to Julie he said, "Another, Julie, dear? It'll help you to sleep."

"Thanks, no," she said. "I'm all right."

Wimpole the man asleep, stirred himself at the sound

of their voices. He straightened his legs until his body looked strong again. Then one hand went towards his head, and he pressed it hard against the side of his face and across the disarray of his hair. He slowly raised one eyelid, and then allowed it to fall again before making the effort involved in peering through both eyes towards Julie. There was a curious precision in his voice when he said, "Good morning. I saw you once when you were weeping."

Peter Carr, as though he was unwilling to commit himself to any interest in a drunken ground-staff officer, moved awkwardly and slightly to the right, so that Julie's picture of the Intelligence man was framed by the authority of the Wing Commander's tall, bending body and that of the Group Captain's on her left. Group Captain Savory, who could be a hard man, said, "You're drunk. And it isn't morning."

Possibly Wimpole didn't know what he had said, or to whom he had said it, but at the sound of the Group Captain's voice a flicker of fear came to his good face. Julie saw it as his eyes went up from where he lay on the chair to Savory's face, and then across and up to that of Peter Carr. He smiled rather stupidly, and, with considerable effort, he raised the watch on his wrist into the line of his vision; and then, allowing his tired arm to fall back on to the chair, he looked between them to Julie. He said, "Technically speaking it's morning. Isn't it?"

She was silent. They all were. Only Peter Carr moved uncomfortably.

"Isn't it?" Wimpole insisted. His voice, for want of real assurance, slipped down to touch the undercurrent of aggression which is in all men, and Julie, looking at him slumped low between the tall, strong pillars of Peter and Savory, felt that he was trying to find somewhere in himself the courage which is not. Quickly, before the Group Captain could speak, she said, "Yes. I suppose so."

The muscles of Wimpole's face, which had been stretched, allowing him to look upwards without moving his body, suddenly slackened, and he lowered his eyes again to Julie. He uttered one syllable of laughter then, and said, as he raised himself towards her, "In spite of life, I live."

"Why, man? . . . Why?" Savory said.

"I don't know why . . . sir. But she could be polite."

Instinctively the Group Captain laughed as he turned towards Julie to say, "Ignore him and his bloody drunken aphorisms at three o'clock in the morning, Julie."

But she, looking at Wimpole as he sank back in his chair towards sleep, to soothe him, said "Good morning."